WHERE ARE YOU, WALLY BEARSTONE?

WHERE ARE YOU, WALLY BEARSTONE?

TOM NORTHAM

TABLE OF CONTENTS

FREMONT COUNTY, WYOMING

Wally turned on his straw-tick mattress. Despite the cold fall Wyoming morning, he didn't feel the chill. No need to hurry, he thought, he was already dressed except for his boots. Sleeping in his clothes was a habit he had started while still quite young.

He placed his hands behind his head and gazed at the water-stained boards supporting the sod roof of his mother's home. Outside, he could hear the rattle and clanging of activities which signaled the beginning of a new day.

He heard the laughter and swearing as the buckboard was being hooked-up. In the distance a rooster's crow said it was time to get up and get started...but not for Wally. Not this day. He was leaving.

This had been a decision he had made without much thought or consideration of the impact. This was his normal mode of operation. Thinking was what others did. Meditation was what his Pa had called it, and he seemed to have a monopoly on it.

In his later years, Pa had his meditation times a goodly portion of each day encouraged by his best friend...*Four Roses* whiskey. They became acquainted when he was working in Louisville, Kentucky on his way west. The two of them generally solved the problems of the world together, or Pa thought so.

While Pa was meditating, Ma would chop the firewood, tend the "Victory Garden," and do the laundry, clean their lean-to, prepare the meals for the four of them , as well as her regular job...cooking and doing laundry for the other hired hands on the ranch. This provided the family with a place to live and its sole income.

On the other side of the burlap curtain separating his bed from the rest of the small dwelling, Wally could hear his sister grunting as she hoisted the cast-iron skillet and banged tin plates and other cooking pots around. From the kitchen smells he knew the morning coffee was almost ready.

Earlinda, his younger and overweight sister, had a routine which rarely varied, which varied about as frequently as she changed her clothes. She had told Wally that she only had a couple of pairs of underwear so while one was drying, the other's flying. Then she would nudge him with her elbow and come out with raucous laughter. The truth was she never moved fast enough to dry anything. She moved at a slow and deliberate but steady pace, much like a "hod" carrier transporting cement.

He reckoned that he should get up, but why should he? Wasn't this his "special" day? Wasn't he going to Paris, France, like his Pa, to fight the Krauts and then maybe the Japs? He was keeping it all a surprise to his family because he didn't know what to tell them. He did not really understand what it all meant and could only wonder, for the only world that he had ever known was Fremont County.

He'd briefly been to a school and had developed limited reading skills. He'd made his way through a few newspaper articles, seen pictures in magazines on his one trip to the barber shop in Lander, but it was all just names and places. He had no way of identifying with them. They meant nothing. In his entire life, he had never been more than a few miles from the ranch.

Wally's only real contact off the ranch was with the few children from nearby ranches, or in the small town on shopping days or during his limited school which ended when he could hoist a few bales of hay. Otherwise, his exposure was mostly to ranch hands. More often than not, the conversation was centered on their exaggerated female exploits rather than anything of substance or wiser than swearwords.

When he was younger, he had heard his Pa talking about a place called Chicago, and another one called New York City...and the great war across the water. He had listened intently when Pa had talked about fighting the Krauts and going to Paris, France... wherever that was?

Wally's world consisted of the only things he had ever known...oil cloth table covers, tin plates, greasy-cast iron skillets. The only smells of home that he knew were those of coal oil lamps, budding potatoes, decaying onions, and the acrid smell of a wood-burning cook stove. Now the smell of fresh coffee and frying sausage and eggs filled the air of the dank, small, sod-covered shanty. These would soon be replaced by those of the barn...the urine saturated straw, the manure and sweat of the horses and cows...and the farmhands. This was Wally's world.

Lazily, the eighteen-year-old lad lifted his massive hulk from his bunk and turned to the wall. He pushed the tin can lid nailed to the wall aside which exposed a hole in the calking between the logs. He unbuttoned the fly on his Levi's and relieved himself through the hole into a muddy pile of unmelted and well-ambered snow outside.

Thus, his day began in Fremont County, Wyoming in November of 1944.

CHAPTER TWO

OLIVIA MAE HOLLERS

Olivia Mae Hollers, called "Ollie," was born in Sheridan, Indiana, around the turn of the twentieth century. Both her mother and father contacted diphtheria and left her and an older brother orphans. Ollie was a large-boned and gangly girl who looked much older than her thirteen years. The brother, two years older, took a job in a logging camp in Washington, Indiana, leaving Ollie to be taken in by a great-aunt with her drunken and abusive husband along with three of their own, but older children. She was required to work on the farm, feeding chickens, hogs, three cows and a couple of horses. Her days were long and hard and at night, she retired to her room in the attic where she spent the night on an old mattress made of straw ticking on the floor.

One Saturday, while picking up supplies in Sheridan with one of her cousins, she met a striking young man, Earl Bearstone. He had just arrived from Louisville, Kentucky and Paris, France…where he had served in the army during the World War.

She found him to be charming. He was an attractive man of thirty-three with a flashing smile and beguiling personality. He had ample means and was totally fascinating. He also had the ability to spin a yarn, and totally enthralled her with his worldly knowledge. When he told her that he was the son of a Cherokee Indian chieftain, that was all it took to make her fall madly in love…all over a sarsaparilla.

Although twenty years her senior, she fell head over heels in love with him, believing all he had told her. She succumbed to her own desires and his pressure and that was that. Her great-aunt gladly and happily granted her blessing to the union, relieved of not having an extra mouth to feed. They were married and off they went. Ollie was filled with visions of wearing a beaded buckskin dress and moccasins; the maiden-bride of some great chieftain's son.

They took off for Chicago where Earl learned that the government was virtually giving land away in Wyoming. Failing to find work in Chicago he thoroughly convinced Ollie that they would thrive on his native and natural-born instincts for hunting and fishing and guaranteed survival while living in the wilds, they left for Wyoming to claim their fortunes.

The two of them worked their way across the country doing odd jobs for bed and board always knowing that greener pastures lie just ahead. After nearly a year on the road and in the wild, they arrived at Lander, a small settlement in Fremont County, Wyoming.

Ollie had learned that a bird in the hand is worth several in the bushes, albeit temporarily. By this time, she was now heavy with child when they heard about a temporary job on the McAllister Ranch...this would supplement their dwindling resources until they struck it rich. They had learned that Mr. McAllister was looking for a cook for the ranch hands. So, on hearsay, they hiked the seventeen miles to the ranch.

As they dredged up the dirt road to the main house, they passed through numerous outbuildings. The sprawling and expansive complex was constructed entirely of logs and stone. There, on the top of the hill stood a large, two-story house with a veranda spanning the front and both sides of the house commanding a spectacular view of the great valleys and mountains beyond.

As they stood waiting for someone to answer the front door, Ollie said to Earl, "Gawd...Wyoming must be the most beautiful place in the whole world."

Mrs. McAllister was a slight woman in her mid-fifties. She answered the door and escorted them to meet Mr. McAllister who handled the affairs of the ranch. McAllister, who was approaching sixty, took an immediate liking to Ollie. She was straight forward, sincere and gave all appearances of being a hard-working young woman. These qualities, which he admired in anyone, would overshadow the fact that she was one of the homeliest girls he had ever seen.

Her large boned and very pregnant body weighed down by more than ample breasts supporting a short neck and large head with a larger flat nose and a high forehead. These physical attributes were obliterated by a beautiful smile and warming laughter that won the old man over. When she laughed, so did those who surrounded her.

Her husband Earl had not impressed him favorably; however, he hired the two of them for forty-five dollars a month plus their own living quarters and board. Ollie, who assured him that she could cook and Earl would be a good hand around the ranch. McAllister figured that the ranch hands would decide whether she could cook, and the foreman along with the other hands would also decide the fate of Earl. Ollie rewarded him with a generous smile and a gleeful giggle of delight.

McAllister accompanied them to their quarters pointing out various buildings and points of interest. When they arrived, he pointed to an added lean-to attached to the main barn constructed of logs. It ran the full length of the barn extending out a little more than twelve feet. One door serviced the windowless structure from one end. A double door opening from the interior gave access to the interior of the barn. It was being used for storage, and probably at one time had been used for berthing of calves, colts, or lambs as there was a small pot-bellied stove for warmth. The floor was hard-packed clay and traces of residual muck from the barn. The roof was sod, completing the structure which housed all sorts of boxes, equipment, and a miscellany of debris.

Ollie, who had illusions of living in a teepee as the maiden-bride of some chieftain's son weaving rugs or beating deer skin was thrilled. At last all the hardships of the past year had a reward...a home. A real home of her own which could stand up to the elements and a door with a hinge-lock to protect her from the wilds.

After McAllister left, Ollie immediately grabbed a muck rake from the barn and began. Both she and Earl set about cleaning the rubble from the lean-to. They shoveled and pitched the old straw and dung onto a heap outside of the barn. Earl took a shovel and leveled the bumps and pits out of the floor and Ollie then sprinkled dry cement over the hard-packed clay. She then sprinkled well-water over the powdered cement and let it dry. She repeated the process until the surface was smooth, hard and clean.

She cleaned and dusted the log walls, packing new caulking where needed. Earl hauled in fresh straw from the main barn along with an old canvas tarp to fashion their bed. Tired and hungry, the two curled up together on their new bed, covered with blankets provided by Mrs. McAllister for their first night. Earl went immediately to sleep and was soon snoring.

Ollie, listening to the rhythm of his nightly routine, smiled to herself and thought, "It's a beginning."

The next morning, they began to make it a home. Two sawhorses topped with planking served as a table upon which Ollie placed a lantern from the barn providing the sole light to the otherwise dungeoness dwelling. Inverted empty nail kegs and boxes would serve as stools and storage for their limited belongings.

Earl constructed makeshift shelves to be used for their future dishes, cookware and supplies, and inserted pegs to hang their sparse wardrobe.

On the afternoon of the second day, Ollie walked the thirty yards to the long bunkhouse and the adjoining cookhouse. She entered without knocking, for she knew the hands were on the range for a few days.

"Gawd Almighty!," she said as she saw what the opened door revealed.

The room was about twenty feet square and housed eight bunk beds, various sized trunks, and boxes, and was strewn with litter that only careless men can create. Loose bed rolls and blankets were dangling from mattress pads half off the bunk beds. Wash pans half full of scummy water, along with razors, brushes, and soap, cluttered the wooden shelves beneath broken mirrors.

Ropes, saddle gear and old boots covered with mud and dung were all over. Dirty socks and clothes were strewn and hung upon any and everything that would support them.

She walked into the adjoining cookhouse of nearly the same size. The two long tables with side benches were set end-to-end and covered with dirty tin plates, cast iron pots and pans containing various levels of unidentified substances and cultures. Cups, utensils, bottles, opened tin cans, dried foodstuffs, wads of paper and cigarette butts and cigar butts were in profusion.

The nearby cook tables and hutches were equally cluttered, and the black cast-iron cook stove was covered with blacked and crusty remains of forgotten meals in cast-iron containers. Shelves on either side and above the stove were filled with tins and jars of either labeled or containing enough of their former substance to identify what they were intended for, flour, sugar, salt, beans, coffee, tea, and other staples.

The plank floor was covered with mud, dirt, leaves, twigs, cigar and cigarette butts and more unidentifiable substances. There were a few spittoons or old cans, or bottles used for that purpose, and cobwebs throughout. The windows were so dirty one was not sure it was a window.

"I think their mother's dead!," smiled Ollie, "I got three days before they're back to make this place fit to live in. No need standing here an' gawking, girl, better start hauling crap out of here."

"Earl!," she bellowed. "We got work to do."

They spent the remainder of that day and the next two, cleaning, washing, scrubbing, sweeping, and organizing. She put Earl to work chopping firewood, hauling water from the large spring-fed galvanized container by the barn and dumping the trash.

Ashes were carefully dumped into a half-barrel to save for making potash to blanch corn for hominy, grits and soap making. By the end of the third day, the floor was clean and scrubbed, clothes washed and neatly folded on one of the bunks. They could sort out whose was whose, and the amber colored windows were clear and clean...as was everything else in the large two-room dwelling.

Ollie had taken an inventory of what was there and what was needed. Early on the morning of the third day, Earl hitched up the buckboard and made the seventeen mile trip to Ambrose General Store in Lander as McAllister had directed and picked up the long list of needed supplies. Upon his return, Ollie sorted and stored the supplies neatly in canisters, bins and on the shelves. The cookhouse now looked like a cookhouse.

Ollie sent Earl back to their lean-to with what she saved from the food supply: a small portion of the staples and borrowed two plates, cups, and utensils along with two or three pots and pans for themselves in their own quarters. Unknowingly, she began her life's career that very day.

In the late afternoon of the same day, the ranch hands returned from the range. Loud, raucous, laughing, yelling, swearing and crude. After taking care of their horses, they swung their saddles and other gear over their shoulders and headed for the bunkhouse. Mounting the four steps that lead up to the front door, they entered one by one. Frivolity ceased and was replaced by stunned silence.

"Holy Shit!," remarked one of the hands.

"Holy Shit is right," responded Ollie as she entered from the cookhouse. "...And anybody who dares to flop their butt down in here before they've been to the bathhouse is dead meat!"

"Now, get in here and sort through that pile of clean clothes, take a set with you and get your butts to the bath house. Get out of those filthy rags you call clothes and get cleaned up...and since I'm a lady, there'll be no running around here in your all-together neither. And...one more thing...leave your boots outside on the porch until you've cleaned the mud and crap off 'em."

Ollie's tone of voice and size eliminated any chance of negotiation or protest. The mighty cowboys of

McAllister's Ranch left to do what they were told. They returned to the sweet aroma of fresh beef stew, hot biscuits and fresh churned butter, and hot coffee. So went their first encounter with Ollie Bearstone.

CHAPTER THREE

THE BIRTHING

The Bearstones were about to have their first child in their first home together. Ollie was less than a month away from giving childbirth and had as her first priority...heat. The unseasonably warm fall had given relief to what she guessed would be a grueling winter. McAllister had approved her request for a larger cook stove in the cookhouse and permission to put the smaller one in her own quarters. It was installed with the smokestack extending the entire length of the lean-to before rising to the outside through the roof. This, coupled with the smaller potbellied stove, would heat their entire quarters.

In spite of Ollie's iron hand and rough manner, the ranch hands accepted her without question. She became their mother, sister, and friend. There was little they wouldn't do for her, and they soon had closed the opening between her own quarters and the barn. They also installed a wood plank floor in the Bearstone's quarters and two windows.

Jake, who was fourteen and the youngest ranch hand on the McAllister Ranch, was the same age as Ollie, although no one would ever have guessed it. He was so excited about her having a baby that he built a small bed from two-by-fours, strung them with rope and made a tick mattress from straw and canvas. Ollie had saved the flour and feed bags which had accumulated, and with thread from Ambrose General Store, had made baby clothes, curtains and quilts. The quilts were more for warmth and comfort than possessing any great artistic design. She made clothes for herself, shirts for Earl and saved every scrap of fabric to make additional quilts or braid rugs for the floor.

Wallace Earl Bearstone II, was born in the late afternoon of December 24, 1926. Late that afternoon, Ollie was baking a gooseberry cobbler in the cookhouse when she felt the twinges and knew her time was near. She told young Jake that it was time to go for Doc Chambers. Jake, already excited about the baby, ran around in an almost nervous frenzy before Ollie straightened him out and shooed him on his way. She calmly sat the cobbler to cool and started walking toward the lean-to. She yelled for Earl who was working on something in the barn, entered the lean-to put a kettle of water on the cook stove, lit the coal oil lamp and took to her bed.

When Earl entered, she told him that her time had come and that he'd better go fetch Mrs. McAllister, "Just in case Doc Chambers don't make it."

Earl ran from the lean-to towards the big house. As he passed several of the ranch hands, he shouted, "Ollie's birthing."

Pandemonium spread throughout the ranch. Mrs. McAllister, hearing Earl's yelling from outside, decided she was going to help. This in spite of the fact that her only exposure to children had been in being one herself. She informed McAllister that she was going down to assist Ollie in giving childbirth.

McAllister, knowing that his wife knew nothing about such things, took off looking for his foreman Lon Bishop, who had helped with the horses and cattle on such occasions. Lon, a weathered-faced man in his late forties, had had no formal training in birthing; however, he had learned on the job and brought many fine specimens into the world.

Lon, who was digging post holes with Ole Geezer, when McAllister found him. He listened to the problem, spat a wade of chewing tobacco into the post hole, wiped the trailing yellow slobber onto his shirt sleeve and the dirt from his hands onto his jeans. He mounted his horse and headed for the barn.

Meanwhile Jake, after riding his horse at full gallop, found Doc Chambers in the local watering hole, the *Eagle's Nest* about three sheets to the wind. Half lifting him, he led Doc over to Ambrose Store for some coffee to help sober him up. He and Ambrose poured several cups of strong thick coffee into Doc before they dared taking him to Ollie. Jake hooked-up Doc's buckboard while Ambrose kept pouring coffee down his throat. Finally, they headed back to the McAllister Ranch.

Mrs. McAllister arrived at the lean-to wringing her hands calling for boiling water and towels. She had no idea what to do with either, she only knew they were needed. Lon, boots covered with mud, once again wiped his hands on his jeans, entered the former stable where he had delivered several colts and many a calf. He grabbed the kettle of boiling water, a dented dish pan, the butcher knife, then pulling a soiled towel from a peg, he threw it over his shoulder and went to Ollie's bedside.

Earl, seeing that all was in good hands, headed back to the barn to commence an early start of the impending celebration. He fished a bottle of *Four Roses* from a water trough where he'd stashed it earlier and took a couple of swigs. The burning whiskey hit his stomach and he realized that he was about to become a father. He had a couple of more swigs to ease his nerves, then on less steady legs, returned to the lean-to.

The buckboard came bounding up the drive with Ambrose at the reigns. Doc Chambers was holding on to his hat with one hand and the side of the wagon for support and his life with the other. He was still in a daze and not totally aware of what was happening. Jake, who was on horseback, had kept leaping ahead of them and would constantly turn back as if they didn't know to follow and catch up.

Ambrose pulled the buckboard up to the barn where he and Jake tugged Doc Chambers down to the ground and with one on each side physically carried him towards the lean-to door. As they were dragging Doc and close to the door, the remaining ranch hands pushed ahead of them into the lean-to and were crowding around the burlap curtain separating them from the bed.

Lon called out to Mrs. McAllister to fetch some more hot water and soap. Mrs. McAllister obediently did and went behind the curtain. Soon, a baby's cry was heard and Lon calmly came forth looking no worse for the wear announcing to Earl that he was the father of a fine baby boy.

"Hey, Lon...does he have hooves?," yelled one of the hands.

"No," replied Lon, "but he's damned near the same size."

Doc Cambers passed out from the spirits and excitement, and as Ambrose and McAllister kneeled down to revive him, Mrs. McAllister pushed aside the burlap curtain for the waiting crowd to see.

There, before their wondering eyes sprawled Ollie, covering the straw-tick mattress, holding her newborn son. He was wrapped in a feed-sack quilt, red faced and bawling. The bleary-eyed father steadied himself against the wall and grinned with pride. Ambrose, rising from his kneeling position above Doc Chambers, reached into his shirt pocket and pulled out a blue tasseled bottle of *Evening In Paris* cologne he'd brought from the store. He gingerly handed it to Ollie.

"This is a special day, Ollie," he said. Ollie responded with an all-knowing nod and a smile.

She announced, "I'm naming him Wallace Earl Bearstone the second, in honor of the two men who ever meant anything to me: Wallace Hollers, my father, and Earl Bearstone, my husband." She added, "I added the "II" because there were two of them."

In the distance, the cry of a lone wolf could be heard as it howled into the clear Wyoming sky filled with millions of bright and shining stars.

CHAPTER FOUR

EARL BEARSTONE

Earl Bearstone was born Earl Archibald Harvey to one Maude Gladys Harvey, a single mother on August 16, 1891, in Louisville, Kentucky.

His early days were usually spent in a one-room schoolhouse or spending a little time with his mother. Most of the time was spent...alone in their single rented room near the docks in Louisville. His mother said she worked at night across the river in New Albany, Indiana, in a Sanitarium on Silver Hills. Truth be told, she worked at night in the red-light district in Louisville near the Ohio River.

She would fill his young mind with stories of a better place and how someday she would meet and marry a very rich business tycoon and the two of them would be living happily ever after in some mansion is Chicago or New York...or maybe Paris, France. She would tell of the great houses in New York and Chicago and describe them in great detail. She told of the mighty palaces in France.

As he became older, he began to question the existence of an absent father which was explained away as he was a soldier fighting Krauts in France in a great war. Just which one, Earl didn't know. He never knew his father either. He realized he was darker skinned than most people. He also had very curly black hair and dark brown eyes. He would pretend that his father was an Indian Chief. Maybe a Cherokee or Seminole, and told the other children that his father was a great Chieftain who was needed to guide the United States Army to battles in France. After telling himself and others this story so often, he began to believe it as well. Both Earl and his stories grew. Rarely were any true.

After his limited schooling, he worked for several years at odd jobs in the warehousing district of Louisville or on the docks at the river. He made his way by gaining people's confidence. He developed a keen understanding of what the other person wanted to hear and then convinced them it would happen. Make them like you and you can do anything. He learned much of this from his mother who had the talent to make every man she ever met think she loved him above all others...at least for a few minutes.

An older Earl knew what his mother did for a living, and that he had no father...or a least not one who knew it or would ever claim him. He knew that whatever he was going to have, he had to get it himself. When his mother died, he kicked around for a few years, and then decided he would follow Horace Greeley advice and head west.

Being a procrastinator, he could always find an excuse to avoid leaving...but when he had saved enough money, he would leave. There was never enough money saved to start his trip West. When he turned thirty-three years of age, he figured it was time to do something.

The day he left, he was transporting the weekly payroll for his boss and just happened to take the bridge from Louisville across the river to New Albany, Indiana and beyond. He headed North for Chicago. Just before reaching Indianapolis, he stopped in a small town in Hamilton County, named Sheridan. There he met a thirteen-year-old girl named Olivia Mae Hollers, who desperately wanted to get away from her adopted family.

The day they met, Earl Archibald Harvey became Earl Bearstone...son of a great Cherokee Indian Chieftain. A few days later he was married to a girl young enough to be his daughter named Olivia Mae Hollers. Together, the two headed West towards a land that neither knew any better than they did each other...or themselves.

CHAPTER FIVE

EARLINDA OLIVIA BEARSTONE

Since most of their forty-five dollars a month went to Ambrose General Store, Ollie had learned to make her own clothes from the flower printed chicken feed bags. Earl, who seemed content to fade into the background, added to their monthly expenses by increasing his bill at the *Eagle's Nest* when in town. His monthly supply of *Four Roses* was growing little by little.

Yet, despite it all, Ollie had created a home. Two days after Wally was born, Ollie was back in the cookhouse with her newborn baby wrapped in a feedbag quilt nestled in a tomato basket next to the cook stove.

The winters were hard and long. Days were dawn to dusk and while the Lord had rested on the seventh day, the ranch hands didn't. The only social life was day-to-day with each other and an occasional get-together at the *Eagle's Nest*...Doc Chambers' place.

Once a year, the families and hired hands from nearby ranches would assemble at the Grange Hall for a meeting and dance. Most of the music was local: jug-puffing, guitar-strumming, a harmonica player, and maybe a banjo or a spoon player. There was usually a visiting fiddle player, who was traveling through the area. This was the big annual event and one that was rarely missed by anyone.

One night after the Grange, in a stupefied state of meditation, Earl had mustered up enough manhood to father a second child. Nine months later, Earlinda was born. Like Wally, she was a very large baby, not unlike their mother.

Although Earl wasn't much of a provider nor was he a father, in the general sense, but he did spend time with the children. He was a good storyteller and had a willing audience by two wide-eyed children in an area that had little else to offer. Electricity had yet avoided the rural areas in Wyoming, of which the McAllister Ranch was a part. Although there were battery-operated radios available, they were not a commodity known, or needed, by the ranch hands.

The only forms of entertainment were doing or teaching how to do practical things...which required talent, patience, and time...all of which were luxuries. Reading was something that neither Earl nor Ollie were proficient at, and anything musical like singing or playing were voids.

Storytelling presented a great opportunity for Earl to make up stories. He was good at that and he would create characters and situations which were exciting to the kids...and mostly suited his own life stories. Few, if any, were true.

Earl would talk about his childhood living in the teepees of the Cherokee Indian village where the great braves taught him to hunt and fish. He would relate his adventures hunting for game and wild turkeys or pheasants in great detail. He would relate his encounters with bears and mountain lions with their terrible claws dripping with blood, fighting them wearing only a loin cloth and feathers. He told how, though frightened and threatened, he would bravely kill them with a spear which, being the son of the great Cherokee Chieftain, he had developed the skills to make. He could do most everything he was called upon to do.

He would tell of life in the Cherokee Nation and share stories of his Ma, who was a squaw, weaving Indian blankets, making pottery, and pounding deer hides with rocks and making beaded dresses, shirts and moccasins. He told of the advantages and hardships of being an Indian living in the wilds. Both

Wally and Earlinda would listen with wide-eyed interest.

He told how he had been called upon by the President of the United States of America to lead the military through the great world war in France...a nation of great kings and queens. He would tell of living in the great mansions of New York and Chicago...there was nothing that he didn't have a story about. None, of course, were true. However, the kids grew up hearing and believing it all. They were so convincing, even Ollie believed most of them.

When both children should have been playing, they were working. Ranch life was difficult and presented many challenges. There were always chores to do, regardless of their age. Both did them. Both had an extended family on the McAllister Ranch which offered little time to get into trouble...except that which had been orchestrated by the ranch hands. The children, like the adults, belonged to the McAllister Ranch.

Both Wally and Earlinda never knew anything except the extended family which consisted of Ollie, their Ma, Earl, their Pa, Lon Bishop the foreman, Ole Geezer, Little Jake, Tracker, Jimmy K, George "Big Boy" Taylor, Bobby Blake and Jimmy D. Both Mr. and Mrs. McAllister were kinda like the distant patriarchs of the family. Mr. Ambrose of the General Store and Doc Chambers constituted their entire circle of acquaintances.

At an early age, Lon Bishop, the foreman, took Wally under his wing and taught him the practical side of living in the rough life that was Wyoming. He taught him how to stretch fences, bale hay, hook-up the buckboard, saddle a horse, rope a calf and use or operate the various tools and equipment used throughout the ranch.

Earlinda was taught and learned nearly everything from her Ma. At ten she could wring off the neck of a chicken with her bare hands and pluck it bare in minutes. She could cut up the pieces of chicken, flour and fry them in melted lard in a cast iron skillet for dinner. She learned how to take the horse corn and blanch it in potash lye until it puffed up into hominy, then wash and dry it and grind it into grits. She could make lye-soap. She learned how to make quilts and braided rugs, do laundry, till a garden, blanch and can vegetables and make jelly and jams and a great variety of other domestic things. She also learned how to handle the raucous ranch hands and by the time she turned thirteen...they almost feared her.

Unlike Earl, Wally took to any challenge. Especially, if presented by Lon Bishop. He learned to build from the materials that were there; turning trees into logs, and how to turn the logs into lumber, and how to use that lumber to make structures. He learned how to turn the rough soil into gardens or make sod for roofing; rocks to walls and foundations. He soon understood that all things are useful. He also learned the riggers of ranching and cattle; roping and branding; the berthing, and breaking and care of animals. He was like a sponge, always seeking more. He would tackle any chore regardless of the tedium or risk. He became Lon's right hand.

By fourteen, he'd outgrown the hand-me-downs from even the largest of ranch hands and was content to wear whatever he already had or could obtain from Ambrose' store for protection from the elements. He had no concern about his appearance and had no fear for he developed the confidence of achievement and success in day-to-day living in an environment that placed a greater importance on survival above all things.

His honesty became one of simple truth untouched by the corruption of social graces. He also developed a sense of humor, largely based on various gaseous or excremental bodily functions and the sexual exploits of others. He also took great pleasure in practical jokes, regardless of who it was on, or what the result might be. He became loud, raucous, and crude...not unlike his many mentors.

Although he was rough as the land that surrounded him, he still saw unexpressed beauty in the world and he would marvel at even the smallest of nature's creations.

Earlinda, like Wally, had been adopted by the ranch hands who took her as their little sister. She too, knew no boundaries. She was an overly large girl with rapidly developing breasts and would compete with most of the ranch hands at twelve. She was a tomboy, who went from a little sister to a person equally loud as the rest of them, and very much respected.

As the years passed, Earl, though only in his fifties, was suffering from advanced arthritis and showing signs of his lifestyle. He had become even more convinced that the good life was just around the corner. He had resolved himself to spend his productive hours meditating about what to do with all his great wealth...when it finally came. He knew it was close. He just didn't know what was even closer. One day, while meditating with his good friend *Four Roses*, the son of the great Cherokee Indian Chieftain went to the Happy Hunting Grounds...he died.

Earlinda found him and slowly walked back to the cookhouse and yelled, "Hey, Ma...Pa kicked the bucket. He's in the barn."

"Well, he can damn well wait!," replied Ollie, "I've got rhubarb pies in the oven."

CHAPTER SIX

THE FUNERAL

T he news of Earl's passing rapidly ran through the ranch and the adjoining community into Lander. There weren't that many people living in Wyoming, and everyone knew everyone locally. There weren't many strangers.

McAllister was deeply moved by Ollie's predicament. He'd grown fond of the big girl-now woman. He liked her kids and all that they did. However, he was never fond of, in fact he disliked Earl and all that he did. He found himself debating on setting aside a special day for Earl's funeral or just letting things happen as they may.

Ollie, after setting her pies to cool, went to the barn with Earlinda, and there found Earl, hugging an empty bottle of *Four Roses,* dead as a doornail. She briefly reviewed their fifteen years together.

"Well, he died dreaming 'bout getting rich...that's for sure," she replied.

"How can you tell?," asked Earlinda.

"He looked troubled...couldn't figure out how to spend it all."

Ollie had long ago gotten over her infatuation over Earl. She realized he was not who he said he was and less the person that she had believed him to be.

Lon Bishop entered the barn and saw Ollie and Earlinda standing and staring at Earl. He said, "Gee Ollie, I'm sorry for what happened...can I help you?"

Ollie replied, "Yeah, you can get him out of the barn and into the buckboard, if you would. Needs to go to Doc Chambers before he gets too ripe." Doc Chambers, also served as the undertaker in Lander.

Earlinda asked if she could go with Lon to watch what the undertaker did to a dead body.

Ollie didn't think that was a good idea for a twelve year old and was about to say so when Wally came in. "What happened to Pa?"

Earlinda replied, "He died."

"That's what I heard…what you gonna do with him?"

Lon said, "I'm gonna take him to Doc Chambers in Lander."

"What are you taking him to Doc Chambers for, he's not sick, he's dead!," said Wally.

"Doc is also the undertaker," commented Lon.

"I wanna go and watch," replied Earlinda, "But Ma won't let me."

"I can help you Lon…come on, let's get him to the buckboard," said Wally, grabbing Pa by the feet waiting for Lon to grab the hands.

Together, they dragged the remains of Earl Bearstone, son of a great Cherokee Indian Chieftain from the barn to the buckboard where they heaved him into the back of the wagon. Once in, Lon threw an old canvas over his carcass.

Ollie prepared a ham sandwich for each of them for the nearly two-hour trip and Lon grabbed a couple of beers and off they headed for Lander.

They bounced along the rutted road in the full moonlight. The fall was falling fast, and the night was cold. Wally watched as the frost gathered on the surrounding countryside and wrapped himself in the rawhide blanket.

"Why are we taking Pa to Lander?," Wally asked, "We're just gonna have to wait the rest of the night or drive back to get him and drive him back to bury him on the ranch."

"That's what we have to do. He needs a proper coffin to be buried in...it's the proper thing to do," replied Lon.

"Says who? I can build a box to bury him in and with the ranch hands carrying him to the grave, we'll give him a right proper funeral at home," stated Wally.

Lon, after consideration said," You're right, Wally, that makes sense." He reigned in the horses, turned the buckboard around and headed back to the ranch.

Wally worked diligently in the barn nearly all night building a box for Earl. He used wood from the ranch and fashioned a right proper box to house the remains of Earl Bearstone. When he finished, he grabbed his Pa like a sack of potatoes and flopped him into the homemade coffin. He had an idea, smiled and then picked up the empty bottle of *Four Roses* and placed it between his Pa's folded hands. He placed the lid on top, but didn't nail it closed in case anyone wanted to pay their respects...or make sure Earl was really dead. He blew out the coal oil lantern and closed the barn door.

Satisfied with the box he'd built, he entered the lean-to, pulled off his boots and crawled into bed. He was proud he had the opportunity to do the right thing. His Pa would have been proud of him and all the ranch hands would think he had pulled off a great joke.

As the sun came up, Ollie was in the cookhouse. It was Earl's funeral, but it was no different today than yesterday. She was a big woman with large breasts and a larger heart. She had a practical sense of humor and would joke with the ranch hands on their level. If she ever had a down day, she never let it show.

Through the years, age had taken many of her teeth and arthritis had given her a distinctive waddle when she walked. Although twenty-eight, she looked twice her age. The ranch hands loved her.

Today, she wasn't going to let it show that she was any different. Her boys needed to eat.

"Ollie...you're walking like you've got a load in your britches," yelled one of the hands.

"I do…it's your breakfast," then she threw back her head and guffawed, "Didn't expect that one did you… hog breath?"

This was the world that Wally and Earlinda had grown up in. Work hard, play hard and worry about tomorrow…tomorrow.

They loaded the casket with Earl in the back of the buckboard and slowly drove the team of horses up the hill to the burying ground. Ollie, Earlinda and Wally, along with Mr. and Mrs. Allister trudged up the hill behind. When they reached the freshly dug hole for Earl, the ranch hands gathered in a solemn group and carried the casket towards the open grave. Wally was disappointed that no one wanted to see Earl and thus, see his *Four Roses* bottle. He nailed the lid down after quickly slipping the whiskey bottle out and four of the ranch hands lowered the casket into the grave on ropes. Mrs. McAllister gave a little sniffle which was due to the golden rod rather than any emotion and Mr. McAllister gave a few words from the Bible about walking in the shadows of death. They all said, "Amen," and each threw a handful of dirt on the box.

Wally and Lon stayed and buried Earl, slapping the shovels on the last few scoops to pack it down.

"Glad we got that done before the ground froze," said Wally.

"Me too," said Lon, "It would have been a real bitch to dig if we hadn't."

The memory that Wally would carry the rest of his life...it was a beautiful funeral for a wonderful man in the magnificence of Wyoming.

CHAPTER SEVEN

EDUCATING WALLY

Wally was never a little boy, he towered over the other kids from the time he started school at the age of seven. He was already a year behind, which didn't matter as they were all in the same room together. He felt intimidated and out of place. The other kids knew how to print their names and read the words on a page. He didn't know how to do those things, but he knew things that amazed them.

Because of his size, the teachers forgot he was only seven and had never been to school before. Therefore, they expected more from him than he was able to do.

He wasn't used to sitting for any length of time and easily became restless. Wally's teachers did not understand that his days began at five o'clock in the morning when he was expected to milk cows and carry the containers and dump the fresh milk into the big container in the barn. He would gather eggs and bring them to the bunkhouse and then bring in firewood for his Ma to cook breakfast for the ranch hands. He did these things before breakfast.

Then there were rules which he didn't understand. There were things he was not allowed to say...for they were "not nice." There were other things that he said that were "bad." Where did that come from? That was the kind of talk he'd always heard from his Ma and Pa and all his friends. They are nice folks. They are not bad. Why would the teacher say those things about them?

The other kids would make fun of him for his size or how he looked. One girl, Shirley Rodman, said he looked like a Teddy bear and then laughed. Many would laugh at the way he was dressed. Why did they do this? At the ranch no one ever said anything about these things. If he wasn't right...wouldn't his Ma tell him?

Wally was confused and filled with misconceptions. Why were some things good at home but not at school? Why were some things acceptable at school but unheard of at home? What is *really* good and what is *really* bad? Wally was not tainted by social mores, but he knew what was real and what wasn't. So, at an early age he began to experience the falsehoods and shallowness of sophistication. A lesson that he would carry with him throughout his lifetime.

In the world of education, Wally was extremely shy. He quietly did what he understood and had more trouble with those things that he considered to be useless. He excelled in arithmetic. History left him void of thought as there was nothing, he could do to change it and he wasn't mature enough to understand that indeed, history repeats itself; that there is a lesson to be learned. Reading was not something he excelled in either...except *The Adventures of Huckleberry Finn* and *The Adventures of Tom Sawyer* and Robert Louis Stephenson's *Treasure Island*. He did not like the *McGuffey's Reader* at all, too much technical talk.

He developed a live and let live attitude about most everything. Kids would laugh at him and he would go along with it...after all, a joke is a joke. If he had been a bully, they all would have run as fast as they could to avoid contact with him. Most of his classmates learned to respect him for his size alone.

Wally also developed a strange gesture that he used to hide behind. He would hear something and then cover his mouth with his left hand...like in shock or had said something that he shouldn't have said. It was completely incongruous to his immense size and something he used whether it was a joke or a serious matter.

At nearing fifteen, he was already six feet, four inches tall, and weighed in at about two hundred forty pounds with little of his weight in fat. He didn't know his own strength, which was a good thing for his arms were the size of nail kegs. He had learned to hoist a bale of hay with little effort. There was no fete he would not tackle for his mind was filled with exploration. He was a curious boy filled with an untainted wonder.

He lasted in school until he was fifteen, then figured he'd learned all there was to know and had had enough of that! After all, he had already seen Chicago, New York and Paris, France, through his father's eyes...or so he thought. He quit school.

There was one aspect of life that he was uncertain about. The ranch hands were constantly talking about it and they all seemed to think it was the old cat's meow. Sex!

There was a girl in Lander that had quite a reputation for sleeping around. This fact had also come to the attention of hands at the McAllister

Ranch. In fact, it came to the attention of the same girl that someone at the McAllister Ranch was quite the big-boy.

Wally had heard none of this and he knew of nothing that was going on. He had, however, heard some things that made him feel like he had a special attraction. He remembered Shirley Rodman's comment about looking like a Teddy bear. His rationale was that everyone loves a Teddy bear, so took it as a compliment. Many of the kid's cruel comments could be taken in different ways. Wally, always the naïve one, judged everyone with the character of people he knew at the ranch. He never considered any comment as anything but complimentary.

Jake, being the youngest of the hands, was in his late twenties. He was the one who heard about the girl and took it upon himself to learn her name… Virginia Bland. Virginia had no shame in what she did…she enjoyed it. She lived with her grandmother who could barely hear and never looked at anything long enough to see it. A natural habitat for Virginia's talent.

Jake told the ranch hands…all except Lon, about an idea he had, to set Wally up to experience his first sex. He would make it a point to meet the girl and tell her about Wally's enormous hands and feet. She could figure the rest out for herself.

One day, the hands were all talking about the benefit of women and their attributes and Jake mentioned Virginia's name and what a set of tits she had. All the hands went along with the game and made all the appropriate gestures and comments. Wally, who was fifteen, grinned and thought that tits were the most important part of the female anatomy. They all agreed that it was...and told Wally he should meet Virginia.

Jake said he could arrange it if Wally wanted him to. Wally, who wasn't sure that was what he wanted or not, but was curious. With a little trepidation, he agreed to an arranged meeting.

The days, then weeks went by. At the end of the third week, Wally asked whether Jake had made any contact with Virginia. Jake said he had and that he loved her tits and wanted her for himself...as his girlfriend. He said people would see her hanging on his arm, and he would be the proudest man in the county. All the others said he was being a real prick. They said he was a selfish asshole because she had the biggest most wonderful set of tits in the county... if not the whole state of Wyoming.

Poor Wally had never really seen anything close to that beautiful and said so. The other hands told Jake, in front of Wally, that he had promised Wally he would fix him up with Virginia. That he had the duty to do what he had promised...if Wally still wanted him to do that.

Wally, who by this time was totally enthralled, dumbly shook his head in agreement and said he did. After much feigned thought, Jake reluctantly agreed.

Wally dreamed that night of beautiful tits...or at least the best he could conjure up as beautiful tits. He'd seen Earlinda's and his Ma's...both quite by accident, but they certainly were not beautiful. He couldn't even vision something so beautiful as what he had heard.

Of course, Jake had not yet met Virginia, but the next weekend when they were at the *Eagle's Nest*, he went out of his way to meet the young vision of loveliness. She was a short girl, with a short neck and even shorter legs than her torso called for, but had the most enormous tits Jake had ever seen. In spite of her peculiar construction, she had a pretty face and smile. Jake walked over to her.

"Hi," he said.

"Hi, back, big boy, what's on your mind?"

Jake, who hadn't expected someone so forward, replied, "I, ah... I have someone who wants to meet you...a lot."

"Where is he," she asked?

"Well...he's a young guy...fifteen, and...well... he's...a bit shy. But he's a big boy."

"How big?"

"Oh...he's over six feet tall...maybe three or four inches...over six feet." He replied.

The under five-foot girl replied, "That's really big! What does he look like?" She had no compunction about knowing what Jake wanted and what she did.

"He's no beauty but has a good heart and enough manhood for two or three men." The latter part Jake was only speculating about, but thought it was equally intriguing.

It did the trick for Virginia asked when and where, and if what he said were true, there would be no charge. That part was even better than Jake had hoped.

They arranged for her to come to the McAllister Ranch for a meeting the following weekend. He'd come in and pick her up and take her to the ranch. Whether she stayed was up to her...otherwise he'd bring her back to town. She agreed and they set a time.

On the return trip from the *Eagle's Nest*, he had to admit that she wasn't bad looking…at all. The boys all hooped and hollered and made the inevitable gestures and subsequent comments.

The following week, Jake told Wally that Virginia was coming to the ranch to meet him on Saturday night. Wally panicked.

While he had hoped for a long time "it" would happen, now that the day was near…he wasn't sure he wanted to go through with "it." All he wanted to do was see her beautiful tits, and now Jake had complicated the whole arrangement…with "IT."

What would he do? How would it all work? He'd seen the cows and horses' mate, but this was something else. It wasn't the cows and horses…it was him!

He didn't dream about beautiful tits that night. In fact, he didn't sleep to dream. He was really panicked and even thought about running away from home but had no place to go. How could he…he didn't even know her? Would she like him? Would she think he was a Teddy bear? This whole thing was traumatic for Wally.

The next morning, Earlinda commented, "What's the matter with you, you're acting odd?"

"What do you mean?," he snapped. Looking around to see who was looking.

"What are you lookin' for? Someone to blame for farting."

"Leave me alone," he said, and left for the barn.

Finally, Saturday came. Wally had enough presence of mind to take a bath. He ate what he was able to eat and put on a clean pair of jeans and a shirt. He waited.

The hands all went to the *Eagle's Nest* for the night. Wally waited.

The sun went down. Wally waited.

It was getting cold outside. Wally waited.

He was about to give up when he heard the sounds of the tack jingling on the buckboard as it bounced down the road. She's coming. He waited.

Finally, he could see the buckboard coming in with Jake and the prettiest girl he's ever seen in the seat... Virginia. In the rear, the rest of the hands, minus Lon and Ole Geezer, who had decided to remain in town.

Wally stood with his mouth open as Jake walked over towards him with Virginia. "She's really short!," Wally thought as she approached.

"Hi there, handsome." Virginia said.

She'd called him "handsome." This was something he had never been accused of before.

"Uh…hi," he grinned and then fell silent.

"Aren't you the Teddy bear," said Virginia.

That's it, thought Wally, "She loves me…I just know it" he said to himself, as he puffed up his chest.

Jake said, "Wally…this is Virginia. She's come to see if it's true…how manly you are."

Wally turned beet red.

"Ah…shucks, why'd you say that, Jake?," mimicked Virginia, "we're just going to sit and talk awhile." She grinned at her own cleverness.

Jake said he had chores to do and left. He went to the barn and gathered the rest going to the loft for a better view.

Virginia walked over and took Wally's gigantic hand, "come on, let's go sit a spell," then looking up at him said, "my, you are a big one. Let's go see."

Wally was totally tongue-tied. She led him like a lamb to slaughter into the barn where they sat on a bale of hay. "Come here, Sugarbear, and give me a little smooch." She pulled him down to her level and planted a kiss on him.

Wally didn't know what a smooch was but liked it. He'd never seen anyone kiss before. It was different for sure, and "smooched" her back.

Then Virginia took over and applied her trade. She rubbed in all the right places and sighed and grunted and when she got to the right place, she said, "My God!"

Above, in the loft, there were many eyes watching the whole event with great joy and a few giggles. When Virginia said, "My God!"

She wasn't the only one. Enviously, none of them had seen anything like it either. That evening, Wally became the big man on the ranch. Virginia decided to spend not only the night, but the next night as well. Jake assumed that she didn't need to be paid.

Wally was in love…and he wasn't the only one.

CHAPTER EIGHT

THE GREAT FAREWELL

This morning, Wally was going to venture out into the world. The ranch hands had convinced him that joining the army was the best thing for him to do: "See the World." It sounded like a dream come true to Wally, he'd believed it all.

At eighteen, Wally was taller than ever and had filled out to become a true giant of a man...the perfect specimen. The only exception to this fact was that his face still remained a round, flat face with acne scars and a large, flattened nose, small eyes and a halo of brown, kinky hair. When he smiled it was filled with teeth that were neglected and unkempt which he disguised with his childhood habit of covering his mouth with his left hand.

None of this seemed to bother him or Virginia, for he would strut around places with her hanging on his arm as proud as any peacock could be. She was his prize. He was the prize. After all, hadn't he taken her from the ranch hands. He had saved her from them all. She told him that she was a virgin, and he believed her. They had been dating now for nearly three years. Ollie had accepted her and Earlinda was neutral but never let either Wally or Virginia know it.

During the week, Virginia still lived with her grandmother in Lander and she and Wally would only get together on Saturday and Sunday nights at the Ranch. She still helped granny financially by whatever means were available, which may be the reason they were still getting along so well. He was hers, and she was his. Neither questioned that fact.

After peeing through the hole in the wall, he let the tin lid close, pulled on his boots and parted the curtain to the kitchen area.

"Well General...you ready for breakfast?," asked his sister as he ambled in.

"Yeah," he responded as he swung his leg over the small stool and dropped his massive body with the grace of a bull.

Earlinda placed a tin plate full of biscuits covered with thick sausage gravy topped with a fried egg in front of him, "how'd you sleep?"

"Okay...I guess. Wondering how to handle Virginia when I leave. She knows I'm leaving...but she don't know I ain't coming back."

"Neither did I...what do you mean you ain't comin' back?," replied Earlinda.

"Well, I was thinkin' that once I get to Paris, France...I may take up with one of them fancy can-can's, you know, Frenchy dancin' girls and settle down. At least for a month or two. Got any more biscuits and gravy left?"

He takes the remaining biscuit and scoops it around the plate and stuffs it into his already full mouth.

"Virginia don't know nothing about this? Don't you think you should tell her?," asked a perturbed Earlinda.

"Naw...didn't want no trouble with her."

"You don't think she'll be upset? Don't you think she'll miss that ugly face of yours?"

"Yeah...she probably will. Hey, Sis, I got somethin' for you as a going away present."

"What?"

"Give me some more biscuits and gravy and I'll give it to you." He takes a slug of coffee.

Falling for his prank, she flopped two more biscuits and his plate and blobbed a large ladle full of gravy on top. "Well, what is it?"

As she flops the plate in front of him, he hoists his buttocks and explodes a roaring fart, "Fart perfume, to make you smell better!" He threw his left hand to his mouth and burst into laughter at his own joke.

"You pig!," stifling a laugh, "Who's going to put up with your crap when you're gone?"

"Virginia's goin' to join me when I get settled."

"When you think that'll be?"

"Someday...four o'clock next summer, maybe?"

"You can't do that...that girl hangs moony-eyed all over you, all the time. Don't ask me what she sees in you?"

Grinning, "It's my personality...the one in my jeans." He grabbed his crotch with his right hand and once again, the left hand flew to his mouth. They both guffawed.

"Yeah, right!" Earlinda knew all about the escapades in the barn for she'd overheard the ranch hands talking about it but had never mentioned anything to Wally about it.

"I guess we'll get married 'cause she said she can't live without me." There was no question in his mind that they'd marry. He had his own rules of honor, and after all they'd been doing, it was the proper thing to do. Someday.

"Sure she ain't marrying you for your money?"

Believing her question to be sincere, replied "Naw, we're in love."

Affection was something never expressed at home and even his feelings for Virginia were more animal instinct than the fulfillment of any emotional need. He had thought about all of this and the money he was going to make in the army. He already knew he was going to buy a new house.

"Virginia's goin' to be living like the Queen of Sheebee, but I'm savin' some for you. Goin' to buy you and Ma some fancy clothes so you don't have to look like a sack of Purina waitin' to feed the chickens."

Wally will miss Earlinda even though he didn't really know why...it was something he had never thought about. Time never permitted any feelings except enjoyment of living for the moment. Grab pleasure when it presents itself.

"You said bye to Ma?"

"Naw...she'll know I'm gone when I ain't here for supper." His response was not one of bitterness but matter of fact. Wiping the last of the gravy from his chin with the back of his hand, then wiping it on his jeans, he rose with a grunt and returned towards his sleeping area, pushed the burlap aside and entered.

He reached under his bed and pulled out a dark brown, cardboard suitcase from Sears Roebuck and Co. and placed it on the bed. There he opened it waiting to pack his limited belongings. He removed a large brown envelope containing his eight-grade school record and placed it in the suitcase. He then withdrew the small empty *Four Roses* whisky bottle he'd retrieved from his Pa's coffin and stuck it in one of his socks. This was his memento of his father and then he brought out a bar of his Ma's lye soap and added some underwear and socks, along with his shaving gear. He closed the lid. He had gotten most of the mud and manure off his boots already, so he grabbed the red-flannel plaid jacket from the wall peg, grabbed his cowboy hat and placed it on his head. He briefly looked around the area and pushed aside the burlap curtain, excited.

Looking straight ahead, he passed Earlinda and said, "Bye, Sis." Then walked out the front door of the lean-to, down the two steps and onto the dirt road that lead to the waiting buckboard. He called out for Lon who soon appeared from the barn and climbed on board. He climbed into the seat, placing the suitcase at his feet. Lon, released the brake, whooped the horses, and they were off.

Earlinda stoically watched as he grew smaller and smaller and finally disappeared into the vast and majestic scenery that was Wyoming.

CHAPTER NINE

PROMISES

One hour and a half later, they pulled up to Virginia's grandmother's house. As Wally was getting out of the buckboard with his suitcase, Virginia opened the torn screen door and stood watching from the front porch.

Lon Bishop tipped his hat towards her, shook hands with Wally and rode off in the bouncing buckboard.

As Wally walked up the dirt path towards the house, Virginia threw her arms open and said, "Hi Sugarbear, been 'spectin' you." She put her arms around his waist and snuggled into his massive chest.

Then she said, "I was hopin' you'd get here sooner so we could...you-know-what."

Wally reached down and pinched her nipple as naturally and playfully as a schoolboy pulls a pigtail. "Would've liked that," he grinned, placing his left hand to his mouth and shrugging his shoulder, "I had to pack all my clothes and stuff."

Looking at his suitcase, "Did you get it all?"

"Think so," replied Wally.

Virginia lovingly said, "Oh, Wally, you're goin' to be so handsome in your uniform." Then added, "My hero."

Wally, looking a little sheepishly responded, "You gonna be proud of me?"

"Oh yes, darlin'"

Compliments were something he was never comfortable with and for good reason, he rarely got them. Standing there in his old cowboy boots covered with mud and manure, his dirty jeans and shirt and old red-plaid jacket, the young cowboy grinned at her with his neglected teeth and said, "Gawd you're bootiful."

"And you're my handsome, prince charming. I'm gonna miss you like nothin' I missed in my whole life. You're my King Dong…that's what you are."

Wally rubbed his bulging groin with the heel of his hand and responded "Gawd I wish I'd got here sooner. But…we gotta go, the bus will be here soon."

They walked the short distance through the small town to the place where the bus would arrive and take him to Fort Leonard Wood. They passed the granary and mill, the gas station, the old building which served as Doc Chambers; office and funeral parlor in the rear and the *Eagle's Nest* bar in the front. Somewhere in the middle of the building was Doc Chambers living quarters. As they passed in front of the *Eagle's Nest*, Virginia, looking across the street from the building said, "Oh, Wally, look at the beautiful tree over there," drawing his attention away from her part-time working place.

When they arrived at Ambrose General Store, which served as the main hub of the town. It was the post office, the meeting hall, the supplier of all goods and necessities of life in this remote mountain valley town. It would have served as a temporary courtroom for a traveling circuit judge if they ever had one, which they didn't. Hard work kept most from straying into trouble and if one did, they took care of it themselves.

The store also served as the Greyhound bus stop. This was city life as Wally knew it. Wally and Virginia sat on the porch of Ambrose General Store sharing a Hires Root Beer in silence. Neither knowing what to say. Although they had been together for nearly three years, they had little in common outside of their barn activities. Wally broke the silence.

"Guess you can come when I get settled in and we'll get married."

"Oh Sugarbear, won't that be great? Just think, our very own house just like we want it. I'm so excited! How long do you think it'll take?"

Wally, speaking as if he really knew, said, "Oh, two, maybe three weeks."

The rattle of an old Greyhound bus coming down the road broke their private thoughts about what the future held.

"Got your ticket?," Virginia asked.

Wally pulled out his billfold, wiped it against his jeans leg as if to polish it. The wallet was genuine leather and brand new. In it was $35.00 and the bus ticket which he had placed there for safe keeping. The ticket had been sent by the army and it was the first mail he'd ever received. Lon Bishop, Geezer, Little Jake and the other hands had taken up a collection and gave it to him as a going away present. It was the first billfold he had ever had. In fact, it was the most money than he had ever had as well. He opened the wallet and carefully removed the ticket. He showed it to Virginia with a little flair, picked up his suitcase and stood waiting for the bus as if he knew what he was doing. The butterflies in his stomach told him otherwise.

The wheezing bus pulled alongside the couple and the door opened.

"Git in if you're going," called the voice from inside, "got a ticket?"

"Yup," replied Wally.

Virginia grabbed Wally around the waist pushing her gigantic bosom against him and looking up, "Oh, Sugarbear, I'm gonna miss you somethin' fierce! I promise I'll wait forever. Write when you get there 'cause I won't sleep 'til I know you're there!"

Wally awkwardly kissed her and said, "I'll send for you, I promise."

"I'll be here waitin' for you, Sugarbear...I promise I will," she replied.

He then turned and shyly and cautiously entered the bus. The door rattled closed behind him, accelerated, and he was off to see the world.

Virginia watched as the trail of blue exhaust disappeared down the road.

CHAPTER TEN

THE BUS TRIP

Wally, having never been in a bus...or car for that matter, wasn't quite sure as to what to do, but since there were seats, he assumed he was to sit. He sat behind the driver holding his suitcase in his lap.

"You can put your suitcase in the rack overhead," commented the driver.

Wally did as he was told and sat back down. He looked out the dirty window at the scenery passing rapidly by. This things' sure faster than the buckboard...someday, I'm going to own a bus, he thought.

There were eight or ten other people towards the rear of the bus other than the driver and Wally. None of them looked like they were going to Fort Leonard Wood, so I guess they will be getting off somewhere in between here and there. Within an hour, he was already further than he had ever been from McAllister Ranch.

Everything was an adventure for Wally, seeing the countryside, experiencing the ride, watching the driver shifting the gears and coordinating pushing the foot pedals as he reached hills and going into valleys; he watched everything with curiosity. If he was going to get a bus, he'd need to learn how to drive. Little escaped Wally's attention.

After a couple of hours, the bus pulled into another small town and approached a lone figure standing by the road. The driver pulled to a stop and opened the door. A young guy entered and handed the driver his ticket. He sat down in the seat across from Wally. Wally, who had been staring at him, thought he was about his age, although smaller. Everyone was smaller than Wally.

The young man smiled and looked at Wally, "Hi."

Wally, not too good at socialization answered, "Hi."

They rode a while in silence so the young man asked, "Where you going?"

Wally replied, "Fort Leonard Wood, Missouri."

"Me too," replied the young man, "Matt Carver."

"No, ranch hand," answered Wally.

"My name's Matt Carver...what's yours?"

"Wally...Bearstone."

"Travel much?" asked Matt.

"No, I'm joining the army."

"Me too, I've never been anywhere...ever," said Matt.

"Me neither, but I learned about Chicago and New York and my Pa was in Paris, France, in the army."

Matt, duly impressed, said, "Did he talk about the war much?"

"Oh, yes...he told me all about it...and the can-can dancers," boasted Wally.

Matt, even more impressed, "Gol-ly! Bet they was somethin' to see." Not that he had any idea what they were talking about.

The driver interjected, "I heard they were really raunchy!"

Wally, now the center of attention, "Oh, yes...and when I get to Paris, I'm gonna find me one of those Frenchy girls and settle down."

"I wouldn't know what to do," said Matt, "I don't have a girlfriend."

The driver said, "Bet you would…comes natural."

"I got a girlfriend," boasted Wally, "Were gonna get married when I get settled…she's got the most beautiful tits in the whole state of Wyoming."

Matt didn't know what to say. While he was no simpleton, he knew enough to know you didn't talk about something like that to others. He noticed the bus driver was amused.

They drove along the side of mountains and into valleys. After a while, it was just road…mile after mile, after mile. They saw some Burma Shave signs and would read them out loud and snigger. And so the time passed.

Pulling into a small General Store, the driver announced "We're stopping for a short break. You've got twenty minutes to do what you need to and get what you want."

Wally hadn't realized how much he had to go to the outhouse. He practically ran toward the privy he saw behind the store. He jerked open the privy door and burst out with, "My Gawd."

The fumes were making his eyes water ,and he was gagging, for the hole was nearly filled with excrement and wads of paper. The stench was nearly unbearable, but he couldn't wait. He closed and hooked the door, dropping his jeans and blasted with a loud explosion what had been last night's dinner onto the steamy pile of waste. He waited 'cause he knew there was more. When he felt he was done, he tore a few pages from the Sear, Roebuck and Co. catalog to clean himself, then repeated the process several times until he was sure he'd got it all. He reached down and took a scoop of lime from the bag on the floor with the old can left for that purpose and sprinkled it on the heap. He pulled up his jeans and opened the door to see all the passengers on the bus quietly waiting in line.

Wally, smiled and said, "Didn't mean to take so long." He was sure they had heard all the commotion he was making. He hoped they didn't think he was responsible for all that was waiting for them to see. He sheepishly passed by the line and headed for the store.

In the little General Store, he bought a bottle of *Nehi* orange soda and a fried bologna sandwich with raw onions, dill pickle slices and *French's* mustard on it. The battery-operated radio in the store was playing "Harbor Lights," and he thought of Virginia. Some of the other passengers came in and would look at him and snigger, but he was unaware. Matt came in and also ordered a fried bologna sandwich and had his with some homemade piccalilli on it. He bought a

Coca-Cola, and the two walked back to the bus together.

Wally ate his bologna sandwich and the *Nehi* orange then drifted off to sleep. A few hours later, he woke and looked around. At first, he didn't recognize his surroundings, but then remembered he was on a bus. He looked over at Matt Carver who was looking out the window at total darkness.

"Where are we?" he asked Matt.

"Dunno...somewhere in the middle of where we started and Omaha, Nebraska," replied Matt.

"How long are we going to ride on this thing?" he asked.

Matt said, "'bout twenty hours."

"Holy Crap...that's a whole day. How long have we been?" said Wally.

"'bout twelve hours, I reckon."

Neither had a watch and the hours dragged on. Wally thought they should be stopping again for a privy-break. The thought was still in his head when the driver announced they would be stopping for a break and something to eat. A few minutes later they pulled into a small town to a cafe.

"We'll be here for forty-five minutes to stretch your legs and to do what you need to and get what you want to eat. This will be the last stop on my watch. Have a good trip." He opened the door to allow the passengers to get out.

"What do you think he meant by his last watch?" said Matt.

"Hell, I don't know," said Wally.

The driver heard them and said, "There'll be another driver to take you on into Omaha, Nebraska. I've been driving for fourteen hours."

Wally, who didn't feel any great urge to go to the outhouse, delayed and let the other passengers go first. He went into the diner and Matt followed. They looked around and then ordered a couple of Coney Island hot dogs, a boiled salt potato with melted butter and a paper carton of milk. Wally said it felt good to stretch his legs as he stretched them under the table to the other side. Matt, who was smaller by at least a foot and a half, marveled at how Wally could even handle the cramped bus.

After they ate, Wally said he had to take a leak and went to the outhouse. Matt followed. When Wally pulled the door of the privy open, then stepped back, turned around, and commented, "You can go in there if you want…smells like the last one! I'm going in the bushes." He then went into the shadows and pissed against a tree. Matt followed and did the same.

They entered the bus and took their seats. The new driver was a younger man of maybe forty. He turned and announced, "I'm Josh Peters and I'll be your driver for the remainder of the trip to Omaha. The approximate time will be eight hours. The estimated time of arrival is five a.m." He did a headcount and being satisfied, closed the door. Started the engine, turned off the lights, shifted into first gear and drove off.

There was absolutely nothing to look at but darkness. Wally maneuvered in the seat and tried to get comfortable. He couldn't. He then stuck his long legs into the aisle, wishing the arm rest wasn't there, but it was, and he soon put his legs over it and let them dangle into the aisle. The humming of the engine and the long day took its toll. He drifted off into a half sleep, constantly shifting trying to find a position that wasn't painful. He never did. After two to three hours of this, he sat up and began to dream of what was to come. This was all an adventure to him, it never occurred to him that he might be killed in action. He wouldn't…he'd survive! It was a given. He was indestructible. This too, was an attitude that would follow him his entire life.

They pulled into the Greyhound Bus Terminal in Omaha, Nebraska at 5:15 a.m. Wally marveled at the fact that after all that time, the driver, Josh, knew what time they'd get there.

He said to him, "How'd you figure out how long it would take?"

"I've driven it many times," replied Josh. It's about 320 miles and, baring accidents or flat tires, we average about 40 miles an hour. We did alright."

Wally was fascinated by his ciphering and amazed at the same time. As they departed the bus, he grabbed his suitcase off the rack above and exited. Matt grabbed his bag and the two left the bus, meeting on the hard, cold ground where they followed the others into the terminal. Both were amazed at the size of the building filled with long polished oak benches and electric lights. Neither had seen anything like it in their lives.

There was a short order stand with workers preparing food and people all over the place. They gawked like a couple of backwoods mountain hicks... that they were.

They asked where they could take a leak and were directed to a room marked "Cowboys." When they entered, they saw three men standing in a row staring at a wall pissing into a trough going from high to low and out. Wally remarked, "Ain't that the damndest thing you ever saw?" Matt agreed, and they both went and did the same.

When they had finished, Wally stood and watched to see what happened to it as it drained down the trough to a hole in the wall. Where, he could only guess, probably into the snow outside, like his pee hole in the wall at home.

He watched the other men walk over to white sinks fastened to a wall with spigots coming out of the wall. They turned the spigot, water came out and they'd just let it pour while they were washing their hands. Then they'd turn it off and dry their hands on a big towel that they'd pull from a box and the bottom would go back into the box. This was Wally's first exposure to indoor plumbing and a modern toilet. Both he and Matt stood in utter amazement.

They returned into the terminal and were amazed at all the activity. There were boys selling newspapers yelling about the war. Other people were drinking coffee they purchased from vendors. You could buy most anything you wanted to eat. The whole scenario was like seeing into the future. Wally liked what he saw. He also caught a couple of girls who were cleaning and sweeping the floor. One had noticed

Wally as well. Wally was hard to miss. She had tits almost as big and beautiful as Virginia's.

The two boys were there taking in all that was to be seen when they were approached by a soldier who said, "You boys going to Fort. Leonard Wood?"

"Yeah. We're joining the army."

"That's right."

"Well you'd better be moving out. The bus is ready to leave and they don't wait for anyone."

"Oh gawd, what do we do, where do we go?" replied Wally nearly in panic.

The soldier told them the door to exit and the number of the bus which was about to leave

Wally and Matt grabbed their gear and ran towards the exit to the busses.

"It's the bus to St. Louis," called out the soldier."

There were busses everywhere. They were lined waiting to leave. Passengers were already onboard and the driver was shutting the storage doors beneath the bus.

Wally knew he had to get on the right one. He had to get there. But which one?

One bus left and another pulled in behind it.

Finally, Matt saw the one with the St. Louis sign above the front window. "There it is!," he shouted.

They ran for the bus and as they entered, the door closed behind them. The driver, a woman, said you were going to St. Louis…or Fort Leonard Wood?"

They said at the same time, "Fort Leonard Wood, Missouri and the army,"

"Well, you're on the right one, Sweetie, have a seat."

They took a seat. Both were amazed at the difference between the bus they had gotten out of and what they got into. This bus was bigger, better and seemingly brand new.

"Hardly want to dirty the seats by sittin' on 'em," remarked Wally.

"Gawd, this is fancy," said Matt.

After inspecting their surroundings and testing the various buttons, they settled back for the ride.

The lady driver said "My name is Katie Summers, and I'm your driver to St. Louis, Missouri via Fort Leonard Wood Army Base. The travel time is approximately ten hours. The ETA to Fort Leonard Wood is six hours and twenty minutes. Have a pleasant drive and God Bless our Troops and God Bless America." All aboard yelled, "Hooray for the army!"

Wally, for the first time realized he was really going to the army. He was going to be a part of something bigger than the McAllister Ranch. He was going to be a soldier. His chest puffed a little with pride.

The time went by fast as he gazed at a new part of the country. The rising sun revealed a land that was flat and plain. No mountains with spectacular views. Just endless miles of fields of dried corn stalks, gathered and standing in shocks. Once in a while a farmhouse with outbuildings and a barn would appear, then more fields of corn shocks. There were cars zooming by in both directions on the paved highways. In a few hours, he noticed that the soil was red, like brick.

Matt said, "Gawd, look at the ground…it's red!"

Wally, all knowingly replied, "Yeah, that's where bricks come from."

Matt said he didn't know that and marveled at all the Wally knew.

Wally farted into the soft new bus seats and was amazed how quiet it was. He couldn't hear it himself.

"Phew...what's that?" said Matt, fully aware of what it was.

"Dunno, but it's sure terrible smellin' ain't it? replied Wally with a straight face. Then he put his left hand to his mouth and grinned. He too, marveled... Matt didn't even know a good fart!

The driver announced the arrival at Fort Leonard Wood, Missouri, "Welcome to the home of the Army's Engineer Replacement Center, Fort Leonard Wood and the pride of the army."

So, after a nearly thirty-hour trip, the two boys from Wyoming, arrived at Fort Leonard Wood, Missouri. Each was about to become a man. Each had his destiny. Each had no idea what in hell was about to take place.

God Bless America!

CHAPTER ELEVEN

INDUCTION, DAY 1

The Greyhound driver opened the door and twelve men disembarked. One towered above the rest, which they all noticed. Wally looked at the group of guys who had arrived together. They were as varied as their numbers would imply. No two were the same, not in size, heights, weight, clothes, attitudes, hair, eyes, nothing was the same about any of them. He wondered how they were ever going to make soldiers out of this disorganized bunch of underbrush.

He and Matt weren't even close, yet he felt as if Matt was his only friend. He didn't know if Matt felt the same way 'cause he hadn't said anything since they arrived. None of others had said much either. They were all alone in a crowd. Wally felt the same butterflies in his stomach that he had felt in Lander.

There was a soldier there who yelled out to the new arrivals and told them to line up. Which they did... eventually. None of the new arrivals had a clue as to what they were doing. All seemed lost. Once in a line, someone yelled, "Attention!"

Everyone drew themself upright, sucked in their stomach and tried not to move. Wally heard someone snigger but joined the rest in silence and waited.

A different soldier marched in. Wally was amazed how all the soldiers marched and turned right or left like they were afraid of running into a glass wall that wasn't there...or...they were avoiding stepping in a nonexistent cow dab.

The new soldier, who was less than six feet tall and maybe twenty-five, said, "I'm Sergeant Johnson and I'm going to make men out of you slovenly creatures. You can call me Sergeant Johnson, and before we're done here, you're going to hate my guts. But by god, you're going to respect me. Did you hear me?

A few men grumbled.

The Sergeant yelled so loud it made Wally jump, "DID YOU HEAR ME?"

The new arrivals meekly replied, "Yes"

"WHAT DID YOU SAY?"

"YES."

"YES WHAT?"

"YES, SIR!"

"YES, SERGEANT!"

"YES, SERGEANT!"

The Sergeant spoke softly, "Now, wasn't that better? See how that works?"

"YES, SERGEANT!"

"Now, LEFT FACE!," shouted the Sergeant.

Some of the guys turned left, some right...it was a disaster.

"THE OTHER LEFT, YOU IDIOT! NOW...FOR-WARD MARCH!"

The guys were running into each other, out of step...some looking at each other's feet and tried to get in step with one or the other, and others just stumbled along.

Somehow, they made it to a wood-framed building that was painted a cowshit-green/brown color with a sign above the door, "Induction Center."

The Sergeant yelled, "HALT!" Some did, and some didn't, "HALT means stop, assholes."

Wally wondered why the Sergeant didn't like some of the guys. They just got there and already he was mad at them.

The new arrivals were told to line up and enter the Induction Center and re-form into two lines facing the American Flag when they got in the building. Once again in lines, they stood waiting.

The Sergeant, who loved to stomp on the floor, entered and marched to the back wall and stopped just short of running into the wall that no one could see and turned right. He stomped the floor again and marched directly in front of the new arrivals and stomped again. He turned and faced them and stomped again.

Wally noticed he was dressed in a cowshit-colored uniform and smiled. Maybe he was trying to stomp the cow shit off his feet.

"Atten-tion!" The men complied.

The Sergeant spoke in a normal tone of voice and all knew he was serious. He began reading from a piece of paper,

"The Oath of enlistment is something that every service member must promise and adhere to for his entire military career. From

the Oath, you can see that you will be defending the Constitution – not a person. Discipline and accepting orders is sworn to. Finally, you vow to face the Uniform Code of Military Justice should any disputes arise.

Raise your right hand and repeat after me...

I...[say your legal name..., and there was a bunch of noise that no one could understand], do solemnly swear,

that I will support and defend the Constitution of the United States against all enemies,

foreign and domestic;

that I will bear true faith and allegiance to the same;

and that I will obey the orders of the President of the United States,

and the orders of the officers appointed over me,

according to regulations and the Uniform Code of Military Justice.

So help me God."

Wally was impressed. He'd never said half of those words…and hoped he said them okay.

The Sergeant then said, "Congratulations, gentlemen…your ass now belongs to Uncle Sam."

"RECRUITS, ATTEN-TION! RIGHT FACE…FORWARD MARCH."

They marched through a door into a huge room. Piled in front of them were what seemed to be thousands of gray-stripped mattresses, blankets…in that same cowshit-brown color, pillows, and white sheets and pillowcases.

"Line up and each Recruit take what is handed to you." The Recruits did as they were told. They were handed a mattress, rolled up and tied with twine, two cow--hit brown blankets, one pillow, one pillowcase and two sheets, and two sets of towels and two washcloths. Laden down with all of this plus their suitcases and other gear, they were marched through a door, onto a gravel path and down through a bunch of buildings called barracks, into one of them and told to find a bunk.

The barracks was a twenty-five feet wide wooden building about one hundred feet long. There were rows of bunks on either side of a central aisle. The bunks, which really were beds, were made from bent pipe with wire fencing stretched by springs stuck through holes in the pipes. They were painted cow-shit brown too. Next to the center aisle, and next to the head of each bunk, depending on which way you laid, was a box with a lid. It, too, was painted cow-shit brown.

In fact, the whole building was painted cow-shit brown, thought Wally. He'd carried his stuff in without a problem; however, Matt hadn't fared so well. He was struggling but made it. They were bunked side-by-side.

"Everyone put your bedding on a bunk and unroll the mattress."

They did.

The Sergeant had a bunk placed in the center aisle and said, "Now listen up and follow what I say. Private Wilson here is going to demonstrate how to make a bunk up...the right way...the army way!"

Private Wilson, a quiet slight type, spoke softly and said, "Once your mattress is on the bed..."

"SPEAK UP, PRIVATE WILSON, I CAN'T HEAR YOU!," shouted the Sergeant.

"YES, Sergeant!"

Private Wilson, a little red-faced, said loudly, "PUT YOU MATTRESS ON THE BED AND TAKE ONE OF YOUR SHEETS AND STRETCH IT TIGHT OVER THE MATTRESS..." He went through the entire process of making a bed, showing how to fold the corners, using one blanket for cover and the second, folded to cover the top half and stretch it all tight. Wally wondered how the poor Private had any voice left.

The Sergeant spoke, "Don't forget any of this. You will be expected to remember every bit, and you WILL make your bed up any time you are not in it. You got that?"

"YES, Sergeant!"

Good, then do it now and assemble outside in ten minutes. Leave what gear you brought with you on the bed." With that he turned sharply to keep from hitting the wall and stomped out the door.

Everyone was rushing to make up their bed; trying to remember it all. Wally didn't see the point in making it all that fancy...it was just a place to sleep but did the best he could. Matt succeeded in doing a better job. Neither did it well. They threw their gear on the bed and a whistle blew and they all went outside to "fall in."

The Sergeant reappeared and started yelling again, telling them to march to another building. When they arrived, once again forming a line they entered. They were handed two duffle bags which were big cow-shit colored pieces of canvas sewed with handles and some metal hardware at the top, which Wally hadn't figured out yet.

As each of the Recruits went down the line with soldiers passing out stuff, there was another Sergeant sizing them up and yelling, "Small, or Medium, or Large...or extra-large. Regular, short, long, etc." Whatever that meant. It was like Christmas. The soldiers were passing out pants, socks, shirts, coats, underwear, T-shirts, belts, rain gear, belts with brass buckles. The Recruits were stuffing them into the duffle bags as fast as they could. When you got one full, you would start on the other one and drag one and pull the other as you went down the line. One soldier asked if you knew your shoe size, if you didn't, they measured it and handed you a pair of shoes and two pairs of boots. The next asked if you knew your hat size, and so it went.

When the soldier that was sizing up the Recruits tried to size up Wally, he said, "Extra-large, extra-long, extra everything...I think." All eyes turned towards Wally and did double takes. "Buddy...you're going to be a challenge!," said the soldier who was sizing the Recruits up.

With the duffle bags overflowing with cow-shit brown clothes, the Recruits were marched back to the barracks and told to take their things, unpack them, put on the khakis, whatever that is, put boots on and put your civilian clothes in the suitcase or bag that your brought with you. You will turn it in later. Straighten out what you got left and put them in the foot lockers at the head of their bed.

"You have two hours to prepare for inspection, "DIS-MISSED!"

The Recruits, dragging their bags into the barracks. Wally picked his two duffle bags up like they were nothing, walked to his bed and dropped them. One by one, he began to dump and empty each of them on the bed. He'd never seen so many clothes in his life.

The other guys had done the same thing and began talking and trying to figure out what was what. They were laughing at each other and pointing and finally one said, "The clothes that look like pajamas are the khakis." Most agreed.

Wally whispered to Matt, "What are pajamas?," Matt shrugged his shoulders and replied, "Damned if I know." They watched the others and soon got the idea.

Wally put on the khaki pants which were at least six inches too short. The long sleeves on the shirts were maybe three inches too short as well. He put on the long socks and dull looking brown boots, which were the only thing not looking like a cow pie. The khaki belt fit fine as did the rest...around the waist. Other portions like the thighs and upper arms were too tight. The boots fit but the hat didn't...it just sat on top of his head.

There were two sets of tan outfits, one with long sleeves and pants and the other with summer short pants and shirts, two sets of khakis fatigues, two dress uniforms, two dress shirts, two ties, two dress stocking, two long stockings and two wool long stockings, two belts, a winter overcoat, and a raincoat. Also, a hip-length jacket in khaki.

After downing the khaki fatigues, Wally waded the remaining clothes into the footlocker. He took his clothes from home and waded them into the suitcase, except for the *Four Roses* bottle and the lye soap, and his new billfold. He hid them in the foot locker in his socks and underwear. He figured he still had some time and went to find the outhouse. There wasn't one. He'd held it for more than five hours and really needed to go.

One of the guys said, "I've got to take a leak," and walked into the next room. Wally followed.

There, in the latrine, as Wally learned to call it, were two rows of toilet bowls, facing each other. There were no dividers. There were also sinks beyond either side of the toilets and along one wall there were a dozen urinals. To the right were numerous shower heads in one gigantic shower stall. Of course, Wally, had never seen anything like it.

The first Recruit walked over to the urinal, unbuttoned his khaki's and pissed into the white bowl. When he was finished, he shook himself and backed away. He reached up and pushed a handle above the urinal and water washed the urine away. Wally said to himself, "Wow, ain't that the damnedest thing?"

When the other guy had left, he did the same thing. "This is great!," he thought.

Wally returned to his bunk just in time for the Sergeant to enter.

Someone yelled into the barracks, "ATTEN-TION!"

They all complied and the Sergeant came stomping in. Wally still couldn't figure out why he did that. He guessed that's what you do in the army...you stomp.

"Aren't we a pretty bunch," sarcastically remarked the Sergeant, "What a sorry-ass bunch of shitheads we've got here."

Wally had heard all the words the Sergeant used before, but never directed to himself. What had he ever done to the stomping Sergeant to deserve that?

"You are the sorriest ass soldiers I've ever seen in my life. We've got a helluva lot to do here...we've got a war to win!," he bellowed. Then he turned to one of the two Privates he brought with him and said, "Let's see how well they packed up their gear and made their beds, Private!"

Once again, Wally wondered what does how you pack your footlocker have to do with beating the krauts?

He yelled in some faces and dumped their locker out and tore other's beds apart. He walked up to Wally, and looking up in to Wally's face and asked,

"Where you from, Giant?"

"The McAllister Ranch, Fremont County, Wyoming...Sergeant."

"So I guess you know what an asshole is, don't you, 'Cruit?"

Wally caught himself short of saying, "Yeah, just lookin' at one," but thought better of it, and replied, "Yes, Sergeant, I've seen many."

"I'll bet you have," replied the Sergeant and then, after berating nearly everyone in the room, stomped out. Fifteen minutes later, the lights went out.

Wally looked over towards Matt and whispered, "This ain't what I expected, did you?"

Matt, who was fading fast replied, "No...he's a loud-mouthed son-of-a-bitch."

Wally was pleased to know that he wasn't the only one who thought so.

So...after an exhausting thirty-hour bus trip, being sworn in to defend the United States of America and being told "you're a sorry shithead," was not the glory and honor that Wally had anticipated.

He lay there thinking about the most exciting part of all of it...pissing in a bowl and having it disappear by pushing a handle...whoosh! That was exciting!

With those memories locked in his mind, he closed his eyes, and although his feet were hanging a foot over the bent pipe at the bottom of the bed, he went to sleep.

Thus, ended the first day at the Induction Center in Fort Leonard Wood, Missouri.

CHAPTER TWELVE

INDUCTION, DAY 2

Wally had slept like he'd rarely slept in his life. At five a.m., he heard a strange sound like someone blowing a happy horn. Simultaneously, some asshole yelled out, "Everybody Up...Off and On 'Em!"

Wally wasn't ready to get up. Then the same asshole yelled, "You got fifteen minutes to shit, shower, shave, dress, make your bed and be in formation outside!"

"Holy Crap!," cried Matt, "That ain't enough time to do anything!"

Another Recruit commented, "Hell, I ain't got time to piss and shake it."

Others just jumped out of bed, pulled up the covers, tucking them in, putting on their khaki fatigues, pulling on their boots, grabbing their gear and rushing toward the "latrine." Wally was reminded that was the name the army used for the out- and bathhouse.

The entire barracks was in pandemonium. Panic seemed to be the prevalent mood.

Wally suddenly realized that all in life that mattered was at that moment! He shot from his bunk and began struggling with clothes, socks, boots and everything else. He barely had his bed remade when the same asshole yelled again.

"All out in formation!"

Wally was tucking in his shirt which was half in and half out, running down the aisle with unlaced boots, through the door, and almost down the steps when he realized he didn't have his hat on. He rushed back and was last to join in the formation...not unnoticed by the stomping Sergeant.

"You're a sorry-ass soldier, 'Cruit...what's your name?"

Wally stood there all six feet, six inches tall, with his fatigues six inches too short and arms protruding from the sleeves of his shirt, sporting a hat that was too small for his head and hair. He slightly grinned, standing at attention, and meekly answered, "Bearstone...Sergeant," then grinned with embarrassment.

The Sergeant, who was almost six feet tall, marched over and stood directly in front of Wally, and looking up into the face of a giant towering over him, "You think it's funny, do you? Wipe that smile off your ugly face and give me ten."

Wally, who didn't have a clue as to what he meant, said, "Ten what?"

"Ten what? TEN WHAT? TEN WHAT...SERGEANT!"

"Ten what, Sergeant?"

Realizing the giant kid sincerely didn't know what he was talking about, said, "Get down on your hands and knees...you sorry-ass."

Wally did as he was told.

"Now, kick your legs back and push yourself up and down with your arms...ten times."

Wally thought the whole things was kinda stupid, but threw his weight onto his hands, flexed his arms and lifted his entire up, including his extended legs and effortlessly raised and lowered his entire body ten times. He finished with his arms extended, holding his body at right angles in the air and said, "Now what, Sergeant."

The Sergeant, realizing that Bearstone had unintentionally made him look like a fool, said, "Just get up and get back in line, Bearstone!" He stomped, turned, marched, stomped and turned again just before running into the invisible wall, stomped again, returning to the front of the troops.

He yelled and told them to, "Right Face," and they marched off, arriving at the Mess Hall, which was where they were going to eat their breakfast.

It was a repeat of something they had done last night when they had a plate full of something that looked like someone had already eaten it, between getting their uniforms and the inspection. He wasn't sure exactly when, as he was too exhausted from the trip and everything that had taken place. He did remember it wasn't half as good as his Ma's...but it ate. At the time he thought they had named it right - Mess Hall.

This morning's breakfast was what they called, "SOS." It was a white gravy with some salty meat in it poured over toast. Someone told him it was called "SOS," meaning "Shit on a Shingle." Wally thought so too.

"Today," reported the Sergeant after breakfast, "You are going to do many things: First, you will go through a medical exam, get shots, get your eyes examined, have your teeth checked, get haircuts and learn to march." Then added, "not necessarily in that order."

After returning from breakfast, they went through a berating over the conditions of everything by the stomping Sergeant. He then marched them to the parade grounds where they were going to learn "*How* to march." That seemed to be important in the army.

There they learned to march, along with the commands needed to direct a formation. "March, Halt, Right Face, Left Face, About Face, Left, Right, Parade Right, Parade Left and Parade Rest." Wally thought it was all kinda neat. He learned something new. Then they tried it all out as they marched with a little pride, in step, back to the Mess Hall for lunch.

Lunch was a hamburger sandwich with mustard, ketchup, all the trimmings, potato chips, and carton of milk and a big, red apple. It was good.

Next, they marched to see the doctors who poked and prodded every hole in their body, had them cough, took their temperatures, checked their throats and ears and everything else. Other doctors asked them to read the letters on a chart with each eye. And while they took blood from one arm, they poked needles in the other squirting stuff in..

In another building they filled in paperwork and were given a number they said was important. It was the number that they called "your serial number... and started with the letters US," which Wally guessed meant your ass belonged to Uncle Sam. You were advised to memorize it. He did.

While some were seeing the doctors, and filling out papers, others went to see the barber. "You went in one end of a building and came out the other. While in there, they sat you in a chair, the barber wrapped a piece of toilet paper around your neck and wound you in a sheet and asked how you wanted your hair cut. Then ran the clippers over your head leaving you bald. Wally recalled shearing the sheep on McAllister Ranch and as he watched the massive amount of his kinky hair fall to the floor. He wondered if they saved it like wool or what they did with it? Since there were no mirrors in the place, he'd have to wait to see how he looked sheared bald.

After the afternoon's activities, they once again assembled. Everyone there was bald. All were looking at each other, laughing and making fun of each other. Wally hardly recognized Matt, who said he only knew it was Wally because he was so tall. Everyone was laughing and all was well.

After dinner, which was ham, macaroni and cheese, a green salad with Miracle Whip, a carton of milk, and followed by a piece of cherry pie. It all was delicious.

The troops were marched back to their barracks and dismissed. Some went in and stripped to their skivvies, grabbed their towels and headed for the showers. Others went to the latrine for the toilets, which are purposely set in the middle of the room where all can watch you wipe and clean yourself. This, to break any self-consciousness about being seen doing private matters. Others shaved, and for the first time saw themselves bald. Wally guessed that's what he'd look like when he got old. All were in bed with most asleep by "lights-out" at nine.

The sound of Taps signified the end of Day 2.

CHAPTER THIRTEEN

UP THE HILL

Five a.m. was no different this morning than yesterday. The same happy horn blower and the same asshole yelled in the barracks door, "Up and at 'em. You got fifteen minutes to shit, shower, shave, get dressed, make your bed and be in formation."

Wally slept the best he had for days and had trouble clearing the fog but was determined he wasn't going through what he did yesterday. He rolled out of his bunk, pulled the covers up and tucked them in. He pulled on his fatigues, socks, boots, shirt, stuck his hat in the rear pocket of his fatigue pants, grabbed his washcloth, headed for the sink and washed his face with hot water, pissed, but couldn't help himself...he stood and watched the water wash his urine around the bowl and through the hole in the bottom. Amazing.

He headed back and was out the door. He wasn't the first in formation, but he wasn't the last either, and stood at attention even before being told.

A whistle blew, "ATTEN-TION," and the stomping Sergeant arrived with his same pissed-off attitude.

Wally, remembering what he had said when they met him and agreed. Everyone hated his guts...or thought they did. They went through the same routine and marched to the Mess Hall for breakfast.

This morning, as they lined up to take their food trays, utensils and approached the cafeteria counter, they heard they were getting something special. They were treated to fried *Spam*, dry tasting scrambled eggs, cold and soggy toast with yellow-colored lard on it, canned orange juice, and coffee. Most ate in silence, a few spoke quietly to their closest companion.

Matt said to Wally, "If this crap is special, I'd hate to get punished!"

Wally mumbled with his mouthful, "It's okay." Then scuffed the last up, wiping the tray with a scrap of toast. It was food. He was accustomed to eating three to four times the amount served. Taste wasn't one of his priorities.

They were marched back to the barracks where they were allowed thirty minutes to do what they had to do...which was clear to all. Make their bunks, police the area of debris, shave or shit and get ready for a full day.

They lined up and marched to the parade grounds. There, they marched, and then they marched. After marching, they marched some more. Wally couldn't figure why they needed to march so much but he was soon to learn. He just didn't know it yet. All toll, they marched three hours. Then marched back to the Center.

They were lined up to receive more shots. Both Wally and Matt figured they were getting shots for any disease that there was...which was right. They just didn't know it. Matt allowed that his arms were going to be leaking like salt shakers.

Next, they were indoctrinated on what it means to be an American soldier and how to respect and handle the nation's flag. They all gave the Pledge of Allegiance to the flag.

Then they were given their metal "dog tags." There were two, one on a short beaded chain which was attached to the long chain holding the other. On the tags was their name, serial number, blood type... Wally's was type "A." It had the persons' religion listed...in Wally's case, since he didn't have one, they assumed he was Protestant.

They were then introduced to the technology of why the notches were in their dog tags...to wedge a person's teeth over them and then to kick their jaw shut...in case they're shot dead. "If they are, you take the tag on the short chain and turn it in to your leader. It was designed to give the troops some reality of war and why they were there. It worked.

Next, they were indoctrinated to the ranking systems for the army enlisted men, concluding with Officer ranks. They soon learned that Officers were almost next to God himself.

They were then introduced to members of the Gideon Society who talked about the Society and then gave out small Bibles. It was the first book that Wally had ever been given to keep. He thumbed through it with the thin pages and tiny print. He'd never been exposed to any faith but did recognize the smaller version of the Bible that McAllister had read from at his Pa's funeral.

They marched to the Mess Hall. Lunch consisted of navy bean soup with cornbread, coleslaw, milk, and another big, red apple. Wally gobbled it up thinking it was delicious.

After lunch, they were marched again to another building where they lined up. One by one, they were handed a small khaki colored canvas bag. By this time, Wally had learned to call it khaki instead of cow-shit brown. The canvas bag was filled with toiletry items: shaving soap in a tin can, a shaving brush, a safety razor, a package of razor blades, a tube of toothpaste, a tooth brush, a comb, a bar of soap in a container and a small metal mirror. All were in containers which were khaki colored. They were told it was a Dopp Kit and described it as something you will use the rest of your life.

Matt said he didn't think there was enough stuff in there to last that long but, "Maybe they know something we don't."

They were once again marched back to the same building where they had received their dog tags and Bibles. There they were instructed by an older Sergeant about how to use each of the toiletries. Most Wally knew, but some he didn't. Matt on the other hand was familiar with each but didn't need the shaving gear...yet.

As they were sitting in the classroom atmosphere, Wally began to feel the impact of his lunch. Not only did he have to piss like a Dutch's Uncle, he was feeling the pressure of gas brought about by the navy bean soup. They were sitting on folding wooden folding chairs and he had to fart. There was no way he could silently relieve himself. He'd just have to hold it.

The old Sergeant described the way to use toilet paper. All that either Matt or Wally had ever used, were sheets torn from the Sears, Roebuck & Company catalog. They listened and watched as the Sergeant said in the "C" Ration containers, whatever they were, there were five squares of toilet paper rolled into a small packet. It had to last all day. He said the proper way to use It is to fold one square into fourths and tear a small piece from the middle creating a hole in the center of the piece of toilet paper. He demonstrated and stuck his middle finger through the hole.

He said, "Use your finger to wipe, then grab the toilet paper and gather it around your finger, lifting it off to clean your finger. Take the remaining piece from the center to clean your fingernail."

Most of the troops laughed; however, Wally listened intently. He was learning something new. His awe was jerked back to reality when someone farted... followed by several others. Everyone broke out into laughter.

The old Sergeant laughed and commented, "My point, exactly!"

Wally, assuming it was alright to let go, did. He was disappointed it was silent...but destined to be deadly. There was a brief period before the stench drifted to the others.

Then someone sitting behind him said, "Jesus Christ...Bearstone! Hey Sarge, he needs toilet paper!"

All but Wally laughed. He forced a smile but was humiliated.

After the training class, they were told to march with the Dopp kit in their left hand and went to the Mess Hall. Dinner consisted of two slices of roast beef, tasting a little like cardboard, powdered mashed potatoes dented in the center and filled with a ladle of greasy gravy, canned green beans, a roll, a carton of milk, and a cardboard container of orange sherbet.

Marching back to the barracks there were numerous toots with the appropriate sniggers and moans. These were later referred to as "The Marching Farts."

They arrived at the barracks and were standing at parade rest when someone blew a whistle and yelled, "ATTEN-TION!"

Here came the stomping Sergeant. He said, "At Ease. Today, you are going 'Up the Hill.' Our time together has been a pleasure and is completed. Go into the barracks and pack all your military gear into your duffle bags. Take all your civilian items and pack them with your civilian clothes. Take a name tag from the pile as you enter, print your name on them, attach them to your bag and leave them on your bunk. They will be picked up and held in storage until you have completed basic training. Now, go and prepare to depart at 1700 hours. DIS-MISSED!"

Then he added, "Bearstone...remain in place!" The troops disbanded and went into the barracks.

Wally, wondering what the hell he'd done now, anxiously awaited.

The stomping Sergeant approached him and said, "Bearstone, you look like hell. We don't have any uniforms that will fit you so we're going to measure you to special order them for you." He turned and called out, "Corporal, approach."

A short Corporal approached and, taking a tape measure, measured Wally's inseam, arm-length, bicep and thigh dimensions, waist, hat size, etc. The Corporal asked, "How tall are you?"

Wally said, "Six foot, six inches...I think."

The Corporal made several notes and then finished. He nodded to the stomping Sergeant and left.

The Sergeant said, "We will send the new uniforms Up the Hill when we get them. Dismissed." He turned, without stomping and left.

Wally turned and went in. He didn't really hate him, after all.

"What did they want?," Matt asked.

"To measure me," remarked Wally. "They're making me new uniforms. Ones...that fit."

One of the other troops said, "Oh...thought maybe they'd thought you'd shit yourself." Several laughed.

Wally just laughed. It was a joke, and a joke is a joke. This was the type of razzing that he had experienced at the ranch. It kinda made him feel at home. His thoughts briefly glanced at what he had come from.

Most had speculated that Up the Hill meant they were going to "Boot Camp." This led to all sorts of tales spun about what was going to happen and what they had heard about it.

The next two hours passed by getting ready. The recruits were toileting, taking showers, shaving, or whatever they needed to do. By this time, the shots were starting to take their toll. Their arms were getting sore. It was becoming increasingly difficult to pack their things, roll their mattresses and tie them with the twine still left from checking in. Blankets were folded around their pillows, sheets, pillowcases and towels. All was gathered and piled on their bunks.

When the time arrived, they began carrying out their gear and piling in on the ground. It took several trips for some and less so for others. They were standing around when a parade of trucks began to arrive. They were flat-bed trucks with wooden side racks on them and a back-gate entrance.

As the trucks came to a halt in front of each of the numerous barracks, a soldier from each said, "Alright, using the 'buddy system,' get in and get your gear in." Wally and Matt agreed that they were being herded like cattle. Once in the bed of the truck, they were surrounded by bed rolls, duffle bags and all the bedding. There was barely room to move.

The loaded trucks rolled over bumpy roads, turning and twisting to an unknown destination. After fifteen or twenty minutes, they began to stop in rows at the center of a large quadrangle with barracks on all four sides.

Standing on the top of a stand with stairs stood a mean looking Sergeant with folded arms. He had a look of "You Don't Want to Mess with Me."

He didn't stomp...he just stood there looming and finally spoke in a booming voice, "Welcome to Hell, you bald-headed bastards!"

This got everybody's attention and drew comments from the new arrivals. Common among them was, "Oh Shit!"

"How many of you guys got Bibles?"

Since everyone had one, they tried to lift their throbbing arms.

"Well...you can pack 'em away, 'cause I'm your little Jesus from now on!" It was not a warm, welcoming speech. "I'm Sergeant Baker, your Drill Instructor, and I'm going to make men out of you bunch of Sissies. You Got That?"

Having been trained to respond loudly, "YES, SERGEANT!," they replied.

"Good, we've got that straight. Now, unload and as your name is called, you will be directed to a barracks. There are four companies located in this complex. Company A, B, C and D. Within each Company there are four Platoons. You will be assigned to one of these companies. As you hear your name...remember it. These will be your home for the next sixteen weeks."

At this point, another Sergeant began to call out names in alphabetical order. "Adams, Company A, Atkinson, Company B, and so it began. Wally was assigned to Company C, Building 301, as was Matt Carver.

They began the process of unloading there and lugging them across the vast parade area into the barracks buildings. It was a painful experience. They were tired, sore as boils, and if they had any sense at all...scared to death.

They entered their respective quarters which were two-story wooden barracks which are the same at every military base in the country. Both Wally and Matt found a bunk on the first floor and began to prepare it, longing to just drop in place. They untied their mattress, made up their bunk, and began to unpack their duffle bags loading them into their footlockers. The barracks was painted grey and had oak flooring. Unlike the Reception and Induction Center, all was immaculate. They had yet to experience...why?

The hour was approaching nine, when a Sergeant yelled, "ATTEN-TION!" The Sergeant who had yelled, walked in and stomped his foot down.

In walked a Lieutenant. This was the first officer that they had encountered. He seemed like an alright guy and was very sharp looking but had an arrogance about him that told you not to mess with him either. Regardless of how he sounded, he didn't seem like someone you wanted to hang around with.

He told them his name was First Lieutenant Powell and he was the Commanding Officer of Company C. He made some other remarks, most of which were unheard by the young soldiers as they were dead on their feet, and he left.

The Sergeant, after snapping to attention and saluting him as he left, remained.

"I'm Sergeant Swain, and I'm the Company C First Sergeant. You WILL be answering to me," he said. "Tomorrow is a big day, get some sleep, guys."

A Corporal yelled, "ATTEN-TION," and after dutifully stomping and everyone saluting, they left.

Wally got his area mostly finished, went to the latrine, watching with wonder how everything went down the hole in the bottom of the toilet when he flushed, and went back to bed. Matt was already sleeping. He flopped on his bunk, closed his eyes, and instantly went to sleep.

He didn't know whether the lights went out or not and definitely missed hearing Taps...which signaled the end the third day.

CHAPTER FOURTEEN

BOOT CAMP OR BOOT HILL?

"The same damned horn player's here too!," thought Wally, as he opened his eyes.

However, the guy who yelled in the door wasn't there anymore.

A booming voice from within the building called out, "Haul your lazy asses out of the sack, you meatheads!"

There stood First Sergeant Swain with his hands on his hips, fully dressed without a spot or wrinkle and boots shining like a glass bowl. "You got fifteen minutes to do what you need to and get your ass outside. Today's going to be a full one, so step lively, lads."

It was five a.m.

Wally knew the routine...they all knew the routine. Fifteen minutes later, they were standing at attention in front of their barracks, at o-dark-thirty, exhausting steam into the freezing air in front of Building Number 301 – Company C.

First Sergeant Swain, less stompy than Sergeant Johnson at the Induction Center, was sharp, disciplined and definitely someone you didn't want to mess with. "My job, along with the Drill Instructor, the DI, is to turn a bunch of undisciplined renegades into a fighting force capable of defending our country and the nation." This, in part, was his opening speech.

The difference between Sergeant Swain and the asshole at the Induction Center, was Sergeant Swain had sixteen weeks to do an unbelievable and near impossible task. Worse yet, he had to live with what he was able to create. There is a fine line between fear and respect. This was the line he had to walk to achieve his goal. The new recruits could feel the difference.

Sergeant Swain called the Platoon to attention and marched them to the Mess Hall. Where they had a choice of fruit, hot cereal or grits, scrambled eggs, fried potatoes, sausage or *Spam*...no decision here, hot biscuits or toast, and coffee or milk. Never in his life had Wally seen such a spread. Amazingly, it was as good as his Ma's cooking.

They were marched back to their barracks where they had one hour to get themselves showered, shaved, their bunks made, and everything in their foot lockers for inspection.

"This is alright," muttered Wally.

Matt agreed, "I thought this was going to be rough."

The other guys had similar comments.

When the hour had passed, each recruit was standing at the foot of his bed, next to his footlocker at attention...as ordered.

A whistle sounded, someone yelled, "ATTEN-TION," and in marched Lieutenant Powell and First Sergeant Swain. The lieutenant marched and stopped at each of the recruits and looked them up and down. That was the nice part...then he berated and yelled at each, criticizing each, tore through their footlockers, dumping in on the beds that he tore apart, yelled at the conditions of their boots and shoes, and so it went.

No one escaped the fury of the lieutenant, when he left, Sergeant Swain took over, making Lieutenant

Powell look like the good guy. There wasn't a would-be soldier in the room that wasn't trembling.

"You guys have humiliated and embarrassed me to death!," he yelled. I've been nice and what do I get? YOU KNOW WHAT I GET!"

"NO SERGEANT!"

"I'm going to get the shit beat out of me on my record. You guys have cost me everything I've worked for, for twenty years." He was red-faced, "You bunch of incompetent, ill-prepared, and undisciplined assholes don't know shit!"

He walked over and yelled into one of the guys, "Take a look at yourself...your boots look like you've been marching through pig shit, your gig-line is all over the place, you're a disgrace to the entire company!"

The berating went on for a while, then the Sergeant said, "We're going to spend the next day learning how to pass an inspection. We're going to spend the next day learning how to dress, we're going to spend the next day learning how to make a bed, we're going to spend the next day learning how to display your clothes and everything else!"

Then he walked in front of Matt and said, "You know what we're going to spend the next day doing, Private?"

Matt, not knowing how to respond, meekly replied, "No, Sergeant!"

Sergeant Swain yelled in his face so close that you could see the spittle spraying Matt's face, "WE'RE GOING TO GET YOUR SHIT TOGETHER!"

Having made his point, Sergeant Swain, turned and left.

One guy said, "That went well."

They were so terrified, that few, if any commented, let alone, dared to laugh.

Wally was certain he'd never seen anything like that in his life...which he hadn't. Probably, none of them had.

After a while, the guys started to get reorganized and back together, they earnestly began to take an interest in what they had been told and tried to remember what it was that they were shown. They had been humiliated by the one they didn't want to go against. Each questioned himself, "How can I make it better...how can I do better? I must succeed."

Sergeant Swain gave them enough time to do exactly what they were doing before returning. He arrived with the usual fanfare, this time with two more...a Sergeant, and a Corporal, and he began, "This morning is an example of what happens when you don't give a crap. This morning is an example of what happens when you think it's all a joke or a game. This morning is an example of not following orders and doing what you're told. There is a reason behind everything we do here, and that is to save your life!"

The recruits he was talking to had a hard time making the connection between "how you roll your socks...and saving lives." Wally and Matt both fit in with them.

Sergeant Swain continued as if he had read their minds, "What does all this have to do with saving a soldier's life, you ask?"

He paused and looked around and then continued, "Everything we do in the army is planned and has a purpose. Each activity in life has a purpose, but there is a time and a place for everything. It must...I repeat, it MUST be followed to the letter of the law. It must become routine and automatic. You must know where everything is, how it got there and what it is used for. You must get to the point where you never question yourself or others. Your life may depend on it!"

Everything he said was beginning to make sense to Wally. He had never thought about any of these things before.

Stg. Swain went on to say, "We are going to spend the rest of today learning about the way the army wants you to do things. What you think, or want, or how you want to do it...don't count. You're in the army now...and by god you *will* do it the army way."

He had made his point. The Sergeant who came with him said, "I'm Sergeant Smith, and we are going to learn how to dress and how to *properly* store your uniforms and the other accessories."

He walked around looking at each of the young recruits while he spoke. "Each of you go to your bunks. Dump all your clothing articles on them."

The recruits did as directed. Some groused at a quiet level, especially after just getting it all packed back in the footlocker.

Sergeant Smith went through each and everything in their footlockers, piece by piece and instructed them on how to fold it. They were told how to fold each sock and store it. Every T-shirt and skivvy bottom, their long underwear, their shirts, slacks, uniform tops, the tans, the fatigues, their jackets... nothing was overlooked.

Matt made the observation that there was a lot more room in the footlocker by doing it this way, to which Sergeant Smith responded, "That's why we do it, recruit...if it were pitch black in here, could you find your skivvies?"

Matt replied that he could and when he was asked "Why?," he replied, "because I knew where I put it and where to look...and how they were folded."

"Exactly," replied Sergeant Smith, "Corporal Riggs is going to go around and assist those who are having trouble."

Everyone worked at what they were doing, wanting to learn the "right" way. Some had problems, others didn't.

Then, Sergeant Smith said, "You were each issued a laundry bag. It is to be tied to the left leg of your bunk. You have two towels. One is to be in your footlocker, and the other...neatly folded in thirds over the foot of your bunk with your washcloth. Now, empty the contents of your Dopp kit on your bunk."

Each of the young recruits did as directed.

"In this kit are the basic necessities of every soldier for grooming: you have soap for bathing, something you *will* do every day. You have shaving soap, a brush and safety razor with spare blades...you are expected to shave every day, whether you think you need to or not. You have a toothbrush and toothpaste for brushing your teeth. You are to use it twice a day... every day. You have a comb and mirror...neither of which you need right now."

The last comment drew a snigger for all.

For most, this was not a new requirement, but for others, it was new. Those who come to the military come from all walks of life. Some never knew any of the above, Wally among them.

"You have two sets of towels and washcloths. When you have used the one towel and consider it dirty, let it dry overnight on the foot of your bunk until it is dry. Do not put damp cloth into your laundry bag. It mildews and stinks! You will turn in your laundry bag once a week which will be marked with your name and serial number and will include one pair of sheets and pillowcase, your dirty fatigues, skivvies, T-shirt and socks on Monday mornings on the way to the Mess Hall. Returning from the Mess Hall, you will pick up a clean laundry bag with one towel, one washcloth, and a clean set of sheets and a pillowcase. All of your uniform items will have your name and serial number on them and will be picked up at the same time the following week. When you return to your barracks, you will put them in their proper place before formation." The Sergeant was exacting in all things.

Wally liked it all. For the first time in his life, he had a positive direction. He was learning things that he didn't know...and why it was necessary. This was true for many recruits in Building 301, Company C... he wasn't the only one, of that he was sure.

Corporal Riggs also aided each of the recruits in the learning process of properly making a bed. They learned to make them tight enough to bounce a quarter on them. They showed them how to display their toiletries, cleaned and located in a specific location on a folded towel with the empty Dopp kit, opened and cleaned, displayed on their bunks for inspection.

They were instructed on how to polish their shoes and both sets of boots for inspection and how to neatly tuck in the shoe laces and place them under their bunks for inspection. They were taught how to polish their brass belt buckle and what was expected.

All in all, it was a very productive morning. They broke for lunch and were marched to the Mess Hall.

Lunch this day consisted of a bowl of soup, either Cream of Mushroom or Chicken Noodle soup, a ham and cheese sandwich, potato salad, a carton of milk, and either a banana or an orange.

Sergeant Swain informed them that they were issuing weapons to each of them when they returned. He marched them back to the barracks where he dismissed them for a latrine break and told them to stand by their bunks. They entered to find two guards standing on either side of a large wooden crate.

The recruits gingerly walked past this and went to the latrine. When they returned, they milled around their bunks.

Being called to attention, Sergeant Swain said, "At ease. We are now going to issue you with an M-1 rifle. Every recruit will have one, and each is responsible for that rifle until they are turned in after graduation from Basic Training. It is to be maintained in excellent condition at all times. It is the property of the U.S. Government. It is also a deadly weapon. It is used to kill the enemy."

"Over the next many weeks and the entire training period you will learn how to properly handle, use and care for this deadly weapon. You will learn how to take it apart and put it back together, even in the dark. You will learn how to fire it, clean it and handle it as if it were your own. When it is not in use, it will be safely stored on the racks which are designed to hold them. They will be under lock and key. Know the serial number on your assigned number and don't forget it." There was no doubt about this in anyone's mind. This was serious business.

Many there had never handled, or seen, a rifle. Wally had and was well trained by Lon Bishop who had trained him well. Matt, too, was trained and knew how to handle it. Other recruits were not from Wyoming.

"Guard! open the crates and stand by to distribute weapons," ordered Sergeant Swain.

"Yes, Sergeant!" The guards did as ordered with precision turning and foot stomping.

The guards opened the crates and as the men's names were called out, they approached and were handed an M-1 rifle, US Army issue, owned by the U.S. Government...just like them.

Sergeant Swain said, "Never, I repeat, Never...point it at anyone. Whether you think it is loaded or not. Always be aware of the direction of your weapon."

And so, it went for the remainder of the day. It was an afternoon of learning how to handle, disassemble and reassemble the weapon. They had brushes and swabs to clean and properly oil the barrel and clean the stock. They were becoming familiar with a heretofore-unknown factor to many and new respect for weapons by others.

Each had a storage slot on the rack. Each night they were secured under lock and key. Each was accounted for. Each had a responsibility to "stand guard" in two-hour shifts to ensure nothing happened to them. Everyone was instructed on how to become a guard, what was expected and to always be alert. They were also instructed on what would happen to them if they failed to follow every step and procedure.

They then practiced marching with their weapon. Several hours were spent on the parade ground marching, which many were still having trouble with, and now they had something else to worry about as well. They had a gun.

They marched directly to the Mess Hall with their M-1 rifles. They were taught how to properly stack them in triangles and Sergeant Swain "volunteered" guards to stand watch.

Dinner that night consisted of fried chicken, mashed potatoes with gravy, canned corn, a carton of milk and a piece of apple pie, all of which the men scarfed up without a complaint.

When they finished, they selected their M-1 rifles, and were marched back to the parade grounds where they spent another hour marching until the sun was starting to set. They marched back to the barracks and the first row of the platoon was "volunteered" and appointed to serve in shifts for the first night of Guard Duty.

The troops were dismissed, and Sergeant Swain, entering the barracks with them, supervised them finding their individual slots for their rifles and ensured each was in place before securing them. A padlock was inserted, and it was locked. Only Sergeant Swain had the key.

They came to attention, saluted and Sergeant Swain left. The troops headed for the latrine, showers, etc. They returned to a much more organized place, removed their fatigues placing them where they could be immediately accessed and hit their bunks...well exhausted, yet feeling a little more like soldiers.

In the distance, Taps could be heard.

Wally lay on his bunk listening to the strains of the now familiar tune and drifted off just before the lights went out.

CHAPTER FIFTEEN

THE CALM BEFORE THE STORM

Reveille sounded and the lights came on. There stood Sergeant Swain, and once again, all spit and polish...not a spot or wrinkle with shiny boots.

"Up and at 'em!," he yelled in his booming voice, "You got fifteen minutes to be in formation." He turned and left.

Wally was up like a flash, as was Matt and most of the others. There would not be a repeat of yesterday. Bunks were made right and tight. There was a dash to the latrine to wash their face and brush their teeth. Some took a leak and beyond. All made a dash and a quick review of the place and went outside to formation.

Those guarding the weapons were relieved by two Corporals, and they joined the formation.

They were called to attention and then marched without their weapons to the Mess Hall. Breakfast was once again a choice of fruit, today it was prunes or pears, grits or oatmeal, scrambled eggs, sausage, biscuits or toast, orange juice or grapefruit juice and coffee. It rapidly disappeared.

After breakfast, served in the Mess Hall which was a massive facility with hundreds of other recruits and was always well organized. There was no standing around so there wasn't any chance to get to know any of the other troops. The entire procedure was get in and get out. You got in line, you made your decision before you got there, took what was handed, went to your table, sat down, ate, policed your area, emptied your tray and returned to formation. Most of the time in the Mess Hall was spent standing in either the food line or the mess line waiting to get food or to turn your dirty tray and utensils back in.

Although Matt and Wally didn't have the chance to talk much, they were like Mutt and Jeff, always together. Of course, there are always comments between them, but seldom heard by others. They were becoming "buddies." Birds of a feather are always together...they were both green and from

Wyoming, and that's all it took. That was all they really knew about each other as well.

Sergeant Swain called the troop to attention, right faced them and marched them off. They had no idea where they were headed. This was not new, they were seldom advised. They would know when they got there. Today, it was a classroom.

As they entered, each took a chair in their habitual location and were seated. They waited.

An older Sergeant entered and stood before them with a chalkboard behind him. "This morning, we are going to address rank, uniforms and markings, insignia, proper gear and identification."

This was something that Wally was confused about. All the titles and markings on their uniforms... what were they and what did they stand for. Would he ever learn what they all meant?

The Sergeant droned on. "You guys are recruits... you got slick sleeves, which means you got nothing because you ain't nothing. You're the property of Uncle Sam and until you are fully trained...you will remain nothing."

"So much for how important I am," thought Wally.

"You are just a recruit, but some people will refer to you as Private. They are just being nice...polite, for you still are nothing. When you have finished basic training, and passed, you will be a Private, and have a chevron or insignia for your sleeve. It will look like this," he said and made a chevron on the blackboard.

"The next rank is called Private First Class and is identified by a rocker on the bottom," and made another mark on the blackboard.

The next rank is Corporal," and so it went. He droned on through the litany of ranks to Sergeant Major.

Somewhere between Staff Sergeant and Sergeant Major, Wally, who had been fighting going to sleep, finally lost the battle and drifted off.

Matt elbowed him, and Wally bounced up and said, "What?"

The Staff Sergeant replied, "The Sergeant Major, you will soon discover, is God himself! Did you get it this time? Recruit, and address me as Staff Sergeant in the future...did you hear that, 'Cruit?"

"Yes, Staff Sergeant," replied Wally, who was now... wide awake.

Once again, the Staff Sergeant began droning through the Officer ranks, markings, and insignia from Second Lieutenant, to First Lieutenant, Captain, Major, Lieutenant Colonel and full-bird Colonel. Then into the General ranks. The Sergeant had done it so many times, it is doubtful that he even had to think about what he was doing, and he couldn't care less about how exciting it was or wasn't.

The recruits had sat there for two hours right after breakfast, which was a killer, and all fought sleep.

Finally, the Staff Sergeant said, "We will have a ten-minute break to stand and stretch your legs. Dismissed."

No one moved as they weren't sure whether he had spoken to them or in their half-awake/half-asleep, it was a dream. When they did, they couldn't get out of there fast enough.

The next session covered what they could expect for their own uniforms. This and a quick break inspired a little more alertness. They were informed that the next building to the present one was a small PX or Post Exchange where they could get their uniforms altered to fit better, have their name tags sewn on, order hard name tags, and purchase brass insignia for their dress uniforms and hats. He went through where each item was to be placed or sewn on their uniforms. He also told them they could order a rubber stamp and ink pad for marking their uniforms with their serial number. Since everyone had similar clothes, identification was really more for their benefit than that of the soldiers.

The Staff Sergeant also advised them how to get the finish off of the brass belt buckle and other brass insignia so that they could keep It really clean by using *Brasso*. This too, was available at the PX.

"What items you need to purchase you may do so by giving your name, rank, and serial number and identify your Company and building number. The amount will be deducted from your first paycheck.

"Hell, that's no different than charging stuff at Ambrose General Store!," thought Wally, "We'll end up owing them more than we make."

When Staff Sergeant finished, First Sergeant Swain went to the front. He turned and addressed the troops, "You guys are about to enter the most difficult week that you have encountered so far. I'm not going to sugar coat it…it's a bitch, and when you think you can't do any more…you will…and then more and more after that. You've come a long way these last few days, but the main event is about to begin."

Sergeant Swain paced back and forth in front of the troops. He had a riding crop which he produced from god knows where and snapped it against his other hand. "Today, after we go to the Mess Hall, we're going back to the barracks, and since it's Saturday. You have the rest of the day off as well as tomorrow... Sunday."

The troops cheered. Wally hadn't even thought about what day it was. At McAllister's Ranch, there was no difference between one day to the next... except he would see Virginia on Saturday night.

"Oh Shit!," he thought, "I didn't let her know I was here."

"Take the time and use it wisely," the Sergeant went on.

"Explore the PX, pick up things you need like your insignia, order name tags, cigarettes, candy or anything else you want. Take a walk around Fort Leonard Wood and see what's here. Go back and polish your shoes and boots, clean your brass. Get ready, for Monday, first thing, you are going to have an inspection. We'll see how much you've learned and accomplished," stated the Sergeant.

"The Mess Hall is open for all meals throughout the weekend, but note the hours of operation. You can eat, or not eat...it's up to you."

"There is a chapel service at 0900 hours tomorrow at the base Chapel for both Protestant and Catholic's. It is voluntary; however, you'd be wise to be seen there," Sergeant Swain said, "Now, let's break, and we'll see you at 0515 hours Monday."

Someone yelled, "ATTEN-TION," all rose, the Sergeant left, and they were on their own for the first time in over a week.

Matt said, "You hungry?"

"I'm always hungry...Let's go," replied Wally.

They headed out for the Mess Hall. When they arrived, the place was two-thirds full already. When they saw what was on the menu board, it said "PIZZA."

This meant nothing to Wally...he'd never heard of it.

Matt had, and said, "WOW! Pizza...man, I love it."

Wally figured if Matt likes it, it must be alright!

They had pizza, three slices, a green salad with Italian dressing, *Coca-Cola*, and a paper cup of orange sherbet. Wally was a convert.

After lunch, they went to the PX and there picked up their brass insignia for their uniforms and ordered their name tags, and a combination padlock for their footlockers. They also bought a *Shinola* Shoe kit containing, brown shoe wax, an applicator, a shoe brush and polish cloth; a can of *Brasso* and a package of cotton balls, some *Mennen* under arm deodorant… Matt told Wally about the deodorant and he needed to get it.

Wally had never heard about it, but he was assured, by Matt, that he needed it so he bought it along with some candy. They also bought fingernail clippers, a pocket knife, a writing tablet and pencils and Wally bought a post card showing the front gate of Fort Leonard Wood. He was reminded by the clerk in the PX that he would need a postage stamp as well.

They returned to the barracks with their treasures. Most of the other recruits had done the same thing. After putting their things away, and inserting and setting their combination locks, Wally and Matt took off to explore Fort Leonard Wood.

They walked for miles exploring the base. They located the movie theatre, the main PX, which was huge, the various Enlisted Men's Clubs including the USO Club, the Noncommissioned Officers' Club, and the Officers' Club...all of which were "Off Limits!" They found the Post Library, the Infirmary and hospital, and other support facilities, including the various hobby and craft workshops...it was an entire city and the biggest that either had ever seen.

Matt commented, "It's like the army has its own world."

Wally found it all overwhelming. It was all amazing beyond his wildest dreams. It was everything anyone would want or need. Everything was neat, orderly organized and there wasn't a cigarette butt anywhere! Everything was raked, no trash, no spare parts lying around. Boy, Lon Bishop would bust if he saw all of this.

It was all new and exciting to Wally, and the only person he had to share it with was Matt. He turned to him and asked, "Have you ever seen anything like this before?"

Matt looked back and shook his head, "Uh-uh."

Wally said, "Me neither."

Matt honestly said, "I ain't never been anywhere. I ain't never seen nothing like any of this."

The two begin to share their lives and experiences. For the most part, it was the first time either had ever told anyone about themselves. Matt and his family had a small ranch many miles away from the McAllister Ranch, in the middle of nowhere. They got a lot of odds and ends from a huckster who came every week or so.

Of course they grew most of their food themselves and the rest they bought from a general store when they took the buckboard into town. They didn't do this too often. They had gone to church on a regular basis, which was something Wally had never been exposed to. Matt had gone to a one-room schoolhouse, like Wally, but had finished.

Wally shared his life on McAllister's ranch and told about Lon Bishop and the other hands and told about Earlinda and his Ma being the cook and how his Pa was dead.

The boys began to bond as they explored and told about their lives, noting the similarities and differences. They each filled in the other on the differences. Wally found himself sharing things about himself, he didn't realize himself. They spent the entire afternoon exploring the military base and facts about each other. They became each other's best friend.

They approached the Mess Hall in time for dinner. After walking for miles, they were both starving. They joined the line, grabbed a tray and utensils and waited until it was their turn. The menu board for Saturday night was grilled cheese sandwiches, dill pickles, baked beans, fruit cup, a carton of milk and a choice of chocolate or vanilla ice cream. After jokes about the beans, the friends ate with great gusto. They finished and returned to their barracks.

When they got there, there was a large package on Wally's bunk. When he opened it, it was his new uniforms and instructions to turn in the old ones to the Company Commander for return.

After getting all of his clothes folded and correctly stored, Wally was a little pissed that he had to start all over, and said so.

Matt said it was no big deal…he'd help.

Wally, unsure whether the new ones would fit, got out of his old fatigues and slipped the new ones on.

"Perfect," replied Matt, "Try the top."

Wally did, and it too, fit. He tried the summer tans and they, along with his dress uniform, were all perfect.

"I guess that runt Corporal that measured me knew what he was doing," replied Wally. "You know...that stomping asshole, the Sergeant? Maybe he wasn't so bad after all. He didn't have to do what he did...but he did. Maybe he wasn't what we thought?"

"Guess all shit doesn't stink, does it?," replied Matt, then grinning said, "You're getting soft, Bearstone."

Wally took all the "too short" uniforms out from his footlocker and together they folded the new ones and packed them away.

They were nearly finished, when another soldier approached and commented, "You two playing house together or something?"

Matt, who was smaller than the recruit who had commented, said, "Why...do you want to play?"

"Naw...but I seen you two all day together and now you're folding clothes and all...what's going on?"

Wally, who had been sitting, got up and towering over the newcomer said, "We're just getting my new uniforms put away...wouldn't you know it, that stomping son-of-a-bitch Sergeant from Reception sent me a present. 'Cause I told him I didn't like what they gave me...too short. So, he begged for forgiveness and bought me a whole new bunch of them. Here, you can help."

He pitched a fatigue bottom at him. "Thanks for asking."

The newcomer, dutifully intimidated, said, "Sure," and began folding Wally's fatigue pants.

Turns out the guy's name was Charlie Yates from Chicago, Illinois. He was lonely, with good reason, and just wanted to be a part of something. He had the knack of rubbing people the wrong way, although not a bad sort.

They polished shoes, and both pairs of boots. Charlie showed them how to spit shine their boots... he'd watched a shoe-shine boy in Chicago do it. He also showed them how to remove the lacquer from the brass insignia and belt buckle and polish it. As it turned out, he'd been in the PX and having no one to hang with had followed them most of the day.

The three soon began to compare stories, kid and joke and build a camaraderie that none of them had ever had. They each had something to teach the other. All were willing to learn and be a part of something bigger than themselves. They talked for hours.

After a while they wore down and started to yawn. It was getting late. So they headed for their own bunks , said "Good night," and headed out.

Wally had his old uniforms neatly packaged in the packaging from his new ones, and had set them aside to turn-in the next day. At Matt's suggestion, he wrote a "Thank You" note to whoever sent them...in case they ran into him again.

Since he had not had a chance to shower since arrival, Wally grabbed his Dopp kit and towel and headed to the showers. He had never had a hot shower with indoor plumbing so was looking forward to it. They were empty when he got there so he stripped, turned on the faucets and as the water began to pour, it was too hot and then too cold and then he learned to adjust them to get the right temperature. He decided he could get used to this. He stood and allowed the warm water to run over his body. He felt himself relax and was satisfied with his decision to join the army. It's a good thing, the army.

He got out, dried off, applied the new *Mennen* deodorant, brushed his teeth, both newly acquired habits and pulled on a clean pair of skivvies and a T-shirt, then headed for his bunk. He hung the damp towel over the foot of his bunk, put his soiled clothes in the dirty clothes bag tied to the left leg. He carefully placed his toiletries on the self to dry and crawled in between the two white sheets.

"This is a good life," he thought, "Good food, good friends, a good, warm shower and a clean bed. I guess it don't get any better than this." He closed his eyes and listened as Taps ended his day.

Wally slept well and was awake before the sun came up but was in no hurry to start the day. He was well organized; he was clean and had clothes that fit, and that was as far as it went. He was well prepared, but no place to go.

Matt, who was also awake rolled over and said, "Let's go to the Mess Hall and go to the chapel, what do you say?"

Wally, who had never been to a church, was hesitant, "Yeah, let's go to the Mess Hall." He got up, got dressed and headed for the latrine.

Matt came in with his Dopp kit and brushed his teeth. He shaved and said, "You didn't say whether you'd go to the chapel...will you?"

Wally said, "I've never been to a church before... won't know how to act."

Matt replied, "I've never been to an army chapel before, so I won't neither. Let's give it a try."

"How long does it last?"

"Don't know...but it can't be that long...anyway, we got all day."

"Okay...if you will, I will."

Charlie entered. "Morning guys, where you headed?"

"The Mess Hall."

"Can I go with you?"

"Sure...we're going to the chapel, too," replied Wally, "You can come with us, if you want."

"We'll see," replied Charlie.

They finished getting ready and they left, walking on the same path they marched on and without being aware, were walking in lockstep with each other. When they arrived, it was not overly crowded. As they viewed the menu board, it was the others' loss. This morning's fare consisted of fruit cup, French toast with maple syrup and sprinkled with powdered sugar, bacon and coffee.

The server even offered extra pieces of French toast if they wanted.

Though two of the three didn't know what it was, but they said, "Yes."

Both Wally and Matt approached the French toast with a slight hesitation but after tasting it, scarfed it down. They casually sat and ate their breakfast without being rushed. It was nice.

Charlie told them how they fixed the toast and pronounced it a good sample. How he knew, they hadn't figured out...yet.

After they finished, the trio walked out into a sunny, but cold early winter day and headed for the chapel. Matt was okay about going, Wally wasn't sure, and Charlie went along to be with someone.

The Chapel was plain, but a very pretty one. It was a white building with a steeple and a set of large double doors in the front. A wing was added to either side.

They entered a small vestibule and then the chapel with a center aisle and saw polished oak pews in rows on both sides, oak flooring with a red-carpet runner leading up to a raised platform with an altar. In the center of the altar was an open Bible surrounded with two lighted candlesticks and a large bouquet of fresh flowers behind it. The platform where the altar was extended across the entire front of the sanctuary and had a two-story high ceiling.

WHERE ARE YOU, WALLY BEARSTONE?

Both sides of the sanctuary had windows with yellow glass and, to the rear of the sanctuary, behind the altar, was a large, round stained-glass window depicting a dove descending with an olive branch. It was beautiful. Soft organ music was playing.

Wally, not sure about being there, followed Matt to the pew. The two sat. Then Charlie appeared. He didn't want to miss out on anything, so he joined them after all.

The Chaplain rose and welcomed them and after an opening prayer, announced the first song, "Shall We Gather at the River" number 723.

Wally noticed a slotted wooden board on the wall in front with a list of numbers and 723 was shown as the first. Everyone around them was singing, including Matt, who had a good singing voice. Wally, who had never sung, and Charlie silently held their hymnal and followed the words.

Then they took up a collection. The boys just passed the plate. They sang "Praise God From Whom All Blessings Flow," and the Chaplain prayed again. When the Chaplain stood to give the morning prayer, he prayed for the President, the Vice-President, and all the generals, and troops in harm's way in Germany and in the South Pacific, and on and on and on.

Then they all sang "The Battle Hymn of the Republic," No. 717, and only Matt sang with the others following the words in the hymnal.

The Chaplain's sermon was about facing fear even in the face of death; that God is with you. He said it is then that Jesus Christ carries you safely in his arms.

And so, went their first service.

As they were leaving, the Chaplain, an army Captain, stopped them, shook their hands and said, "Welcome, men. I'm glad you're with us."

To Wally, it was something he would remember for a long time. Never in his life had he heard the things that were said or the songs that were sung. He wondered how the Chaplain knew him for he was talking right to him in the sermon.

Matt felt good and said it was a good service. Even Charlie said he was glad they went and then added, "What's next?"

They explored more of the base and then headed for lunch.

The Mess Hall was packed. They stood in line for what seemed like an hour. The menu was roast pork and dressing with gravy, mashed sweet potatoes, buttered beets, green beans, milk and a piece of cherry pie.

Charlie announced with great flourish, that it was "food was fit for a king!"

They all laughed and agreed, then left. They ambled back to the barracks.

Wally took the package of his original uniforms to the Company Commander's office. The Company Clerk said he didn't know what to do with it, but said he'd find out and take care of it. Wally returned to the barracks where he decided he'd write the picture Post Card to Virginia, letting her know he had arrived. He did, saying: I have arrived, and addressed the card to Miss Virginia Bland, Lander, Wyoming. He licked the stamp and pasted it on the Post Card. Ready to mail. Then he laid down and took a nap.

The others had taken a nap as well, and all three had slept through dinner. The rest of the evening was spent playing games with the deck of cards that Charlie bought at the PX, while sharing tales of the past and thoughts about the future.

Sergeant Swain had told them it was going to be a difficult week. Little did they know.

CHAPTER SIXTEEN

THE DEVIL OR THE D.I.?

Morning came and so did Sergeant Swain, sharp as usual. The troops were up and quickly in formation by 0515 hours and apprehensive about what the day would hold for each of them. They marched to the Mess Hall and ate whatever was served, and returned to the barracks. Sergeant Swain informed them that they had fifteen minutes to do what they needed to do to prepare for inspection.

Wally wasn't too concerned about that, for he had spent part of Saturday and Sunday both, in getting organized. He went to the latrine, shaved, brushed his teeth and returned, opened his footlocker and displayed all of his toiletries on the bed as instructed and was ready. Matt had done similarly and both were standing in the right spot when Sergeant Swain shouted, "ATTEN-TION!"

Lieutenant Powell, the Company Commander, along with Sergeant Swain marched to the end of the room and with much pomp and stomping. Stopped, turned and looked the first recruit directly in the eye and said, "Are you ready for inspection, Private?"

The recruit said, "Yes, Sir!"

Lieutenant Powell looked him up and down, then at his bunk, his footlocker, looked at the shoes and boots under his bed. All was fine.

Lieutenant Powell said to Sergeant Swain, "Passed."

Then he went to the next one and repeated the process.

It seemed like it took forever until he got to Wally, who was standing at attention. Lieutenant Powell looked up at Wally's face, it was freshly shaved.

"Are you ready for inspection?," he shouted.

"Yes, Sir," replied Wally. His uniform was neat and properly tucked in, his gig-line was correct, his shoes were clean and polished, his bunk was tight, his toiletries and Dopp kit were correct, the shoes and boots under the bed were polished, his towels folded correctly. Each thing that Lieutenant Powell checked, he studied, and Wally sweat.

"Passed," stated Lieutenant Powell, and went to Matt.

Wally let a small sigh and his stomach relaxed and thought, "It's Matt's turn to sweat."

Matt passed as well. Charlie passed. In fact, the entire Platoon passed. Not one demerit, and they were all relieved that last week's disaster was not repeated.

Lieutenant Powell stopped, turned with much stomping, and Sergeant Swain stomped. They both saluted each other and Lieutenant Powell said, "Sergeant, your Platoon has passed. Excellent job." He turned and left.

Sergeant Swain yelled, "At Ease."

The men relaxed, yet unsure as to what to do or say...or just shut up.

"Platoon, you have done a good job. Now, secure your gear and be in formation in ten minutes." He turned and stomped off.

They were all in formation and Sergeant Swain said, "ATTEN-TION!"

They all jerked to attention, and Master Sergeant Baker appeared. He was larger than life and the son-of-a-bitch that had welcomed them the first night...if you could call it that.

"You bunch of pussies have had it easy for a week. Now it's time to begin making men out of you. Any of you cunts know what PT is?"

No one responded.

"Didn't think so. You're a bunch of weak sister's aren't you? Well...we're going to do something about that. From now on, we don't march like you've been doing. We're going to double-time. We're going to double-time everywhere we go. You're going to double-time in your sleep."

The Master Sergeant then shouted out, "Right Face! Forward March...Double Time!"

The men began to double time, which was, as the name implied, half-running, half-marching.

"Left, left, left...left, right, left," and off they went.

After an hour, they were still double-timing. A few of the men were beginning to hurt. Particularly the smokers, a habit that Wally had never started. Some of the men were holding their sides, but they kept on running. The Master Sergeant was running with them, so it wasn't like he was punishing them. They double timed to an area in the middle of nowhere.

They came across an area which was a huge obstacle course. As they entered the area, it was covered with walls that had openings like windows, there were walls ten or twelve feet high, there were poles strung with nets, old tires alternately placed in double rows on the ground. There were hills in the area with well-worn paths up and down. Another area had buildings with no backs. It seemed like it was a large playground...Wally doubted that it was.

Finally, the Master Sergeant should, "Halt! Take ten."

Many of the men were gasping for air and holding their sides. Steam was pouring from all of their mouths. All were glad for the ten minutes break.

Wally, Matt and Charlie were among those who were not smokers, yet they all were beginning to hurt as well. Charlie was hurting the most, but was putting on a happy face. He was not an athletic person. Wally and Matt were ranchers, they were used to hard labor, but not so great at running.

Wally said under his breath, 'That son-of-a-bitch damned near killed some of 'em."

Charlie sniggered, "You mean Little Jesus?"

There would be no Mess Hall. A truck pulled in and off-loaded what would pass for lunch. They didn't have time to check it out for the Master Sergeant called them back and told them what was going to happen. They were given detailed instructions as to what must be accomplished and they began.

They ran, they exercised doing jumping jacks, they twisted, they did push-ups the way you are supposed to, they did sit-ups, they bent over and touched their toes, they squatted. Wally couldn't figure out why all this was necessary but was sure it had a purpose. He easily did all that was required. Towering above the rest, he was easily noticed by all, including the Master Sergeant who had been observing him. He walked over to him and said, "What's your name 'Cruit?"

"Bearstone, Sergeant!"

"Where you from, 'Cruit?"

"Wyoming, Sergeant!"

"I'm putting you in charge of your Platoon. You're the Platoon Guide."

"Yes Sir...Sergeant Major. Thank you...what does that mean, Sergeant Major?"

"That means you got forty-eight recruits you're responsible for...that's six squads. You appoint six

Squad Leaders that will be responsible to you. How you do that is up to you." With that, he turned and walked away. They finally broke for lunch.

The Sergeant Major assembled the men and announced, "Private Bearstone is your new Platoon Guide. He will be appointing six Squad Leaders and each squad will consist of eight men. These men will become a team. You will eat together, you will meet together, you will train together...you will shit together. Now, go get some chow."

The men lined up for lunch. Today was baked beans and franks, canned spinach, milk and a banana.

Charlie announced, "Stand by for the toot line."

Matt asked Wally, "What's all this Platoon Guide stuff?"

"Damned if I know...but I am it," replied Wally, "You want to be a Squad Leader?"

Matt replied, "Yeah, I guess."

Wally called out to Charlie, "Hey...you want to be a Squad Leader?"

"Sure...what do I do?," replied Charlie.

"You lead a squad, asshole," yelled one of the troops.

The Sergeant Major yelled, "Off and on 'em!"

More exercises, only this time they danced through old tires, back and forth, over and over, then they crawled through sewer pipes. Matt's knees were nearly raw, as were his elbows. So were Wally's and Charlie's. Still they crawled. It seemed like this was the favorite of all the sadists.

They worked in the "Playground" until after 1700 hours. Then they lined up in formation and double-timed all the way back to the barracks.

When they were dismissed, Charlie commented, "Man...did you hear the Marching Farts coming back? They were in double-time! Putt, putt, putt."

Matt, getting into the shower said, "God, my knees and elbows are bleeding. What the hell was all of that crap? I gotta get something to cover them with."

Wally checked his, and agreed. They needed something. He heard someone say that Kotex pads would work. He'd heard the ranch hands talking about Kotex. He also knew what they were for. "I'll be damned if I'm going to wear Kotex on my elbows and knees.

Charlie remarked, "That's good, for I'm not going to buy them for you or anyone else."

The trio finished their showers and put on a clean set of fatigues, hanging their dirty set to dry on the foot of their bunk.'

They were in formation and double timed to the Mess Hall. The menu board told them they were having spaghetti and meatballs, a spring salad, which looked like all the other salads, garlic bread, beverage of their choice and Rainbow sherbet. All three ate like horses.

They double timed back to the barracks, were dismissed, and headed for their bunks. The day had been exhausting for all of them.

Wally, asked Sergeant Swain if he could talk with him a minute. The Sergeant agreed and said, "What is it Bearstone?"

"Sergeant, what does a Platoon Guide do?," Wally sincerely asked.

"A Platoon Guide is in charge of the Platoon. He's the boss and responsible for keeping them in line. He's also responsible to listen to them and looks out for their well-being as well. The Platoon Guide is responsible for communicating orders and reporting to me or the DI. The Platoon Guide is their leader and must be someone for them to look up to."

It was a lot for Wally to take in. "How do I pick the Squad Leaders, Sergeant?"

"The Squad Leaders have seven men to do the same thing the Platoon Guide does, except they answer to you. Pick people you think you can trust and ones that have leadership skills. Since they report to you, you have six people to manage and they each have seven. That's called the Chain-of-Command. Like I answer to the Sergeant Major and he answers to the Commanding Officer."

They spoke a little longer about what needed to be done.

Wally, who thought he had it, snapped to attention and saluted Sergeant Swain, "Thank You, Sergeant." He did an about face, and went into the barracks.

He approached Matt and Charlie and told them what the Sergeant had said. They both thought they could do the job, so Wally had two out of six. Now... who should the others be? Imitating Sergeant Swain, he yelled out, "ATTEN-TION!"

The whole barracks drew up to attention, and waited to see who was coming.

Wally, acting like he thought a Platoon Guide should act announced, "My name is Wally Bearstone, and I'm your Platoon Guide." He liked the sound of that.

"I need to appoint four additional Squad Leaders, we already have two...Matt Carver and Charlie Yates. Is there anyone here who would like to be a Squad Leader; otherwise, I will appoint someone?"

There was discussion of what a Squad Leader did, what their responsibilities were, etc. One guy, Lawrence Taylor said he would be willing to lead a squad. He was followed by another Dwayne Duncan.

Wally thanked them and asked if there were any more. No one responded, so he looked around and saw a couple of guys he thought could do the job. He "volunteered" them and that was that.

"We will have a meeting of Squad Leaders in five minutes," Wally said and headed for the latrine.

The meeting was held at Wally's bunk. The six gathered around: Matt Carver, Charlie Yates, Lawrence Taylor, Dwayne Duncan, Ray Green and Lenny Schultz.

He repeated to them what their responsibilities were, and they were to pick the seven men for their squad. How they did it, was their choice or problem. Once they had done that, there would be rearranging of sleeping arrangements so each man was with his squad and their leader. Being the Platoon Guide, he would be quartered upstairs in the room at the head of the stairs.

Wally wasn't happy about having to move away from Matt, but he had his orders too. One advantage, he had his own room. There were going to be a lot of adjustments.

There was a lot of discussion and grousing, some complaining, a lot of activity. Wally hauled his footlocker, rolled his mattress with everything in the middle, and after four or five trips up the stairs, had his room in order. It wasn't much, but it was the first room of his own that he had ever had. It even had a real door!

Matt and Charlie came up the stairs and joined Wally in his room.

Matt said, "Wow, this is neat. Lucky you."

"Good night for us," Charlie commented, "after the baked beans and weenies. The barracks is safe."

They all were laughing, when Wally farted and they rapidly bounded from the room, shouting back a goodnight mixed with other comments and headed down the stairs for their new locations.

Wally dropped onto his bunk. His elbows burned, as did his knees. He wondered how one could keep Kotex in place on your elbows, "Damn...they're sore as the devil."

The now familiar strains of Taps could be heard and shortly thereafter, the lights went out. So did Wally's, but it didn't last. He tossed and turned, and worried about being the Platoon Guide.

CHAPTER SEVENTEEN

LITTLE JESUS

Wally didn't sleep too well. His elbows hurt and his knees rubbed against the sheets. He worried about what was next and how he was going to manage everything. Then he thought about the McAllister Ranch and Lon Bishop, the foreman. Did he go through this? He guessed he probably did.

He just started to drift back into sleep when Reveille sounded and he knew Sergeant Swain would be standing downstairs yelling to "Up and at 'em."

He was up, tightened his bunk, put on his fatigues, socks and boots, grabbed his Dopp kit and headed to the latrine. It was crowded and everyone was dreading the day. Wally was too.

In formation, the newly appointed Squad Leaders, lined up with their squads. With Wally in the front row next to Matt. Sergeant Swain did his usual and they double timed it to the Mess Hall. They had apple juice and gobbled down the sausage gravy and biscuits, fried potatoes and coffee, and doubled timed back to the barracks. Where they changed back into their dirty, but dried fatigues from yesterday.

The Sergeant Major was out in front for formation and they were soon double timing back to the Playground where they began with exercises. Still sore from the day before, they grunted and groaned and silently cursed Baby Jesus. He was a son-of-a-bitch, and there wasn't a soldier there that didn't think so.

If they thought they exercised a long time yesterday, today was even longer. When they did the squats, they could feel their knees rub against their pants and hurt even more. They danced through the rubber tires, and crawled through the freezing sewer pipes.

It was nearly Thanksgiving and the weather was freezing cold, the ground even colder. They painfully crawled over the hard frozen ground, each silently begging for a different exercise, but it didn't come.

They broke for lunch which wasn't nearly as good as breakfast and were back at the exercises and training. With the exception of a ten minute break, they worked solid until time to double time back to the barracks at 1630 hours.

The Sergeant Major ridiculed, put down, and berated them all with a constant string of obscenities and insults. They hated him and they had only just begun. He pushed them to do far more than they thought they were able to do. When they were worn out, he called for more. Wally noticed that some of the men were on the verge of tears.

Wally was worried that some of the men wouldn't make it. He was so quiet that Matt remarked, "What's wrong with you?"

Wally said, "I'm just worried about some of the men."

Matt replied, "Hey, don't get too carried away with the Platoon Guide thing."

Wally said, "I can't help it."

Matt asked, "How much more are they paying you to do that."

"Nothing," he replied.

Matt informed him, "If you're making the same as before, why are you worrying about it? If you don't worry so much, are they going to pay you less?"

Matt had a point. The guys probably wouldn't break. But god, it was tough. Wally, himself, was pushed to the limit and he was in a lot better shape than most of the others. He looked over at Charlie who had a slight frame and was struggling, but working as if trying to prove something to himself. He didn't know much about Charlie, but would make a point to find out.

Meanwhile, they had to get through this day. They did. Then with great effort doubled timed it back to the barracks. Where they headed for the warm showers, cleaned up and were back in formation to double time to the Mess Hall.

Dinner that night could have been horse manure and they would have eaten it. Fortunately it was ham, macaroni and cheese, coleslaw, milk and apple crisp, which was delicious. They ate with much gusto and headed back to the barracks.

Wally went to his room upstairs and sat on his bunk.

"Now what?," he thought and then wondered if he had said it out loud.

He was comfortable with Matt and Charlie and missed being around them. Being a Platoon Guide isolated Wally from the rest. It was a feeling that, only a few weeks ago, wouldn't have bothered him; however, it did now. He enjoyed the camaraderie.

He grabbed his Dopp kit and a towel then headed to the latrine. After using the toilet, he shaved and brushed his teeth. Charlie came in and stood at the next sink to his.

"What's happening?," remarked Charlie.

"Getting ready for bed...I need it," said Wally.

"Man...I hurt like hell. But that bastard's not going to get me down. He may think he's Little Jesus, but he's not. He's one sadistic son-of-a-bitch!"

"Ain't getting to me, neither," agreed Wally. "Hey, tomorrow we take our rifles to the range."

Charlie said, "Maybe we can use him for target practice! Hell, he'd probably enjoy it!"

"At least we won't have to crawl, I hope!"

Matt entered and remarked, "Great minds think alike." He sat down on the toilet. "My butt's the only part of me that don't hurt."

"We were just talking about that," said Wally. "We're going to the firing range tomorrow."

"We're shooting at the Master Sergeant instead of Hitler," said Charlie.

"Good idea," agreed Matt and then farted.

"Say something?," asked Charlie

"That was Moose-a-linni talking," said Matt.

The three all laughed. This was what Wally missed, but he didn't know how to tell them. His feelings were something that he had never learned to share with anyone. It was like a gigantic wall was around him and even he couldn't break through it.

Matt, as if reading his mind, asked, "How's the ivory tower upstairs?," as he was finishing the paperwork.

"Quiet," commented Wally, "No bull shit going on!"

Charlie piped in with, "I miss your ugly face too, Wally," and spit out the toothpaste from his mouth.

They cajoled a little longer and said goodnight.

Wally went upstairs, and Matt and Charlie joined their respective squads.

Taps played and lights were out, but Wally lay there staring into the darkness. He was thinking about everything that was happening to him and finally drifted off to sleep.

Over the next several days, the trainees had their M-1 rifles and after double timing to the range. They learned to fire their rifles which heretofore had been only props for marching. Before this part of their training is over, they will become weapons.

The Sergeant Major pushed them beyond what they wanted. Their arms and shoulders were sore from the butt of the rifle recoiling into them. They ran and dropped to their bellies, and learned to fire with precision. Wally had no trouble with this effort. He was an excellent shot. Matt, too, had grown up with guns and did well; however, Charlie had difficulty. His slight frame and inexperience in handling weapons left him void. He had never fired a weapon. He had to work twice as hard as the others, but felt driven to succeed. He was lacking the coordination necessary to fully achieve what was required. Sometimes, he couldn't hit the target, let alone the bullseye. The Master Sergeant ridiculed and put him down by making fun of him.

By the end of the week, all three of the boys were worn down with every muscle in their body aching. They also had another thing in common, they hated the Sergeant Major.

"I got scabs on my scabs," remarked Charlie, "but I ain't letting that bastard win."

Wally, who had watched Charlie struggle, said, "You're trying too hard. Relax a bit and take your time."

"How can I with that bastard breathing down my neck."

"It ain't going to be easy, but ignore him," commented Matt, "Easy for you two to say!"

They were in the Mess Hall, and he was struggling with his tuna fish casserole. He'd learned that if you didn't like what was served, you went hungry. Tonight he was so hungry he had to try to eat it. He hated fish so added any condiment he could find to cover the taste.

Over the next two weeks they learned to crawl through near freezing mud, in the rain/snow with their M-1's. They were trained to do so under live fire overhead. They had night fire training until nearly 2200 hours. They had "search and cover" and crawled under barbed wire so close to their backs they didn't think it possible. They played war games pitting squad against squad, platoon against platoon.

With Wally's and Matt's help, Charlie finally could hit the target and had a couple of shots near the bullseye.

Thanksgiving came and they had the day off. The Mess Hall had gone all out with turkey, dressing, mashed potatoes and gravy, candied sweet potatoes with raisins, jellied cranberry sauce, green bean casserole, and a choice of pumpkin or minced meat pie. Wally, who had never celebrated Thanksgiving, thought the food was the best he'd ever had in his life.

The weather had turned from slushy rain to snow which didn't help, for they still had training. On Friday, they went into an unfamiliar room with gas masks on, then told to remove them. The room had been filled with tear gas which took them by surprise and their objective was to find their own way out. Staggering outside in the snow, they were gasping for breath and struggling trying to wipe their eyes. And altogether, a totally unpleasant experience.

"I'd bet that damned DI had something to do with this crap," said Charlie.

Matt, who was still coughing, just shook his head.

Wally said, "Uh huh!"

Later that day, they had a training film on frostbite, which showed pictures of people with half of their fingers off and black feet with infection oozing out of them. Charlie said he was glad they'd already had lunch.

Saturday's inspection went well without incident as did the next three weeks. There was talk about getting off for Christmas, but it was only rumor. No one really knew.

They were feeling better about themselves, certainly looking better. All three were solid muscle, filled out and had their uniforms altered to fit. There was a camaraderie between the three that few had. They were best buddies.

On Saturday, after inspection and mail call, it was announced that Leave would be granted during the week between Christmas and New Years Day.

The trio was discussing what they would do, when Charlie surprised them by producing three roundtrip train tickets to Chicago that his parents had sent. He had written to them about the possibility of coming home for Christmas and that Wally and Matt would probably come with him as well.

"My mother and father have invited you to come for Christmas, if you'd like to?"

Both Wally and Matt were overwhelmed and didn't know what to say.

"Come on guys, please come to Chicago with me," pleaded Charlie.

"Oh, Hell yes!," remarked Wally.

"You betcha!," added Matt.

"Good, it's settled. We're heading to Chicago!," said Charlie.

The three were excited. They were going to Chicago in celebration of the birth of the baby Jesus, not the son-of-a-bitch who thinks he is.

CHAPTER EIGHTEEN

CHICAGO, THE QUEEN OF CITIES

It was Saturday morning and the boys, dressed in their Class A Dress Uniforms were all spit and polish with shiny boots. They carried matching bags they purchased at the PX and had them crammed full of underwear, socks, their Dopp kit and other needs.

They took the early Greyhound bus from Fort Leonard Wood to St. Louis. Wally and Matt were silent when they saw the size of the town and especially the Union Station. St. Louis' Union Station is the largest train station on one level in the world. Never in their life had they seen anything like it. To both, it was like going into another world.

Charlie, took charge. He guided them to the large Departure Schedule listed above their heads. They had tickets for Chicago's Union Station on South Canal Street. Charlie noted the train number and they went to the appropriate gate. They waited for nearly an hour and then boarded. The whole thing for Wally and Matt was an adventure from one distraction to another.

They sat in facing seats with the fourth seat occupied by another soldier going home. He, too, was based at Fort Leonard Wood in the Engineering School. They told him they were in basic training.

He introduced himself as "Joe."

Since they had name tags, there was no reason to give your last name. Joe's last name was Olstead. The train was packed with every seat taken. It was December 1944, and most of the travelers were soldiers. The St. Louis Union Station had about 100,000 passengers a day going somewhere.

They talked about basic training and Joe talked about the engineer school. By the time the train left, they were each sharing their experiences.

The trip was passing quickly. They had gone from Missouri into Illinois and stopped in a couple of small towns and then arrived in Springfield. There, some got off. There wasn't much to see and the chatter continued.

Six and a half hours later, they pulled into Union Station, Chicago, Illinois.

Neither Matt nor Wally had any idea of what to expect. Wally remembered his Pa's rendition of Chicago, but like many things his Pa had told him, he'd been wrong. He didn't know what could be there.

When they left the train, they walked into a gigantic facility. Wally couldn't even imagine anything man-made to be that big. As they walked up the ramp into the terminal, Charlie's parents were waiting for them. Mr. Yates was a stately, gentleman with graying hair and most intimidating. His mother was a beautiful woman, the likes of which he had never seen.

"Hi," grinning, his father said.

"Hi, honey," his mother said and threw her arms around her son.

Charlie, proudly said, "Mother, Father these are my friends Wally and Matt."

Mr. Yates shook their hands and said, "Welcome to Chicago."

Mrs. Yates went to each and superficially hugged each saying, "Any friend of Charles' is a friend of ours."

Wally had nearly the same feeling about Mr. and Mrs. McAllister. They were different.

They walked through the magnificent terminal and out to the front of the building where Mr. Yates had a car waiting. It was a long, black Packard. The driver opened the door for them and the four entered. Wally had never seen a car this big. In fact, he had never seen too many cars, and those that he had, didn't look like this one. It seemed like it was almost as big as the lean-to.

It was nearly 1500 hours so the sun shone upon all around them. Neither Wally nor Matt had ever in their lifetimes, ever dreamed of what they were seeing. The buildings were so high, they couldn't see the tops from the car windows. Everything was cement and groomed and polished. The streets were cement and smooth. The Packard glided over the surface like it wasn't even running.

There was a thin layer of snow on the ground, but Wally could tell from the shrubs and trees that the wind was blowing something fierce. He remarked, "It must be colder than a witch's tit out there."

There was an extended silence, and then Mr. Yates remarked, "Yes, it's definitely cold."

Matt, who had remained silent, added, "How cold is it?,"

Mr. Yates said, "It's in the low twenties."

"Like home," added Wally.

"And your home is where?," asked Mrs. Yates.

"Wyoming...Lander, or near there. It's about seventeen miles away from there," said Wally.

"My home is more remote," said Matt, "It's in the middle of nowhere."

Wally said, "We ain't got electricity or indoor plumbing...we use outhouses and Sears, Roebuck catalogs to wipe."

Mr. Yates, who had already sized up the backgrounds and realizing the lack of social graces said, "Did you know that Sears, Roebuck and Company headquarters are in Chicago?"

"No sh...," Wally caught himself using improper language, and didn't complete the sentence. His left hand going to his mouth.

The conversation came to silence and the boys looked out the window at the Queen of Cities, Chicago.

The buildings were huge and beautiful, the city was resplendent with boulevards and parks. People were everywhere. It was hard to believe that there was a war going on. Both Wally and Matt were gawking at everything.

Charlie, who had been quiet, finally added, "Wait until tomorrow, I'm going to show you all through the city. It's amazing," He then added, "Father, may I use the car tomorrow?"

Mr. Yates replied, "Of course you can, Charles."

Wally caught the name...Charles? What the hell's going on here, he thought.

Matt, who doesn't miss much, also heard it. Who calls someone named Charlie...Charles?

They drove north along Lake Shore Drive and entered through an iron gate. They drove towards a house that neither Matt or Wally could believe. It was a large stone structure with leaded glass windows. Everything was immaculate and well groomed. The driver pulled to the front door, exited, and opened the door for the four passengers. One by one, they exited and Mr. Yates went to the door which opened before they got there by a guy in a black, fancy suit.

Wally wondered how he knew they were coming, but didn't ask.

They were shown to their rooms, each had a bathroom, and were expected to dress for dinner. They had on what they brought and that was that. Nothing to choose there. It is what it is.

Charlie lightly knocked on Wally's bedroom door. Wally, never having a door for someone to knock on, wasn't sure what to do so walked over and opened it.

When he saw it was Charlie, he said, "Charles...I didn't know it was you."

"Knock that shit off, Bearstone...I've put up with that crap all my life. Give me a break." He walked in and sat on the foot of Wally's bed. "Everything has to be proper with them...like we're better than everyone else. I'm not, I'm just me. Yet people have treated me like I thought I was, and I don't."

Wally, who never in his life had to deal with that problem, was at a loss, "You didn't say your folks were rich."

"You wouldn't have understood. I've never lived up to their standards...never been anything compared to them. How the hell could I? Father was a star athlete, and mother was always in the spotlight. They never took the time to even change my diapers."

Wally not knowing what to say replied, "Well, you shouldn't have shit 'em."

Both laughed. Then Charlie, realizing that he had said too much, regained control and said, "At dinner, we will have something fancy that will be served by my folks employees. We are not to thank them, and wait until my mother lifts her fork or spoon and starts to eat before eating. No farting is allowed." He then sniggered and said, "No...Go ahead, fart at your own peril."

At dinner, it was as Charlie had cautioned. Everything was proper, or so Wally thought. How would he know? He wasn't smart about those things but he wasn't stupid either. Matt wasn't either. They did the best they could and hoped they didn't make too many mistakes. They both liked Charlie and didn't want to embarrass him.

Mrs. Yates, who tried to be hospitable, was condescending as was Mr. Yates. Both Wally and Matt...and Charlie felt it. They were being tolerated.

Dinner consisted of clear broth, braised squab under glass, served over wild and long grain rice, julienne beets in sour cream, and fresh strawberries in whipped cream over meringue. The wine was a fresh, crisp Chablis, which tasted a little like vinegar to Wally. Neither Wally nor Matt had ever had wine but drank it. The evening was completed by a small glass of *Drambuie.* Neither had ever had it either, but they drank that too.

With dinner over, the two excused themselves and headed for the large staircase leading upstairs and to their rooms. Having never had alcohol they both felt a little lightheaded, but made it up the stairs and into their rooms.

They both went into Wally's room and were talking when there was a tap at the door and it was Charlie. He entered and the three began a dissection of the dinner.

"What was that little chicken?," asked Wally.

"That wasn't chicken, it was squab."

"What in hell is...squab?"

"Pigeon," remarked Charlie.

 Charlie described it all and told them what it was. He was almost apologetic about the entire affair.

"This is the world I came from," he stated. "I was drafted and was happy about it. I wanted to get away and prove myself to me and the rest of the world...I guess?"

He sat for a few minutes, then added, "My father has connections and tried to get me out of the draft, but I didn't want that. I reported as directed. I've never been able to live up to their standards."

Wally now understood a little why Charlie was struggling so hard at the firing range and pushing himself at the other things. He was trying to succeed. The poor guy don't fit in anywhere.

Then he did something that he never thought he could do. He walked over to Charlie, put his hands on both of Charlie's shoulders and said, "You're alright, Charlie." It was awkward, but sincere.

Matt, uncertain what to do, reached over and hit him on the arm.

Charlie had never had friends. He had spent most of his eighteen years in life being catered to by nannies, cooks and chauffeurs. He went to private boy's schools, where he was not well liked, and often made fun of by classmates. He was a "C" student, and because his father's checks were very good and regular, given "B" grades.

Charlie had never really applied himself, for everything he did, he was criticized by his parents. It became a way for Charlie to get some attention. The poor kid wasn't good at anything. His father was on the board of directors of Swift Premium Meats. His mother was a spoiled only daughter of an auto manufacturer. Lack of money had never been an issue, but then again, he never really needed much.

Both Wally and Matt now partially understood why Charlie was the way he was. They couldn't fully understand because they had nothing to compare it to. Both of them had lived in near poverty and without most of their days. The army was definitely an improvement.

This was the first time the three had ever really talked about anything deep. They talked openly and freely until the wee hours in the morning. Wally told about his Pa and Ma, what they did and how his Pa had drunk himself to death. How he had made the box, he even shared his little joke about putting the *Four Roses* whiskey bottle between his hands. He talked about Lon Bishop and Little Jake and the rest of the boys. He stopped just short of telling about Virginia and her big tits and how he'd been screwing her for the past three years. He just thought it was better that way.

Matt, shared his life as well. His parents were a little older and had acquired the acreage from the Bureau of Land Development and started the ranch. It had been a hard time for all, but they were happy. They had been involved in the church all of Matt's life and lived by the standards issued from the pulpit. Like Charlie, he had never had a girlfriend.

They didn't get to bed until after 0300 hours, and none was awake until nearly 1000 hours. They got up and each, having their own bathroom took advantage of it.

Wally shaved, brushed his teeth, and then walked into the shower, which was gray marble and big enough for six people. When the shower came on, it came from all four sides and from the ceiling as well. "My Gawd…it's like it's raining," he said to himself. He put on his uniform and went to the next room which was Matt's.

Matt was sitting waiting, and soon Charlie joined them in civilian clothes. It made him look entirely different. Wally made a comment about him being too small to have anything that would fit him. Matt could almost wear Charlie's clothes…but they'd be a little tight.

Charlie said we'll take care of all of that later. The three went to breakfast. His parents were nowhere to be found.

Charlie told the servant to bring them eggs, bacon, potatoes, biscuits, pink grapefruit and coffee with cream. The three of them sat waiting while the maid brought coffee and each a half of a pink grapefruit with a cherry on top. It was something that neither Matt nor Wally had ever had. Charlie, took the teaspoon from the side and took sugar which he sprinkled on the top. Wally and Matt did the same thing. After the maid had gone back to the kitchen, Wally hoisted one cheek and farted, then covered his mouth with his left hand, "Oops!"

The three of them burst out laughing and were sniggering when the maid returned with a pitcher of cream. The three were giggling like a bunch of school girls.

Breakfast was served. Wally wanted ketchup for his potatoes and asked the maid, "Can I have the ketchup bottle?"

The maid showed no reaction, slowly nodded her head and left. She returned with a silver dish with ketchup, on a silver tray where she had placed a silver spoon.

He looked at Matt, then Charlie, and the three broke out again in laughter. This time, Matt farted, followed by Charlie.

So went breakfast on the first day.

Then Matt and Wally followed Charlie to the garage and entered. There were three other cars. The big, black Packard wasn't there, neither was the chauffeur. Charlie went to the wall and opened the garage door and then took a set of keys from a board and walked over to a smaller and sporty-looking Packard and opened the door.

"Hop in guys."

Matt got in the back seat and Wally sat up front so his long legs would fit. Charlie started the engine and waited for it to warm up, then shifted the gear and backed out. He got out and closed the garage door, returned and drove down Lake Shore Drive towards the city. Wally was impressed.

They drove along and both Matt and Wally were impressed at the size of the buildings, "Gawd... they're all huge!" There were parks galore along with a roadway system that neither had ever thought possible. Although covered with snow, they had never seen anything more beautiful.

Everywhere they looked, it was all manicured. There were people walking in spite of the severe wind. There were cars everywhere. The city went on and on. Wally said, "There must be a million people here!"

Charlie replied, "Several...Chicago is the third largest city in the world."

They saw Sears, Roebuck & Company, which brought comments by Wally and Matt, Montgomery Wards, Marshall Fields, the Furniture Mart, the US Army Consolidating Station. There were double-decker buses on Michigan Avenue, street cars, more parks and then the Chicago Rail Yard. They had never seen so many railroad cars.

They saw the Chicago River winding its way through the city. Wally was very impressed that there were people living in boats on the river...they were like houses. Both boys were overwhelmed at the magnitude of everything.

Wally started to sniff and said, "Alright...who farted?"

Matt said, "Not me."

Charlie said nothing.

So, Wally said, "Okay...who shit?"

"No one," replied Charlie, "It's the Union Stock Yards...you should feel right at home."

"I thought something smelt familiar... cow shit!," said Wally.

Charlie, being the tour guide said, "Chicago's Union Stockyard has 475 acres of animals. We are the butcher's of the world. Among the meat packers are

Armour Meats, Swift Premium Meats...that's my father's company, and several more."

Wally said, "So, your father's a butcher?"

"You could say that, but I wouldn't," responded Charlie.

"Me neither," commented Matt.

When they arrived at the stockyard, the smell was overwhelming. The place was enormous with stalls crammed full of cows, sheep, pigs, as far as the eye could see. Train cars were being emptied and animals were being led to stalls and from stalls to the meat packers.

"There must be millions of heads of cattle," commented Matt.

Charlie said "At least."

They drove from there to Randolph Street which was lined with theatres and restaurants. Charlie pulled up to Pizzeria Uno, and said, "You gotta have this. It's the best pizza in Chicago."

They went in and, after a nearly forty minute wait, they got their pizza. They ate it with great relish washed down with *Coca-Cola*, and once again were back on the road.

Charlie showed them many schools, which were multi-storied buildings. They were a far cry from the one-room buildings in Wyoming. They went to colleges and universities, museums and the Chicago Opera House. All were impressive and all enormous.

They pulled into a men's shop. There, Charlie said, "We're going in here and you both are going to let me buy you some clothes. No argument."

There he bought them a set of civilian clothes so they could spare their uniforms. He bought them each a sweater, a dress shirt, a pair of slacks and a beLieutenant They could wear their army shoes.

They both promised to pay him back, but he said, "Don't bother. My parents won't even miss it. Besides, they won't have to look at something so common as an army uniform. Merry Christmas."

They all chuckled but were still a little embarrassed that Charlie had bought them clothes. Wally had never had anyone buy him clothes or much of anything else, for that matter.

When they arrived back to Charlie's parents home, they were pretty much worn out. Charlie told them that dinner was at eight...he corrected himself, twenty hundred hours. Wally and Matt were glad to get out of their army uniforms and into something less formal.

Wally said, "I can't get the stockyard smell out of my nose. Hope it's gone by dinner." It was.

That night at dinner, which was sharply at 2000 hours. The boys came in. After they were seated, wine was served. Tonight's wine was French Burgundy which was selected to go with braised sirloin tips, a medley of onions, potatoes, and carrots braised with extra virgin olive oil and honey, cantaloupe and honeydew melon balls, and a slice of chocolate cheesecake with little chocolate mouse droppings on top and coffee. Once again, a little glass of *Drambuie*.

"Tomorrow's Christmas," commented Mrs. Yates. "Shall we celebrate it tomorrow morning or tomorrow evening?"

Wally had been so distracted he'd forgotten, "Tonight's my birthday...I almost forgot."

"How old are you?," asked Matt.

"Nineteen," replied Wally.

"How unfortunate for you," said Mrs. Yates.

"Oh, I don't mind...I guess when you're older it matters how old you are, but don't bother me," said Wally.

Mrs. Yates said, "What I meant to say was how unfortunate to have your birthday on Christmas Eve."

Mr. Yates commented, "You probably didn't get both Christmas and Birthday gifts, did you?"

"Naw, I didn't get any gifts anyway," Replied Wally.

"You and baby Jesus was born at the same time," observed Matt.

Wally shook his head, "Naw, he's older."

"Had I only known, we could have had a birthday cake for you," replied Mrs. Yates.

"That's alright. Wouldn't know how to act," said Wally.

Charlie, who'd been really quiet said, "We went all over today, I gave them the grand tour."

"What did the two of you think of our city?," asked Mr. Yates.

Matt relied, "It's big, for sure.

"We saw the meat market where you work, too. Man, it's really big," said Wally, "I never seen so many cows and pigs in my life...or smelt 'em either...all that manure." He was proud he'd used the proper term for cow and pig shit.

Charlie, who was having trouble stifling a laugh, said, "We also went to *Pizzerias Unos* for lunch. Couldn't come to Chicago without having pizza."

"No, indeed," added Mr. Yates.

Mrs. Yates, still recovering from the thoughts of a stockyard being mentioned at her dinner table, said, "Shall we retire to the parlor?," and rose from her seat.

Wally, who had never seen a parlor was the second one up. He was followed by Matt and Charlie. Mr. Yates rose, and offered his arm to Mrs. Yates, and led the way.

The "parlor" was huge with a twelve feet high mansard ceiling in stained glass, Tiffany lamps, polished brass, dark polished wood and elegant leather upholstered chairs all spread out on burgundy colored Persian rugs. However, the central focus was a huge nearly twelve feet high Christmas tree with thousands of lights and glass balls, and ornaments. All topped with an angel with golden wings and a lighted halo. The entire tree was covered with metallic tinsel.

Wally and Matt stood in silence. Charlie, realizing what was happening, said, "Grab a seat guys, make yourself at home."

That was about the last thing that Mr. or Mrs. Yates ever would have said or wanted, which Charlie knew, and secretly enjoyed watching them squirm.

Mrs. Yates said, "Yes, please be seated. We need to discuss our Christmas celebration."

Wally, who was still in awe of the Christmas tree said, "Gawd, that tree is the most beautiful tree I have ever seen!" Truth be told, it was the *only* Christmas tree that he had ever seen.

It was decided that they would celebrate Christmas the next afternoon with a festive Christmas dinner followed by sharing gifts with each other. Mrs. Yates then realized that she was dealing with soldiers who were on leave from the army and probably hadn't brought gifts. She had a wonderful thought.

"I'll tell you what, let Mr. Yates and myself treat you all to Christmas dinner at the Country Club and that will be our little Christmas gift for you."

"Wonderful, Dear…that will be delightful," said Mr. Yates.

"Yeah, sure. Sounds great," said Charlie.

The short remainder of the day consisted of strained conversations and, finally, saying, "Good

Night." The boys headed for their bedrooms and the bedtime consultations.

CHAPTER NINETEEN

CHRISTMAS DAY, 1944

Christmas Day and the temperature outside was near zero degrees, Fahrenheit. The wind was blowing like there was no tomorrow. The boys were up by 0900, shaved, showered, and down for breakfast. Once again, no sign of Mr. or Mrs. Yates.

Wally wondered if they did that on purpose or just slept in late. Matt was in his other outfit and was Wally and then, in walked Charlie. He had on casual clothes as well.

Charlie ordered breakfast and soon, it was being brought to the table and they were served.

The maid also brought ketchup without being asked. Maybe she had an eye for Wally. Although she was a little too old for him. She was probably forty years old.

The three ate with relish and soon finished. Wally blotted his mouth with his napkin like he'd seen Mrs. Yates do, but exaggerated it. Matt saw him do it and sniggered a bit.

"Okay, guys...today is the test. We're going to the South Shore Country Club for early dinner. I need to let you know what you're in for. Up until now, you ain't seen nothing yet. I was hoping we could avoid that scene, but we're not." He was now embarrassed but went on, "What you are going to see is the most pretentious place filled with the most pretentious people you have ever seen."

Guess he was right for Wally asked, "What's pretentious mean?"

"Well, it's when people show off what they have and all the wonderful people...they don't really know," replied Charlie.

Matt said, "Like 'Puttin' on the dog'?"

"You could say that," said Charlie.

"When we get there, my father will run into everyone he knows and so will my mother. They will Oooo, and Aaah, and say nothing to each other. They will expect us to wear our uniforms. Then they will introduce us to everyone, and all the people who don't want to meet us. None of these people care that there is a war going on. That is until it affects the 'bottom line,' and then they care....or maybe their son gets shot!"

"Man, that sounds exciting," exclaimed Wally, "I can't wait!"

"Oh, it gets better," added Charlie, "When we sit down for dinner, my father will order the entire dinner for everyone, while my mother corrects every selection, which annoys him."

"Is that when they start throwing stuff at each other?," said Wally.

"No, that wouldn't be proper. It's the little games they play with each other."

Matt was listening with interest. "Why are we going there? Doesn't sound much like Christmas."

Charlie replied, "Oh, it's special. That's why they're doing it. The South Shore Country Club is one of the oldest in America and it is the one of the most elegant places you will probably ever see."

"Is it as nice as the Mess Hall?," grinned Wally.

"Well...?" after a pause, "no, but close," kidded Charlie.

Charlie couldn't say he never warned them. He didn't blame his parents, they knew nothing else. He knew both sides, and preferred the less pretentious life. He liked Wally and Matt. They were his friends. That gave him a thrill even thinking about it. My friends.

The time went by and it was time to get ready to leave. They all got dressed up in their Class A Uniforms ready to be shown off. They were all spit and polish with shiny shoes and ready for duty.

Mr. and Mrs. Yates appeared from someplace. Mr. Yates was handsomely dressed in a tuxedo. Mrs. Yates wore a beautiful emerald green satin gown that showed off her flowing dark hair and was wearing jewelry the likes of which neither Matt nor Wally had ever seen. Mr. Yates held a grey fox fur cape which he slipped over her shoulders. They were ready.

Mr. Yates opened the door and they went to the waiting Packard limousine and the chauffeur holding the back door. Soon, they were zooming down Lake Shore Drive south toward the Country Club. They passed the Edgewater Beach Hotel on the right, with a spectacular view of Lake Michigan and saw the spectacular beaches that both young men thought would be teeming with swimmers in the summer. Lots of tits, thought Wally.

The driver pulled through massive iron gates and drove onto a roadway with trees lining both sides of the road through hundreds of acres of landscaped lawn. In the distance stood a massive brick building, which got larger the closer they got. He pulled into a Porte-cochere and stopped.

A doorman, dressed in a formal Santa Clause suit said, "Good afternoon, Mr. and Mrs. Yates, Merry Christmas." He glanced at Charlie and said, "Welcome home, Master Charles," and held the door for all.

Wally grinned and said just loud enough for Charlie to hear it, "Welcome home, Maaaster Chaaarles."

Matt sniggered.

And Charlie waved his hand behind his back signaling, "Shut up."

They walked down the *passaggio* which was three hundred yards of splendor. It was a wide ceramic tile hallway with twenty feet high windows supported by Romanesque columns with dark furniture and oil paintings lining the walls.

While in the *passaggio*, they were greeted by others. Mr. Yates said, "Lawrence, I'd like to introduce you to my son Charles' friends, Privates Wallace Bearstone and Matthew Carver, this is Lawrence Hegsworth, the owner of the County Club."

Lawrence Hegsworth said, "Welcome soldiers. I'm glad you're defending our country, and Charles, it is so good to see you again. Are you with us long?"

Charlie answered, "Till New Years' Day, sir." That's one down and four hundred more to go, he thought.

As they slowly strolled through an opulence few see, they greeted and were greeted by several. There were insincere introductions to people no one wanted to meet. They turned into a massive entrance with marble stairways going to some place. There were crystal chandeliers and oil paintings galore. They finally entered the main dining room with twenty feet high windows revealing a scene only seen in pictures. Lake Michigan in all its splendor.

They were seated at a table set with three crystal goblets and water glasses at each place setting. The Damask linen napkins were folded by some magician, at least that's what Wally figured, with a pile of spectacular dinnerware and ornate silver utensils, one for each course. There was a line of forks, knives and spoons. Wally had no idea what one did with all of that stuff. He usually used a fork for everything.

Wally, who towered over the rest, realized he was the center of attention in the dining room of the South Shore Country Club. He knew he had that special attraction. He probably was, but not what he thought. He stood out because most had never seen a taller, more homely man in their lives. Despite his uniform, he was as out of place and anyone could be which was obvious to all. He scratched and picked and gawked at everything.

Mr. Yates, who insisted that he order, looked over the menu. There were no prices on the menu. The waiter came to the table and said, "Good afternoon, Mr. Yates, would you care to hear the specialties?"

Mr. Yates thought for a moment, and replied,"Yes, go ahead."

Wally and Matt both thought the waiter was speaking in another language as he recited the litany of specialities. He did think he heard "turkey" but wasn't sure.

Mr. Yates then began to order. We will start with a half-dozen oysters on the half shell for each, and please inform the sommelier that we are here. I think we will have a dry white wine to accompany our oysters. We will follow the oysters with a watercress salad with bacon crumbles. The turkey sounds wonderful..."

Mrs. Yates interrupted him saying, "Please make sure the turkey is not dry."

Yes, dear. "Please ensure that the turkey is not dry. Then we will have the dressing with plumbs and slivered almonds and ..."

"Please dear, don't order the wine sauce if it has too much fat."

"Yes, dear," then to the waiter, "Please ensure the sauce for the dressing has no fat."

The waiter assured him he would.

And so it went, just as Charlie said it would. Bottom line was they were having turkey, mashed potatoes and gravy, dressing, cranberry sauce, green bean casserole, and pumpkin pie...just like the Mess Hall.

The sommelier arrived with a cup hanging around his neck, and greeted them, "Good afternoon, Mr. and Mrs. Yates, and how are we this afternoon?" Not waiting for an answer he continued, "I notice you are having the oysters on the half shell and recommend a French Chardonnay."

Mr. Yates agreed, and the guy with the cup around his neck left. He returned with a bottle of wine and after opening it, poured a small amount into Mr. Yates glass and stood back.

Mr. Yates lifted the glass, rolled the wine around, smelled it and then sipped the little amount that was there. He shook his head "yes" and the sommelier poured the remaining small wine glasses to an inch from the top.

When the oysters were served, Wally looked down at them and cringed. There were six slimy grey things on a piece of shell lying on silver plates sitting in silver bowls filled with chopped ice. In the center was a little silver dish filled with something that looked like ketchup and pieces of lemon with little forks stuck in them lying on a bed of fresh parsley sitting next to the grey things. He had no idea how to eat them.

He looked at Matt, who had the same confused look, and both of them looked at Charlie. Matt shrugged his shoulders, and Charlie smiled.

Charlie nodded back, took the lemon wedge and twisted the fork in the lemon, while sprinkling it over the oysters.

Matt and Wally did the same.

Then Charlie, taking the smallest spoon, took some of the cocktail sauce and drizzled in over the oyster, picked up the entire shell, and poured it into his mouth.

Wally and Matt had followed him each step until it came to pouring the thing in their mouth. Wally took his wine and guzzled a mouthful, then sucked the oyster off of the shell, into his mouth, bit down, and swallowed.

Everyone noticed, but no one said anything. Wally thought he did real well. He only had five more to go. It took another two glasses of wine, but he made it.

The remainder of the meal went alright and was almost as good as the Mess Hall. Mr. and Mrs. Yates introduced them to other people, and oohed, and ahed, to most saying nothing. They acted just like Charlie said they would, and they wished a hundred or more of their closest friends a Merry Christmas and called for the car. The Packard was waiting for them under the Porte-cochere, and off they went.

"What a divine affair," commented Mrs. Yates.

They all agreed, but divine wasn't what Wally would have called it.

Later that night, they were gathered in Charlie's room for the nightly meeting of Company C where the conversation turned to their Christmas dinner. The three figured it probably cost a years' salary for each of them. Not bad for a butcher, thought Wally.

They all joked about the superficiality of the day at the South Shore Country Club. Wally related his version of the oysters which had them all rolling on the bed in stitches. They talked about the opulence of the place and speculated about how many millions of dollars that it cost. Despite all they laughed about, it would be a day that none would ever forget.

They discussed these things and other related things about manners and of life, and though they were often kidding, it represented one way of life in America. In contrast was the other extreme and it too, was important to others. That's what America is. That is what it's all about. That's what we were fighting in Germany and Japan about. We should each be able to do what's important to us. Hitler was killing Jews and all whom he disagreed with, and the German soldiers, including little boys, were dying for his purposes. The Japanese were torturing American soldiers beyond anything we could ever imagine.

While they were in all of these deep thoughts, Wally scanned Charlie's room. It was all beautiful, as was the whole house, but it lacked any memories. There was something that was missing and he couldn't put his finger on. There was a school pennant and a picture with Charlie and his parents in his graduation clothes, but that was it. There wasn't anything that said, "I live here...this is my room."

"Hell, even I had my pee-hole in the lean-to. Charlie ain't got nothing here except clothes." No wonder he was glad to be in the army. "Me too."

Company C continued its conversations until nearly midnight. All agreed, army life was good, it had a purpose.

They were all learning something about themselves. The three were becoming very patriotic.

What everybody wants is freedom. They were all proud to be fighting for America...the land of the free and the home of the brave.

Wally thought it's just like that song that Kate Smith sings, "*God Bless America.* "

So ended Christmas Day in the year nineteen hundred and forty-four. It was a Christmas that Wally would never forget.

CHAPTER TWENTY

THE RETURN TO HELL

The next several days sped by like none had ever experienced. Charlie showed them everything from baseball stadiums to Grant Park; from horse racing tracks to cathedrals. But the one place he took them was Wally's favorite, the Chicago Zoo. He saw animals that he had only heard about, but never seen, even in pictures. He was amazed by the size of the elephants, the height of the giraffes, strength displayed by the tigers and lions. He saw snakes, and lizards, penguins, and everything that was there. They saw an ape and said it reminded them of someone they knew. They spent one entire day there.

Other days they went to restaurants, some fancy, others not. Despite the cold and windy weather, they studied houseboats on the river. They braved the cold and stood on the banks trying to see inside of one of them, but couldn't. Wally was gawking so much, he lost his footing and was saved from falling in by Matt, who just happened to see him beginning to fall.

"Shit!," said Wally, "I'da drowned for sure...just after my balls froze off."

New Year's Eve was celebrated, once again, with his parents who had treated the three to a dinner and dance in the ballroom at the elegant Elysium Hotel in Chicago. Wally couldn't imagine dancing, let alone dancing in a fancy place. Neither could Matt...or Charlie for that matter. But Mrs. Yates thought it appropriate. Maybe they would meet some lovely young ladies. Fat chance!

Wally was sitting at a table, with a silver-colored, cardboard New Year's hat on. It was a pointed cone shape, and he felt like a jerk...he also looked like one. Six foot, six inches tall and ugly as a mud fence with a little cone on his head. He had a whistle that rolled out with fringe on it when he blew it.

He was sipping on his third glass of champagne when an extremely tall girl came over to him and asked him to dance. Wally wasn't even sure she was talking to him but said, "I don't know how to dance."

"Good, we can step on each other's feet," she replied, "Please? I'm Gretchen."

Wally rose from his chair and joined Gretchen. Matt and Charlie were making comments and laughing so Wally could hear them. People from all around were watching Wally on the dance floor with Gretchen, who was no beauty herself. Wally noticed that she didn't have much in the way of tits either.

"What a lovely couple," commented Mrs. Yates, dead-serious.

This brought another outburst from the young soldiers.

Wally, who was awkward to begin with, was seriously trying to impress Gretchen with his suaveness and carefully avoided stepping on the poor girl's feet. He had almost pulled it off, when... *CRRRUNCH!*

Gretchen screamed, "OW! Ooo!" She fell and was sprawled out on the slick dance floor with the Jolly Giant, and his little cone hat towering over her. Two hundred forty pounds had not only come down on her foot, it was so extreme that it broke the heel off her satin shoe.

Wally leaned over and helped her up. His homely face was scarlet with embarrassment. Her blond hair, which had been neatly coiffed and piled on her head, was now halfway hanging on her face. Unsure as to what to do with the poor girl, he asked, "Do you want me to carry you back to your table?"

Gretchen, who was totally embarrassed herself, replied, "No, but thanks." She gathered her shoe heel and limped away across the dance floor to her table.

Matt and Charlie were totally cracking up. Mr. and Mrs. Yates were pretending that it didn't happen, and Wally returned to the table, bringing all eyes in their direction. He sat and tried to act as if nothing happened.

None of the boys had any more requests to dance. When the hour approached midnight, and the members of Company C were tipsy from too much champagne, the orchestra began "*Auld Lang Syne.*"

Mrs. Yates offered herself for a superficial kiss on the cheek, the gentlemen all shook hands and Wally, blew out the curly whistle. It was a wonderful evening at the Elysium Hotel ballroom.

The drive back to the North Lake Shore Drive home was a quiet one. They all knew this was it. Tomorrow morning they will be returning to Hell.

They made an attempt at small talk, but it fell short. The chauffeur let them out at the front door, they entered, said "good night and thank you" to Mr. and Mrs. Yates and headed up the stairs. There would be no meeting of Company C this night. They had to pack and be at the train station at 0700 hours.

The train was equally as packed going back to St. Louis as it was heading for Chicago. Each of the boys had a slight hangover and the trip lacked the excitement and enthusiasm they had left with. Each wondered just what lay ahead.

The hours passed slowly as the train went from Union Station to Union Station. Mostly they all slept a lot. As they pulled into St. Louis, they gathered their bags and got off the train. There were many soldiers there among them.

They headed for the Bus Stop where the shuttle was waiting to take another load of soldiers back to Fort Leonard Wood.

They off-loaded at the Fort and, after showing their ID's, entered through the gate and walked the road to the quadrangle and barracks Building 301. They lumbered up the steps and entered. A few of the other guys were there, and there was the usual hoopla.

Charlie went to his area, Matt to his, and Wally went through the room and up the stairs to his room. It looked the same. He flopped down sitting on his bunk and remembered an old saying he'd heard Lon Bishop use, "Fly high...and fall in cow shit."

"That about says it all," said Wally to himself.

CHAPTER TWENTY-ONE

NOT THE SAME O, SAME O!

Reveille sounded, and Sergeant Swain entered in his usual spit and shine uniform and gave his same, "Up and at 'em." Nothing had changed. Same O, same O!

They all fell quickly back into the routine of basic training. They ate at the Mess Hall, they double timed to the firing range, they went through the abuse and ridicule of Master Sergeant Baker who was the same son-of-a-bitch as before.

The weeks passed and soon the graduation from Basic Training was in sight. With all the hardships and anguish, the pain and suffering and the bitching and complaining…it was over.

Wally, Matt and Charlie were in Wally's room and just hanging out. Wally, who was by far the best rifleman, was moving up in the world, he was assigned to go to 6th Infantry Army Engineer

Replacement School, in Fort Leonard Wood, Missouri...same damned place. Matt, who also was good with weapons, was going to artillery training at Fort Sill, Oklahoma. The biggest surprise, Charlie, the world's worst shot, was too. Both were going to the 75th Field Artillery Brigade at Fort Sill.

Since the Normandy invasion and Germany's imminent surrender on the horizon, the war in Europe was about over. What was going to happen to Japan was a little uncertain, but since Midway, the American's had won every victory since. The management of Company C, thought it was just a question of time. It would be neat to have occupational duty and see a different part of the world. What was going to happen to Wally after engineer training, who knew?

The three were disappointed that they would be broken up, but made vows to always stay in touch. None of them considered anything other than that, after all, they were best friends.

Graduation was on Friday, February 2, 1945, at 1000 hours. Wally thought it was fitting, as it was Groundhog day. Travel was right after that to their new assignments on February 5th. Mr. and Mrs. Yates were coming to Fort Leonard Woods to the exercises despite the weather which was colder than a witches tit. Neither Matt's nor Wally's family was...nor anyone else they knew for that matter.

The recruits were cleaning and polishing everything they had, their brass, their shoes, and most importantly, their weapons. They checked each other's appearance. They were proud. All were lean and mean and looking the best they had ever looked.

On Friday, they were gathering and in formation with their weapons. Today, they were bona fide soldiers and proud to be an American. They were defenders of the nation. All were beaming with pride.

Mr. and Mrs. Yates, who had never shown pride in Charles or his accomplishments, were bundled up and sitting in the bleachers to watch their only son, marching in formation with precision they never thought possible. Charlie was well aware of that, and as they were marching toward the bleachers and all the bunting flapping in the breeze, he stood a little higher than normal. They all did.

The four companies were in formation, had marched in and were spread across the span of bleachers in front of the guests and speakers. There was a General in all his splendor surrounded by all levels of top brass, including the stomping Sergeant, and the mean son-of-a-bitch, Master Sergeant Baker in his dress uniform. There were the usual speeches and falderal.

Wally, towering above the rest, could see Mr. and Mrs. Yates sitting in the stands. He hoped Charlie could as well. After the ceremony, they all gathered and spoke with Charlie's proud parents.

Wally, Matt and Charlie were all chatter. They shared the barracks with his mother and father. They showed them as much as they could. All the troops were oozing with pride. Wally saw that Charlie realized that his parents were impressed. How long it would last was doubtful. He felt proud of Charlie as well.

They were all sitting in the Mess Hall, which Wally was sure that Mr. and Mrs. Yates didn't appreciate as much as the boys did, having dessert and coffee. The former Company C Privates were sharing stories, when Charlie told his parents that he and Matt were being assigned to the 75th Field Artillery Brigade at Fort Sill, Oklahoma to artillery school.

"Oh, dear," commented Mrs. Yates, "I didn't know you shot things."

"Yes, mother, we're in the army during a war!"

"Yes, but we thought you'd be doing something else, didn't we dear?"

"Charlie's real good," commented Wally, "Damned near killed the Master Sergeant one day."

"Not cool, Wally," scolded Charlie.

Matt said, "We hoped he would, but he didn't."

Mr. Yates said, "Who is Master Sergeant?"

Wally said, "Master Sergeant Baker, our DI...meaner than cat manure." Once again glad for his choice of words.

Charlie took the opportunity to change the subject, "He's the one who did most of the training."

Mr. Yates asked, "Was it really difficult...like they say?"

"Worse," replied Charlie, realizing for the first time that he knew something his father didn't.

"I can not see my son...with a gun," said Mrs. Yates.

"Well, mother, someone could, that's why I'm going to Fort Sill," he responded.

Both Mr. and Mrs. Yates were very uncomfortable in the military environment. It was alien to everything they knew. They were total strangers. Yet, they tried to put on a happy face...much to their credit.

"Father, would you like to see the training ground where we did a lot of stuff?" asked Charlie.

"Yes, I think I would."

"Come on guys…let's give 'em the tour," said Charlie.

They all walked to the "Playground" which took nearly thirty minutes. They told of how they double timed it and ran all the way and all the way back., They showed them the walls they had climbed, the barbed wire they had crawled under, the nets they had climbed and other Herculean efforts they had achieved. They told of the live fire they had crawled through. All was exhausting to the person who had never done them. Mr. and Mrs. Yates must have been impressed that their "do-nothing" son could accomplish so much.

Wally observed the change in their attitude towards Charlie. They were impressed. They were impressed with all of the boys. Mr. Yates, visibly shrank from being pompous to an overwhelmed person. His son had accomplished all of this, while he hadn't even come close in anything he had ever done.

Parents rarely appreciate what their children have accomplished. Little do they realize what it is to grow up in a world governed by their parents' accomplishments. Neither did the Yates'. Charlie had done so much more than either of his parents' would ever accomplish. They were just beginning to realize it.

Matt and Wally let Charlie run the show. They had watched him struggle and hurt. They watched a determined guy, beat the odds and achieve. This is their friend, and they were going to support him?

Wally didn't tell them that Charlie loves fart jokes, or about the time they all had the marching farts. There were a lot of stories that they thought best to let go untold. Even Matt didn't think they would understand.

Charlie was the hero of the day, let there be no misunderstanding. They thought that Mr. and Mrs. Yates thought so too.

So, it wasn't just a same-o, same-o day. It was a splendid one.

After Mr. and Mrs. Yates left, the Privates of Company C gathered for perhaps the last meeting. None knew what the future held. None knew what they were facing. They were all apprehensive. None was willing to say so.

When men have shared so much together in difficult times, it's not easy to walk away. They had each become a part of the other. It was an experience that none had ever expected and one that could never be repeated. It was what it was. There was a bond of love, not romantic, but love none the less. One to last a lifetime.

CHAPTER TWENTY-TWO

SEE YOU, LATER

Matt and Wally said "goodbye" to Mr. and Mrs. Yates and left. They let Charlie say his farewells as he wanted, in private. There wasn't a lot of time to pack up everything. Wally had all the time he needed as he wasn't going far. But Matt and Charlie had to get their butts in gear.

Charlie joined them a few minutes later, and they talked on their way back to the barracks.

Matt said, "That was great of your parents to come."

"Yeah," commented Charlie, "I think they were impressed."

Wally chimed in, "They should be."

"You know guys, I was really proud today," said Charlie, "Proud to be an American, I was proud of us...the whole thing."

"Me, too," commented Matt.

"Me, too," said Wally, "When we were at the Playground showing your mother and father, I was remembering crawling around in all that mud taking shit from that son-of-a-bitch Sergeant Major, just like a bunch of groundhogs."

Wally didn't know at the time, but he had just given them a nickname.

Charlie said, "Neither of them had any idea what we went through."

Matt replied, "Not many do."

They arrived at the barracks and Wally stayed with Matt and Charlie to help. They took their two duffle bags and began packing their clothes from the footlocker, remembering unpacking it all ten or twelve weeks ago. They had both duffle bags packed tight and rolled their mattress, blankets and pillows along with their sheets and towels, stacked on the bunk as directed for return. They had already picked up the civilian clothes they arrived in, most of which they pitched out.

They had their orders, their wallets and their Greyhound bus tickets in a brown manilla envelope. They were ready to leave. Matt said he had to take a piss, so the three went to the latrine and did just that.

Of course, Charlie farted and came up with a few remarks. They washed their hands and returned to their bunks, hoisted their duffle bags and headed out the door.

Wally walked with them helping with their duffle bags. They arrived at the main gate to wait for the Greyhound bus which would take them to St. Louis' Union Station and train to Fort Sill.

They were all silent. What needed to be said, had been. All three were feeling the same thing. None would risk saying anything that could possibly turn on the water spickets.

The big Greyhound bus arrived and the three soldiers stood, shouldered their duffle bags and walked toward the bus where they heaved them on the pile to be loaded underneath. When they turned towards Wally, they stood at attention and saluted him.

Wally saluted them back but could not let them go without saying something. "See you later," he shouted. His eyes began to fill with tears.

Both Matt and Charlie, not seeing too well either, shook their heads in agreement, clinched their jaws and entered the bus. They found a couple of seats together and looked out the window. There, standing with a grin on his face, was Wally. They waved at him through the open window. The bus pulled out and Wally stood waving back until the bus was out of sight.

The two privates sat quietly for quite some time before Matt spoke.

"Wonder if we'll ever see him again?"

"Who knows?" said Charlie, "I'm going to miss the big ox."

"Me, too," responded Matt, "Let's see how the next training cycle goes, maybe we can get away for a few days."

"Good idea," replied Charlie.

The next two and a half hours were going to be very quiet.

Meanwhile, Wally turned when the bus was out of sight, wiped his eyes with his sleeve and headed back to the Mess Hall. He sat alone and had his supper. He wandered back to the barracks and went up the stairs to his room and sat on his bunk. For the first time in nearly three months, he was alone.

He began looking through the clothes that he had arrived in. Had he really worn those things. Was that him...or a bad memory? He thought about all he had seen and done...the places he has gone. Omaha, Nebraska, Chicago, Illinois, St. Louis, Missouri. Lake Michigan and Lake Shore Drive...the South Shore Country Club.

It was hard to remember all that he'd done since he wore those jeans and flannel jacket, filthy as they were. He had a whole new life, and there was nothing about any of that crap he wanted to keep. Not even a memory. He grabbed up the cardboard suitcase which his Pa had brought from Louisville, and heaved it into the large trash can. He noticed there were others in there as well.

There was no Wyoming left.

He decided that he would just see where the future takes him...like the Sergeant said, "my ass belongs to Uncle Sam."

He rambled around in the barracks. There were a couple of other guys there, but as far as he was concerned it was empty. He went to his room and stripped off his clothes, grabbed a towel and his Dopp kit and went to the latrine. There he stood in a steamy shower for a good half an hour, came out, shaved, and put on the deodorant that Matt had told him he should use. Matt was right. He brushed his teeth and was ready for bed. He walked back to his room, pushed whatever was on his bunk to the floor and flopped.

Tomorrow, he would pack up his stuff and report to the 6th Infantry Army Engineer Replacement Training Center, where he could learn how to dig ditches and build things.

CHAPTER TWENTY-THREE

THE GIFT HORSE

Wally lumbered up the steps to the Headquarters, 6th Infantry Army Engineer Replacement Training Center. Dropped his duffle bags on the floor and handed his orders to the Company Clerk.

The Clerk took the papers and read. "Are you checking in?"

"Yes," replied Wally, "Just finished basic and reporting early...if that's okay?"

"Sure," said the Clerk and looked at a clipboard. "That class starts on Monday, the 5th, and you are quartered in Building 434. Let me check to see if the Quartermaster has anyone over there."

He picked up the phone and dialed some numbers. He waited, and then someone answered, "Yes, Sergeant Clark, there's a Private Bearstone here reporting early for the Engineer Replacement class starting on Monday, I show they are quartered in Building 434, is that correct?" He paused, then continued, "Is there someone there who can get him set up? Good, I'll send him over."

He told Wally where to go and gave him directions. Wally thanked him and picked up his duffle bags and left. He walked to Building 434 and walked in and reported to the Sergeant on Duty.

"Are you Bearstone?" asked the Sergeant, "I was told you were on the way."

"Yes, Sergeant," answered Wally.

He took Wally's papers, read them and asked him, "You were the Platoon Guide in Basic?"

"Yes, Sergeant," replied Wally.

"Well, you'll be the Class Leader then. That'll save some time. Grab your things and follow me."

Wally, picked up his duffle bags and followed the Sergeant from his office into the building, which looked like the one he just moved from. They walked through the darkened sleeping quarters and went up the stairs to the same type of room, except it had a desk, a chair and a metal locker besides the bunk and footlocker..

"How's this?" he asked.

"Just fine, Sergeant. I can figure out where to put stuff," Wally grinned.

"Good," replied the Sergeant, "Drop your bags, and come with me."

Wally put his duffle bags and the small sports bag from his trip to Chicago on the floor.

The Sergeant asked where he was from and made small talk. Wally, had not been talked to by any other Sergeant who didn't order him to do something. He was not used to it. They walked to a large store room where the Sergeant grabbed two pairs of sheets, a pillow and two pillowcases, two blankets, and two towels and two washcloths. He handed them to Wally.

"Here you go," he said, "When you're settled in, come on back to the office, and I'll give you office supplies and a Class Leader manual."

Wally thanked him and carried the bedding and towels to his room. He made up his bunk and unpacked his duffle bags, placing the items in his footlocker. He opened the metal locker to find four hangers on one side and a set of shelves on the other. He hung his Class A's and the civilian clothes that Charlie had bought for him in there and put his Dopp kit on the shelves. He sat in the chair at the desk and felt for a minute like he was important. Then he folded up his duffle bags and placed them in the bottom of his footlocker. He put his polished shoes under the bed. And soon, all was ready for inspection. He walked back down to the Sergeant's office.

"Settled?" asked the Sergeant.

"Yes, Sergeant," said Wally.

"Wallace...isn't it?" asked the Sergeant

"Wally, Sergeant," he answered.

"Wally, you don't have to be so formal. I'm only a three striper. You can just call me Sarge," said the Sergeant.

"Okay, Sarge," a little uncertain.

Sarge handed him the Class Leaders Manual, and also had a couple of other binders as well, some yellow tablets, pencils, paperclips, a ruler, a calendar, a stapler and staples. He also had an in/out box and a clipboard. Wally wasn't sure what to do with all of it but figured he'd learn.

"As the Class Leader, you will do pretty much what you did as Platoon Guide. You will form your class and march them to and from class, and report to the instructor. You'll be responsible for attendance, and make an accounting to the Officer-in-Charge."

Sarge, who said he was substituting for a friend that worked for the Quartermaster, told him a lot, for which Wally was very grateful. He wasn't used to the informality of the school...so far anyway. It was totally different from Basic Training. He was aware that the army is still the army, but this was more relaxed. He thought this was going to be alright. Maybe.

"You got an alarm clock?" asked Sarge.

"No...do I need one?

"Yes, and I don't have one to give you. Go to the PX and pick one up. You're going to need it to get the class up and ready." said Sarge, who opened a drawer on his desk, "Here's a whistle for around your neck and a stopwatch. These you'll have to sign for." He had a form on a clipboard and filled it in and passed it to Wally for his signature.

Wally signed the form and said, "Gee, Sarge, I don't know what to say...this is better than Christmas."

Sarge smiled and replied, "Oh, you'll earn every bit of it."

Wally went back to his room with all the "goodies." He put them on the desk and then headed out to find the Mess Hall. It wasn't the same Mess that they had gone to for basic. But similar. He had a hamburger and french fries and a coke. Then went to the PX. This one was much larger and cleaner with more stuff. He bought a small alarm clock which he paid for from money in his wallet. He eyed a small coin purse and thought about buying it as well, but let it pass. He looked at other items in the PX just to know what was there. This was a new luxury for him. He thumbed through some magazines and looked at books. He did buy a small pocket knife and a bag of peanuts before he returned to the barracks.

He went to his room and looked at his treasures. He played with his alarm clock and figured out how to wind it, set it and turn it off and on, then started placing stuff where he thought he'd need it. Then he picked up the Class Leaders Manual and started to read. He saw everything that Sarge had told him and a lot more.

He looked at materials in the two binders that Sarge had given him. They were the curriculum for the course and had tabs for the different classes. He studied them for some time. He didn't know what else to do, so took his Dopp kit and towel and went to the showers. After a lengthy shower, he did his nightly routine and went back upstairs. He thought he should have bought a magazine to look at, but figured he didn't need it. He went to bed.

He was nearly asleep when he heard Taps in the distance. It was a pretty song, he thought, there was something comforting about it. It told him all was going to be alright.

The next day, Sunday, he had nothing to do, so decided to please Matt who'd still be on the train to Fort Sill and go to the chapel. It was the same one he'd been to many times. He went into the now-familiar Chapel with the red carpet and was seated. He looked at the board up front and turned to the first number, 513, he turned to the page and it was "Soldiers of Christ."

As the organist began to play, he followed the words. He knew Doxology and then turned to the third number 526, "What A Friend."

The Chaplain talked about Jesus walking on the Sea of Galilee and trust and faith. It was all about things he didn't understand. When the service was over, he turned to leave and saw Sarge shaking hands with the Chaplain.

He sped up and caught up with him in the vestibule.

"Hey, Sarge."

"Thought that was you, Bearstone," said Sarge, "You're hard to miss."

Wally was at least a foot taller than Sarge. He was accustomed to that as he was taller than most people.

"Yeah, I know," grinned Wally.

"What's on your schedule today?" Sarge asked.

"Nothing...I don't know what to do with myself," replied Wally, "My two best friends have gone to Fort Sill, Oklahoma, and I got assigned here."

The two were walking back toward the engineer school. When Sarge asked him if he had lunch, which he hadn't, and asked Wally to join him. They went to the Mess Hall and took a seat. It wasn't open yet, so they helped themselves to a cup of coffee and waited. Wally noticed his name tag said, Turner.

"You said you were from Wyoming? I've never met anyone from Wyoming, tell me about it."

"Well, there's not too much to tell. I was raised on the McAllister Ranch where my Ma did the cooking and my sister helped her. I never went anywhere till I joined the army. This is as far as I ever been...well, I went to Chicago for Christmas last year."

Sarge told him he was from Kentucky, near Louisville, and told Wally about Churchill Downs, and the Ohio River and the bluegrass. He shared that he had joined the army at Fort Knox. That's where they store the nation's gold. They shared tales and troubles.

The Mess Hall opened and they got in line. The menu board said today was roast beef stew, with biscuits and honey butter, and peach cobbler. They loaded their plates and headed back to the table.

Sarge asked Wally if he'd gone to the Chapel before and was told that he'd gone with Matt and Charlie several times. But didn't understand it all. He shared that his own family didn't talk about that kind of stuff, so he never learned anything about it.

Sarge told him he was a preacher's kid and had grown up in the church. They spent the rest of the afternoon discussing it. Wally had a million questions and Sarge had a lot of answers.

Wally was like a sponge. He soaked up a lot of information. He was obviously not an educated man, but had an inquiring mind. Sarge was impressed and asked where he had gone to school. Wally told him he went to a little school and quit after the eighth grade to work on the ranch. He shared that he had worked with Lon Bishop and had learned how to build most anything. He shared a lot and soon, Sarge, knew why he was in Fort Leonard Wood. The poor guy lacked education, but knew how to build things and had a great mind for making something out of nothing. Very resourceful.

"How's your math skills?" he asked.

"Okay, I guess, if you mean arithmetic," said Wally.

"Yes, I do," he smiled, "I'd like to help you with a few things, if you'll let me?"

Wally sensed that he'd just met someone who could be a friend. He said, "If you can put up with me...I ain't too bright."

"You're smarter than you know," replied Sarge. He liked Wally, although he was the least attractive person he'd ever met, he was God's creation.

"Tell you what, class starts tomorrow and will last for ten weeks. We can't be friends in front of the other guys, but we can use the facilities after hours. You have got a lot more free time here than you had in Basic. I'll work with you with math and several other subjects. We have to get your G-E-D."

"What's G-E-D?"

"It's a General Educational Development...a high school diploma. I think there is time, but you'll at least have a good shot at it," said Sarge.

"If you think so, fine with me," said Wally.

"Okay, let's meet every Tuesday and Thursday night at 1800 hours for a couple of hours and on Sunday afternoons...If that's okay?"

Wally, who had never had anyone offer to help him other than Lon Bishop, wasn't sure where this was going. What does this guy want? This was what he was thinking when Sarge said,

"This is a lot to consider, Bearstone, but you got a lot to offer the army...they don't know it, yet. I didn't say this before, but I'm a graduate of the University of Louisville and trained to be a teacher. This war has screwed everything up. Someone saw something in you, that's why you're here and not going to the war zone. You still could, but probably not. I teach here."

"Holy shit," replied Wally.

"Shit, is not holy, but I know what you're saying," he corrected.

"Why me? Asked Wally.

"Why not?" replied Sarge. He realized he had a lot of his father's gifts for saving people, and this was definitely a challenge.

Lon Bishop had told him to never look a gift horse in the mouth. He didn't know whether Lon was right, but had a feeling that he had just been offered a great gift.

"Why not, Sarge...I'll see you on Tuesday," replied Wally.

"You may see me sooner," grinned Sarge, "I'm one of your Class Coordinators."

CHAPTER TWENTY-FOUR

THE AWAKENING

Wally quickly adjusted to the routine in the Engineer School. Being Class Leader gave him privacy in his room to study, and far less stress from day to day than that of basic training. While the curriculum was difficult, it was also challenging. His private tutoring was also going well. The combination of the two gave him discipline and structure without distraction.

Math, a skill which had always been his strong suit, was being honed. He took to the slide rule, which is a mystery to most, like a duck to water. Once again, he was like a sponge. He absorbed it all and craved more. Sarge had never seen anyone like him. He was almost obsessed with learning. He instinctively knew how things worked.

Of course, Wally was in the army and with it came the usual regime; the inspections, the formations and marching. But school came first and was the most important. They had ten weeks to turn young men into field engineers. To teach them to build rapidly under extreme conditions. To develop a keen sense of logistical support requirements. Wally excelled.

Sarge, who was only four years older than Wally, was challenged to keep ahead of him. The other instructors also were commenting about him as well. He learned how to build on land, regardless of terrain, and the hydrodynamics of building temporary bridges. He learned how to operate heavy equipment, there seemingly was nothing he couldn't do or wasn't willing to try.

The days flew by into weeks. Sarge thought by the end of week five, that Wally should be given the GED test. His reading skills had greatly improved, his ability to calculate were excellent, his writing skills were greatly lacking, but half of the doctors in the country can't write. Social studies were something else, but Sarge thought he could do it. His knowledge of history was improving.

On the social level, Wally had no other interests but the Engineer School and what Sarge was teaching him. Sarge was his mentor, his teacher, his friend. In

Wally's eyes, he was god. Of course he never told him. They talked about the church, God and Jesus Christ. This too, was of interest; however, it did not dominate him.

Sarge made the arrangements for Wally to take the GED test on Saturday, March 10th at 0900 hours. Wally was not overly anxious. It was what it was. He either knew the answers or he didn't. As it turned out, he did…well, most of them. He barely passed the test, but he passed.

Sarge said they should celebrate and Wally agreed. It was Saturday night, so they went to the USO Club on the post. Wally had never been there in the five weeks he'd been at the Engineer School. They served beer, wine and liquor which he really didn't drink. They also had dancing with a few USO girls there; however, he remembered the disaster at the Elysium Hotel and figured he pass on that as well. Sarge, being a preacher's kid, did neither. They ordered a couple of Cokes.

"Congratulations, Wally," said Sarge. "I knew you could do it."

"Thanks, Sarge."

They hoisted their Cokes, clicked glasses and celebrated.

"That was fun," remarked Wally.

"Wasn't it though," said Sarge.

Both men had concentrated so much on teaching and learning, neither had much to say. Socially, they had nothing in common other than the desire for education and dedication. For a nineteen year old and a twenty-four year old, they were acting like a couple of old men.

"Did I tell you about going to the Elysium Hotel in Chicago?" asked Wally.

"No, I don't think so," replied Sarge.

"It was a disaster," commented Wally, "Well, Matt and Charlie and me were in Chicago last Christmas and Charlie's parents, who are kind of uppity, they were treating us to an evening at the Elysium for New Year's eve."

Wally relayed the story of his dancing prowess. Sarge had never heard Wally talk about his past before. And became amused at how he could make fun of himself and tell a story that was remarkable, yet quite believable. He was personable, witty, clever and funny. Soon, Wally had Sarge in stitches. He was laughing so hard he couldn't catch his breath. Sarge could see this homely, six foot, six giant standing on the dance floor with a little hat on and the elastic string under his chin.

When he told the story of building a coffin for his Pa, and the *Four Roses* whisky bottle, Sarge could barely keep up with him. He totally lost it. He saw a side of Wally, that few have seen. Wally, who never had told stories before, became amused at himself. He would laugh while trying to tell the story, which made it even more funny.

What he told, and the manner in which he told it, while appearing to be serious about it...was a rare talent. He didn't tell it to be funny, he simply relayed a story. The conditions in his story were generally preposterous and self-effacing. He was a funny person. His immense size and the awkward appearance added to his stories.

Sarge, told about growing up in church and some of the fun stories about people, about dropping the communion plate, and strange sounds at awkward times always brought laughter.

Both shared stories about basic training and their reactions to various situations. Wally shared stories of Matt and Charlie and even through in a couple of fart stories.

What started out as a nothing night, turned into a fun evening for both. They walked back towards the barracks and agreed they would go to the Chapel the next day at 0900 hours and said goodnight.

Wally went up the stairs to his room and sitting at his desk began to study. He enjoyed learning. He stopped, laid his pencil down and realized he was a high school graduate. That wasn't so hard. What about college? It's possible. I'll have the GI Bill when I get out.

He started thinking about a career. What am I going to do? I like the engineer school. I'm doing well in the army, it's been good to me. Maybe I'll just stay in the army. Sarge had told him he would probably stay in the States anyway. After seventeen weeks in the U. S. Army, he had made up his mind. He decided to stay in the army.

With that decision made, he went back to his studies. He heard Taps, but he had a schedule to keep.

It was after midnight when he finally went to bed and fell asleep.

He was up by 0700 hours, went to the showers, shaved and did his morning routine. He dressed and was ready for Chapel by 0800 hours. He studied until

0835 and left, arriving at the Chapel fifteen minutes later.

He looked for Sarge and finally saw him. He joined him in the pew. Then, looking at the number board up front, turned to hymn 155, "All Hail the Power of Jesus Name."

Sarge sang out with gusto, but Wally never had and probably never would. He followed the words and looked at the music. The latter, he didn't understand…maybe Sarge could explain it. He had learned to say the Lord's Prayer, and contributed a couple of bucks to the plate. The sermon that day was on the widow's mite

Wally was glad that they had already passed the plate. The board said 128, and it was "*He Leadeth Me*." Nice song. The Chaplain gave the benediction, and that was that.

Wally felt comfortable in the Chapel. The Chaplain, who knew him by now, asked him if he was staying for the pitch-in lunch today. He looked at Sarge.

"Sarge, you want to stay?," said Wally.

"Sure, why not."

"Great," said the Chaplain, "It's in the fellowship hall."

Wally had no idea where the fellowship hall was, but Sarge led the way. There were men and women and a few children, all toll about a hundred people. People had brought food from home and the women had it covering three eight-foot tables. Wally had never seen so much food.

They were all waiting for the Chaplain and his wife to arrive, and when they did, they asked him to say grace. He prayed and thanked God for the food, which Wally didn't understand because he thought the women had brought it.

When he finished, people lined up, grabbed a plate and started taking what they wanted. Wally couldn't figure out what he wanted. He wanted a little bit of everything but was sure the plate wouldn't hold it all. It was all good.

They sat with people that neither knew. Everyone was talking to everyone else. Wally had never seen people so friendly. They were like Sarge when he met him. They introduced themselves and shared freely. They asked Wally what he was doing and listened to his response with interest. He was soon talking to other people. Sarge watched with interest as Wally became familiar with a church pitch-in dinner.

After they ate, the organist got up and went to the piano and began to play a faster song that everyone knew and were singing along. They sang for quite a while; it was beautiful. Another new experience for Wally.

Everyone was happy, enjoying themselves and full of good food. Then someone said dessert and coffee are ready. Once again, they took their plates and went back to the tables that now were covered with cakes and pies and other desserts. Wally thought that picking the right food was hard, he didn't know where to start. He had several different desserts and was full.

When it was over, everyone pitched in and helped clean up. The hall was cleaned and they left.

Sarge and Wally were walking back to begin studying.

"That was fun," said Wally.

"Yeah, I had a good time...did you?"

"Yeah...are Christians always that happy?," Wally asked.

"Not always...but we make an effort to be," replied Sarge.

"I never been to anything like that," said Wally, not even the Grange.

"That's how I was raised," noted Sarge. "I've never known otherwise."

"Are all churches like that?"

"Pretty much...some more than others," replied Sarge.

"Easter is coming in April, on the first. That's one of the biggest church holidays in the year. Christmas and Easter," said Sarge.

They discussed it further and arrived at the training facility. Sarge became the teacher of another subject. He began to lecture, prompt and started today's lessons. The two were used to each other, and Wally was respectful of each of their roles. They worked for an hour and a half.

Sarge thought that Wally's Chapel experience counted as social studies. But he was amazed when Wally asked him if he could explain music. This was a new and surprising dimension. He stood at the blackboard and drew a music staff and explained the difference between the treble staff and the cleft staff and the short explanation of *doe ray me fa so la tee doe*, with the difference in sounds.

"How do you know all of this?" asked Wally in total amazement.

"I studied piano for many years," remarked Sarge.

"You...can play the piano?," said Wally.

"Yes...I'm a preacher's kid," said Sarge, "It comes with the turf."

"Gawd...is there anything you don't know?"

"Lots," he chuckled, "but I'll never tell you...I'll just let you think I'm smart."

They called it a day. It had been a good weekend full of great experiences.

"See you tomorrow, Sarge," said Wally as he gathered his materials, "Thanks for everything," and left.

"Night, Wally."

Sarge erased the blackboard so the music could no longer be identified and checked out the room before he turned out the lights.

Wally went back to his barracks and began studying. He wasn't hungry at all, so studied and completed his homework. He thought about the activities at the Chapel and opened his footlocker, pulling out the Gideon Bible. He thumbed through it then began to read, *"In the beginning God created the heavens and the earth."*

An hour later, he was still reading. He tore off a piece of yellow tablet and made a bookmark and put it down on his desk.

He stripped down to his skivvies, grabbed a towel and his Dopp kit and headed for the latrine and the showers. He did his nightly routine. He mulled the events of the day over and over in his head. People don't have to stay where they are or what they are. You can be anything you want. You can become anything you choose.

He went to bed with this in mind. Tomorrow's Monday. Wonder what it will reveal? He went to sleep.

CHAPTER TWENTY-FIVE

THE REUNION

Monday night's mail call held a surprise for Wally. He had never received any mail before. Of course, he'd only sent one post card to Virginia and didn't send his mailing address. When his name was called and the mail was handed to him, it was a strange feeling. Then he saw it was from Private Matt Carver, 75th Field Artillery Brigade, Artillery School, Fort Sill, Oklahoma.

He took it to his room and opened it.

Dear Wally,

How are you. Charlie and me are fine.

We will graduate from Artillery School on Friday, March 30, 1945, and have another graduation. How is your Engineer School? Our's was very difficult with lots of yelling and foot stomping. Ha Ha, but no marching farts.

We have 10 days Leave before we ship out. They will not tell us where we are going, but it will <u>not</u> be Germany.

We are going to come to St. Louis to spend some time there and want to get together. Can you meet us there?

Your Friend, one of the groundhogs,

Matt

"Wow...that's three weeks," thought Wally. "My graduation isn't until April 13th." He was excited. "Maybe they're going to go to Chicago too. Damn, I can't go...too close to graduation."

He looked at his calendar to verify that his graduation is scheduled for April 13.

"Easter is on April 1...if they arrive after graduation, which is on the 30th, then there's 29 hours on the train, say 30. The soonest they could be in St. Louis is 1700 hours Saturday. I could miss Easter Chapel, so wouldn't have to be back until Monday morning, but does the Greyhound run at that time?...Man, that's tight. That would give us Saturday night and all day Sunday. They got ten days. If they're shipping out, I'd guess they're going to Chicago. I wish I could go with them...I'll see what Sarge says."

Wally was not optimistic. He could at least see them for a short weekend. There'd be a lot of catching up to do in a short time. Well, something is better than nothing. It is what it is. It's the army.

He went to supper at the Mess Hall and returned. Stripped to his skivvies, grabbed his towel and Dopp Kit and to the latrine and showers.

Later, in his room where he was studying, he thought he'd get a camera and some film. He'd never owned one, but had seen a lot of guys with them and thought it was time. He wanted pictures of Matt and Charlie and himself as well as Sarge. There were certain places like the basic training areas and like the Chapel, and Engineer School and the USO Club...his room...even the latrines...he sniggered, covering his mouth with his left hand.

The next morning he was up and at it. During one of his breaks, he ran into Sarge, and flagged him down.

"What's up," asked Sarge.

Wally told him about Matt and Charlie and had some questions. Wally said he really wanted to go to Easter services, but seemed like Saturday and Sunday were the only times he would be able to see Matt and Charlie.

"Maybe we could find them some room and the Guest Quarters here at the base....don't know, but maybe. They might be able to come here for a couple of days. Let me check and I'll let you know tonight."

"Thanks, Sarge," Wally, turned and returned to class.

Later that evening, when he arrived at the training facility, Sarge was waiting. Wally entered and they gave their greetings.

Sarge asked when they were coming and Wally said if they left Fort Sill right after graduation at say, 1200 hours he knew the train to St.Louis took about 29 hours, so at the soonest they could be here was 1700 hours on Saturday or later.

"Are they coming to see you, or St. Louis?

"I hope they're coming to see me," remarked Wally, "Not much there anyway."

"Don't tell the Chamber of Commerce," laughed Sarge.

"What I was thinking," said Sarge, "They could stay somewhere here at the Fort, that is if they wanted to, so you can all be together. There's a lot of barracks emptying out from the various classes and there may be a few empty bunks....although not officially."

"I never thought of that, I was thinking of a hotel or something outside of the gate," said Wally.

"You are going to be quite busy up until graduation...which is April 13th. That's one month from today."

"Sarge, you have any idea when my next assignment is coming?"

"...Not really, Wally, I'm sure they will be coming in the next week or so," said Sarge, "Why...did you have a preference?"

"I'd kinda like to stay here. if I had a choice," he said.

"Why?" asked the Sarge.

"I like what I'm doing," said Wally.

"Wally...do you think you could teach others how to do the stuff you do?"

"Why not...just show 'em how it's done," he replied.

Sarge realized just how gutsy Wally was. How unafraid, how sure of himself.

"You've shown a lot of leadership qualities...maybe it's because of your size, but others seem to follow you without question," remarked Sarge, "That's good. Far as space being available, give me a couple of days and I'll get back to you. Now, let's get on with your studies."

Sarge went to the chalkboard and began writing some formulas and figures. Wally went to his normal pause of eating on the back of his pencil.

A couple of nights later, Wally was writing to Matt.

Dear Matt,

Glad you are coming. I am good, too. I am looking forward to seeing you and Charlie. I know the train trip from Fort Sill is 29 hours long, so you would arrive in St. Louis after 0700 hours.

I have only Saturday and Sunday off. That should be enough to get in trouble in St. Louis. Ha Ha.

If you can stay longer, we can come back here. There are some empty bunks here that you can temporarily stay in at Fort Leonard Wood. That is not official, but no one will know. We can go to the USO Club and the Mess Hall.

It will be like old times.

Let me know, the ETA of your train.

Your fellow groundhog,

Wally

He folded the letter and addressed it to Matt, sealed it and put a stamp on it. He stood in on his desk so he would remember to mail it tomorrow.

He picked up his Bible and read for a while. Matt would like that. He smiled. He closed it and wondered if there were any honky-tonks in St. Louis? Charlie would like that. Maybe we all would?

As the days came closer to graduation, so did the days to the reunion. Wally was excited. He was excited about seeing his old buddies and excited to find out where he was going.

At mail call, he received a letter from the Commanding Officer, 6th Infantry, Fort Leonard Wood, Missouri.

This must be it, he thought as he headed for his room. He tore it open and read. "YES! YES! YES!," he shouted.

"Thank you, Lord!" This is as close as Wally has ever come to a prayer.

He ran from the building to Sarge's quarters and knocked on his door. Sarge answered the door to a grinning Wally Bearstone.

"I got my orders, Sarge...I'm going to stay right here!"

Sarge, who already knew, in fact had worked behind the scenes to make it happen replied, "Hey... that's great, Wally. Congratulations. See, hard work pays off."

Wally was like a little boy, all six feet, six inches. This is probably the best thing that had happened to him in his life. What Sarge didn't tell him, was that he was also advanced to an acting rank of Corporal, to be in a place of authority over incoming Privates.

"Gee, Sarge, I was hoping this is what would happen, but I was afraid to think it. How do you think they knew?"

"Wally, you've been working your butt off and doing a great job. All your instructors and trainers have noticed...and people say things,"said Sarge. "Doing your best and hard work gets you noticed in the army."

Five more days and Matt and Charlie would be here, he thought. How could he stand it?

Work soon took his mind off of it and his orders. He still had three weeks of classes. No way could he let up now. He dove in and continued.

On Thursday, he received a letter from Matt.

23 March 1945

Dear Wally,

We arrive on the train at 1723 hours in St. Louis. If you meet us there we can stay there. If you want us to go back to the Fort with you, that will be okay too. We are coming to see you, not St. Louis.

Have the USO Club call in some honky tonk girls for us, Ha Ha. We want to watch you dance some more.

Your Friend and Fellow Groundhog,

Matt

P.S. Both Charlie and me want to hear some St. Louis jazz.

That settles it, I'll take the bus to St. Louis and meet them on Saturday. We can go hear some St. Louis jazz and take the night bus back. We can go to the Chapel for Easter Sunday and meet Sarge.

On Friday, Wally went to the PX and made an investment, he bought an Eastman Kodak Brownie Edition 127, two rolls of 127 film, and a small bag to hold it all. The purchase was $3.49. He had been eyeing a portable radio for quite some time. Everyone was listening to them and he wanted to keep up with the times. He'd been looking at the General Electric. They also had an RCA, but he liked the looks of the General Electric which was $3.00 cheaper. He bought the General Electric. For a person who didn't spend money, this was an extravagance, all toll, nearly twenty dollars.

He took his purchases and returned to the barracks and put the radio on his desk. He fully digested the instructions and figured out how it operated. He also located a jazzy station. He then opened the package with the camera and film and read the instructions. He read the instructions over and over. Then loaded one of the two rolls of film into the camera. He clicked some pictures of his room to get the feel of taking pictures. He was ready.

He went to the Mess Hall and had a hearty meal of tuna and noodle casserole, creamed broccoli, milk, and banana cream pie. He wasn't in a particular hurry, so ate leisurely, then, after cleaning up his table tray, left. The weather was beginning to be quite nice.

He walked back to the barracks, went to his room and turned on the radio. He listened to *Fibber McGee and Molly* and laughed. Then shutting it off for fear it would wear it out, went to the latrine and showers. He shaved and returned, hanging his towel over the foot of his bunk, and put on clean skivvies and a T-shirt, then sat at his desk where he briefly surveyed the way it looked with a new GE Radio...never thinking to turn it on.

He read a chapter of his Bible, turned off the lights and retired.

Hey lay there thinking of how great it will be to see Matt and Charlie and catching up on everything. He had so much to tell them. He was sure they had a lot to tell him, too.

He listened to the strains of Taps, and drifted off to sleep.

CHAPTER TWENTY-SIX

THE BEST LAID PLANS...

Wally arose early, got ready, went to the Mess Hall and after having a hearty breakfast of sausage and scrambled eggs, toast and coffee, grabbed his sport's bag and headed for the early Greyhound Bus for the two and a half hour trip to St. Louis.

There were many there to take the trip, as many were granted leave and had finished their basic training and waiting for additional training. They were alive with chatter and excitement at seeing their families and loved ones. Most were acting like the children that they were...just forced to be men before their time.

Wally was also excited, that is why he took the early bus. He knew he'd arrive many hours before Matt and

Charlie, but he thought he'd rather be there than be late.

He listened to various conversations and speculations about the war. Much discussion was on the Normandy invasion, General Eisenhower, Montgomery, Patton, and others.

Several of the soldiers were expressing how well informed they were. Wally figured they were practicing for their girlfriends. They impressed themselves about how much they knew; how well informed. There were speculations that Hitler was being closed in on and the Allies were about to take him out. It was even speculated that it could happen at most any time.

However, the war with Japan was not being discussed too much. It kept going on and on. Although things had been looking better since Midway, there was a lot of uncertainty. The Japanese were digging in. Most of the men were kept pretty much in the dark, "...Loose lips, sink ships."

His studies had kept him so busy, he hardly had time to study the war. He and Sarge had discussed many things. War was not one of them. It was what it was, and neither could change that. Wally figured that President Roosevelt had things well under control.

He dozed a couple of times and then they arrived at St. Louis' Union Station. Wally swore he'd never seen so many people. Even the Greyhound had accelerated the trips to Fort Leonard Wood. There were tens of thousands of soldiers being processed, trained and shipped out to other forts and posts worldwide.

Wally explored the areas around Union Station. There wasn't a lot to see, or at least what he'd care to see. He looked for Blues and Jazz clubs, but then again, they were nothing that attracted him either. He checked out hotels and all were full. He thought of the holy family...there's no room in the inn. Certainly, St. Louis was not in the same league as Bethlehem. He began to feel bad that Matt and Charlie were coming to a place that wasn't that welcoming. For someone who was studying and supposed to be so good at logistics, he had let them down.

As the time came and was growing near for their arrival, he returned to the Station. He checked the time schedule and the train was on-time. He went to the gate to wait.

When the time came, people began to come into the terminal, and then he saw them. He excitedly waited for their approach. Each was lugging a duffle bag, hats set askew, looking very cavalier. They saw Wally and beamed.

When they were face-to-face, Wally thought, "To hell with what people think!" and grabbed both of them in his massive spread arms and gave them a huge hug.

"Damn it's good to see you guys!"

Both Matt and Charlie hugged him back. They just stood there for a minute or two. None moving.

Charlie, pulling back said, "Let me take a look at you," he studied him for a second, "Naw...you haven't gotten one bit better looking."

The three laughed, "Both of you guys look better and leaner. What they do to you there?"

Matt replied, "Worked our asses off!"

"We needed new ones anyway, our old ones were cracked!," laughed Charlie.

Both Matt and Charlie were well tanned. Somehow, they looked a little older than their nineteen years. They were genuinely glad to see Wally, but not more than he was to see them.

The three waded their way through the throng in the terminal and went outside to a beautiful early-Spring evening. They went to a bench and dropped their bags.

Wally spoke first, "There ain't much here to see," he said, "and I did some looking around. There's not much more to do either."

Charlie said, "We came to see you. There's not a damned thing in St. Louis that I give a shit about."

"Me either," chimed in Matt. "This might come as a surprise...we're not rich, well, not all of us, anyway."

"Moneybags, I ain't," said Charlie.

Wally said, "It's a good thing...there's no rooms available anyway."

"Hey, we'll sleep here in the park, if we have to," remarked Matt.

Wally, puffed up and acted as he thought he would, if he were important, "Tonight, gentlemen, you will be my guests at luxury accommodations at...Fort Leonard Wood."

"How'd you swing that?" asked Matt.

"Connections," replied Wally.

Charlie added, "Wow...great friends."

"Let's head for the bus, guys," said Wally, "Grab your bags and we may make the 1800 bus."

All three ran like hell attempting to catch the bus. They arrived just as the bus was heading out. Without hesitation, Wally dropped his bag and ran after it, grabbed an appendage of the bus and clung on. His body was swinging back and forth like an ape from a vine. He was yelling at the driver.

People on the bus were cheering and yelling at the driver. The driver at first didn't see him but then did and came to a stop. Meanwhile, the other two caught up.

The bus driver opened the door and angrily stomped out yelling, "Hey soldier, you can't do that!"

Wally, grinning, said, "Well I did, didn't I? We gotta get to Leonard Wood."

Soldiers in the bus were cheering and encouraging the three interlopers into the bus driver's space. The confrontational driver, realizing he was fighting a losing battle said, "Alright, grab your gear and get in." He turned, and re-entered the bus.

As he entered the cheering bus, Charlie spoke to the driver, "Thank You, Sir...you're a gentleman and a scholar."

The driver just groused something under his breath, "You got tickets?"

Wally said, "I got mine and turned to the others, do you?"

Both did, reaching for their wallets. "You think we're hitchhikers or something?" remarked Charlie.

The driver took them and plopped them onto a spindle in front of him.

"Bet that hasn't happened before!," commented one of the soldiers.

Another joked, "Bet he thought he was looking at *Tarzan of the Apes*!"

When they arrived at Fort Leonard Wood, they exited. As Wally walked past the driver, the driver remarked, "You got a lot of guts, young man, but I admire your spunk. Good Luck, son."

The three were on familiar territory, but soon left it or a different part of the base. They got to Wally's barracks and entered.

"Jesus, Wally, you got the same room here as you had in Basic," commented Charlie.

"The whole place has barracks like these. They're all alike," said Wally.

They looked around Wally's room, "Damn," commented Matt, "You even got a desk and a locker!"

Wally smiled, "Got a radio, too?"

"You guys got to use the latrine?"

"Yeah, my back teeth are floating," said Charlie.

They dropped their gear and headed down the stairs to the latrine. They finished, and headed out for the USO Club. When they entered, it was alive with soldiers and only a few USO girls. Some were dancing, all were drinking something, though it was 2100, it was Saturday night. Work hard, play hard seemed to be the motto. All were talking, laughing and totally oblivious of rank.

The Groundhogs stood, each having a beer...a first for Wally. He thought it tasted like it looked, but didn't say anything. He would do anything for his friends.

They finally got seats and were having a second beer as conversations turned to experiences. They shared their times at Fort Sill. They talked about weapons, artillery, the principles, and all of the safety measures and requirements. The discipline and everything to do with exploding and firing them. Wally hadn't any idea that there was so much science to blowing stuff up.

Matt and Charlie listened with sincere interest to stories about Sarge, all Wally's lessons, his passing

WHERE ARE YOU, WALLY BEARSTONE?

the GED...which he had to explain and all concerned. He spoke of Sarge often and in depth. He avoided talking about future assignments and church.

Matt and Charlie said they didn't know where they were going as it was "SECRET!" It was one that remained that way, as their surroundings had all sorts of signs and posters reminding them to keep their mouths shut!

Matt asked Wally if he had gotten his orders. Wally, unable to lie, said he had, and told them.

"You lucky shit," said Charlie, "How the hell did you swing that?"

"Hard work and a lot of studying," commented Wally.

"The good thing is, Matt and I are going to see the world," said Charlie.

"If we don't blow ourselves up first," commented Matt.

Wally, sincerely asked, "What's the chances of that?"

"Very little," remarked Matt, "We're in the artillery, we handle the big guns, so we stay a far piece behind the enemy lines."

"Unless you're appointed Forward Observer...which is the unlucky son-of-a-bitch telling the artillery where to aim the guns." said Charlie.

"Holy shit," was all Wally could say.

"Holy shit is right," Matt and Charlie agreed.

In the background the Jukebox was playing the song hits of the day, and they ordered another glass of "Horse Piss." Before they knew it, it was closing time and they headed back to the barracks.

"Where are we sleeping?" asked Matt.

Wally said, "I'm not sure, but we'll take care of it."

Charlie said he could sleep on the floor, a prediction which proved to be true.

When they got there, every bunk was full. Wally, who had keys to the storage room, got a couple of mattresses and a few blankets and returned to the room. He threw them on the floor.

"Make yourself comfortable, gents," he said.

"This is an April Fools joke, ain't it?" asked Matt.

"Nope," grinned Wally.

Crammed in like sardines, after crawling over each other, and finding a spot to go to sleep, the trio slept like logs. They were awake by 0700 hours and went to the latrine and showers. No one even noticed there were visitors.

"Know what day it is?" asked Wally.

"Yeah, April Fools day," said Charlie.

"It's Easter," said Matt.

"Both of you are right!," said Wally, "So, we three fools are going to the Chapel."

No one disagreed, so they got ready and walked to the Chapel, arriving a little early. There, they ran into Sarge.

"Sarge, this is Matt and Charlie...my best friends," said Wally, "Guys, this is Sarge."

Sarge said he knew all about them and welcomed them back to Leonard Wood.

Both told Sarge that he'd done something right with the big ox, they hardly knew him. They added that Wally thought the world of Sarge. On hearing this, Wally stood there grinning.

Both the visitors recognized the Chaplain who couldn't return the compliment. However, he did take a picture of the five of them standing in front of the Chapel. Then Sarge took a picture of Wally, Matt and

Charlie, and Charlie took a picture of Sarge and Wally. Then they took pictures of other points of interest, and each other using the rest of the roll.

The five went to the Mess Hall and had an Easter Dinner of ham, candied sweet potatoes, succotash, rolls, cranberry sauce and coconut cream pie with coffee.

They were laughing and joking and Sarge fit right in with the rest. All young men, who had met during difficult times. They inducted Sarge as an official member of the Groundhogs...then told him why. They were having a great time, when the base sirens began to blow.

Concurrently, the loud speakers sounded,

"All Hear This, All Hear This! Military Personnel are to report to their duty stations. The President of the United States has cancelled all Military Leave. All Military Personnel are ordered to return to their Assigned Units. If you are unable to do so, report to the nearest Military Installation Officer-In-Charge."

"Holy Shit!," commented Wally, "What the hell is this?"

Sarge, who fully agreed with Wally, didn't have a clue. Both Matt and Charlie were totally confused.

"What do we do?" asked Matt

"Where do we go?" added Charlie.

There was pandemonium both in the Mess Hall and as they exited, everywhere. Sarge took charge and left immediately with the trio following him. He went to Headquarters and asked for the Officer-of-the-Day. He didn't have the answers they needed.

After nearly an hour, Sarge reported back to the men, "There has been a major conflict on the Japanese front. You guys have got to get back to Fort Sill, immediately. There are a couple of planes preparing to depart shortly...you can catch a hop with them. Get back to the barracks, grab your duffle bags, there's a Jeep coming for you at Wally's barracks and will take you to the airfield."

The Groundhogs ran like hell and barely got Charlie's and Matt's stuff crammed into their duffle bags and ran down the steps and outside, when the Jeep pulled up. They hopped in, and they were off to the airfield and a waiting plane to Fort Sill, Oklahoma.

Sarge and Wally stood looking after them. Just an hour and a half ago, they were enjoying Easter dinner.

"Look on the bright side, you at least got to see them. You had a great time and a fun night, didn't you?" asked Sarge, "That's more than most get during war times."

"Yeah, but they didn't get to hear any St. Louis jazz on my new radio?" said a disappointed Wally.

"Well," said Sarge, "you ever heard of a Scottish poet named Robert Burns? Back in the 1700's he said "The best laid plans of mice or men often go astray.""

"No. Wonder if he had to drink horse piss to be with his friends? Maybe, that's why he said it?"

CHAPTER TWENTY-SEVEN

BEYOND HELL

While being disappointed with the early and unexpected departure of Matt and Charlie, Wally had had a great time. He caught up on all they had been doing and had shared the recent events of his life, and his accomplishments with his two best friends. Sarge had pointed out it doesn't often happen.

He continued with his studies and working with Sarge, which he enjoyed even more, now that he had met Charlie and Matt. They all four seemed to get along great.

He turned in the film to the PX and was anxiously awaiting to see if they were any good. He listened to his radio and often to see if he could learn anything about what had happened, but so far there was nothing that was reported.

Once in a while he would listen to jazz or just plain music Bing Crosby, Frank Sinatra, Jo Stafford, Peggy Lee, Johnny Mercer, and on and on. One of the jazz songs he liked was "*There Are Great Things Happening Every Day*" by Sister Rosetta Tharpe. It made him feel good. Then there was "*Fuzzy Wuzzy*,which made him laugh and Frank Sinatra came out with "*You'll Never Walk Alone*," which made him tear up a bit. All in all, the radio was a good investment.

Wally was excelling in his grades. Sarge was impressed at how much any one person could learn, but Wally did it. Graduation was just days away, on Friday, April 13, 1945. That's supposed to be unlucky, Friday the 13th. What could happen?

Wally and Sarge were eating at the Mess Hall. Wally showed the packet of pictures he'd picked up at the PX. The two were looking at them and all but a couple were pretty good. One was just great, and that was the one with Matt, Charlie, Sarge and Wally, which the Chaplain had taken.

Both Sarge and Wally though it was the best one… all four were smiling. It was 3" x 5", and Wally said "I'm going to buy a brass frame at the PX and put it on my desk."

Sarge thought that was a good idea. They had just finished a piece of Cherry pie and Sarge said, "Day after tomorrow is graduation."

"I know," countered Wally, "I can hardly wait."

"Looking forward to starting your new job?"

"For sure, do you know what it's going to be, Sarge?" asked Wally.

"I do," answered Sarge.

Like the big little boy that he was, he said, "Tell me, please."

"You'll be working with Major Merriweather as a teacher trainee, but don't say anything. I'm not supposed to know," said Sarge.

"A teacher trainee? How the hell am I going to do that?" questioned a shocked Wally.

"You prepare...just like everything else. Just work as hard as you have been," said Sarge.

He asked Wally if he'd heard anything from Matt and Charlie, and he told him he hadn't heard a word.

They visited more and went back to their barracks. Wally went through his nightly routine and called it a day.

Morning began with the sounds of Reveille playing. He did his usual latrine duties and walked to the Mess Hall for breakfast. When he had finished, he passed in his food tray and reported to the Training Center. There, he joined his class and the day had started. He did the headcount and reported to the Sergeant and returned to his seat. The material presented he was already familiar with, and he whizzed through the assignment.

They were mid-way through the afternoon session, when the loud speaker system came alive with:

"**Now Hear This, Now Hear This! Today, at 1:00 PM, Franklin Delano Roosevelt, the four-term, thirty-second president of the United States, died at his summer retreat in Warm Springs, Georgia. No further details are available at this time. Again, President Franklin Delano Roosevelt has died at age 63.**"

All sat in total silence. What was there to be said? The United States was in the middle of two major wars on two continents. The nation desperately needed leadership, and its only effective leader was dead. Everyone was wondering, what would happen next. To use a navy expression, we are a ship without a sail! What's going to happen? Class was dismissed.

Everything was in turmoil, fortunately, the military wasn't so easily shaken. There was a lot of leadership, the world just didn't realize it. There was precedent to be followed. The world does go on.

The Vice President Harry Truman, a haberdasher from Missouri, was sworn in later that day at 7:00 p.m. in the cabinet room at the White House. An army soldier from WWI and a boy from Missouri was now the 33rd President of the United States of America.

The world mourned for the four-term President FDR and the inexperience of now President Harry S Truman. It dominated the news: however, the graduation of the 6th Infantry Engineer Replacement Training Center, took place as scheduled at 1100 hours on Friday, April 13, 1945.

Wally stood proud as his name was announced, Private Wallace Bearstone. He was even more proud when he was cited as "The Outstanding Trainee of the Cycle." He hadn't any idea of receiving this honor.

Later, when discussing these events with Sarge, he asked, "Did you know about this?"

"Wally, there's little I don't know about what's going on here. Of course I did. You were recommended by every NCO and Officer in the school."

"Holy Shit!" was all he could say and as soon as he had said it, covered his mouth with his left hand.

"It's alright, I won't tell Major Merriweather that you're a dumb ass...who swears," replied a grinning Sarge. "Let's celebrate tonight. My treat."

Later that night the two went to the USO Club. As usual, it was packed full of soldiers who mostly talked about FDR and the new president. Little was said about the war, although it was heard now and then.

Raising his glass of Coke toward Wally, "Well, you did it."

Very humbled, Wally replied, "I wouldn't have, if you hadn't helped me."

"Yeah, you would have. You have a bright future, Wally. Don't ever let anyone tell you otherwise. If you put your mind to something, you do it. You don't see that often, especially in the army," said Sarge.

"Thanks, Sarge," replied Wally. He clicked his glass of Coke with Sarge's, "You know what's nice?"

"No," Sarge answered, "What?"

"You don't like horse piss," Wally grinned.

They stayed for several hours visiting at the Club, then called it a night.

"See you at the Chapel on Sunday?"

Wally replied, "You betcha. Night Sarge."

"Night, Wally."

Later on, Wally reflected on the day's activities. He looked at the brass-framed picture of the Groundhogs and smiled.

"Wouldn't they just shit if they heard...I was the Outstanding Trainee of the Cycle? Then he thought of all that happened over the past several months... unbelievable!

The next day they went to the Chapel, greeted several people that they had come to know and of course, the Chaplain. Wally was becoming quite comfortable among the Christian people there and grew to love the Chapel services. He still didn't sing, but enjoyed listening to music. He and Sarge had a Sunday routine which usually didn't vary. Chapel, the Mess Hall, additional training, Mess Hall and back to the barracks.

Today, at the Mess Hall, Sarge said that he'd taught Wally all that he could. No lessons today.

"What do you mean, 'No lessons today,?'" replied Wally, "You're my friend, I want to hang out with you. Hell, Sarge, I ain't got anyone else."

Sarge smiled at his awkward reply, "Okay...what do you want to do?"

"Can we go to the Training Center? You could teach me about music."

"What do you want to know?" asked Sarge.

"Tell me about those little black dots and what they mean."

"Okay."

He pulled a paper napkin and began to draw. He explained about how each represented a time element, explaining the sixteenth, eighth, quarter, half and whole notes. He spoke about the different time values and the beats to a measure and reminded him of the treble and bass clefs. They spent hours at the Mess Hall discussing music.

"Gawd, you're smart," stated Wally, "I don't know if I'll ever get that stuff."

Sarge went through many paper napkins which were becoming a hefty stack. Wally asked many questions and Sarge gave many answers. The mess crew ignored the two and cleaned around them. Sarge demonstrated about four-four time, versus three-four time. He picked a familiar tune to Wally, "Don't Fence Me In," a new song by Bing Crosby. He demonstrated using the familiar tune to help him understand. Soon Wally gave a glimmer of understanding.

"Now, you're getting it," remarked Sarge. Wally understood the difference between a waltz and the foxtrot.

"It's close to 1700 hours, Wally, and you still got to relocate. Let's go get your stuff and I'll help you move. You know you're moving into my barracks."

They left, but not before Wally grabbed the pile of musical napkins, and they left.

Sarge borrowed a dolly and some boxes from his friend at the Quartermaster's, and they wheeled them to Wally's barracks. They spent nearly an hour gathering stuff up and packing it into the boxes and his duffle bags. When his room was cleaned, they pushed the loaded dolly for the several blocks to Sarge's barracks.

Once there, Sarge took him to a room on the main floor about the same size as the one he had vacated. It was set aside for the enlisted trainees and teaching staff. Within 30 minutes, he was settled in. There were several there who knew Wally and greeted him, congratulating him and welcoming him to the staff.

Just like the rest of the army, people were easily met and spoken to. Most were friendly. Wally noticed that army people learned to become friends and get to know people quickly. It hadn't dawned on him that the reason was they may not be here tomorrow. They were in the army, after all. A fact that he was reminded of when he was told that next Friday was inspection.

Since there was no leave being granted, he began his new job on Monday at 0800 hours. Sarge walked with him to his new office where he was scheduled to go through orientation. He would also meet Major Merriweather. Wally wondered if he was going to yell and stomp, but didn't say so.

Major Merriweather entered and, after being called to attention, he said, "At ease." His manner was straight forward, unemotional and very matter-of-fact.

"Staff, we have lost President Roosevelt, but we are still at war. Our work is still cut out for us. It is our job to train new field engineers how to build effective and efficient facilities under adverse conditions. We need to teach them how to operate earth-moving equipment, to plan for and effectively handle materials and resources, to strategically ensure that what is needed is provided under tactical stress and difficult conditions."

"The demand for field engineers is even more important now that we are engaging more heavily with the Japanese. We have suffered great losses at Okinawa. It is critical that we turn out more engineers."

He went on, "I welcome back our outstanding staff and welcome new members. I look forward to meeting the newcomers." With that, he adjourned the current staff and told the newcomers to remain.

There were five new staff members who had been assigned; one Sergeant First Class, one Staff Sergeant, two Sergeants, and one six foot, six inch, Private Wallace Bearstone.

The Major gave them all a greeting and spoke to each about their experiences, what their levels of expertise was and what their future positions and courses would be to teach.

He then approached Wally, "You, young man, come with a recommendation of my staff, you're the Outstanding Trainee of the Cycle, and from what I hear, excel at everything you tackle. How do you do that, Private?"

Wally wanting to impress the Major said, "Sir, it's kinda like sorting pepper from fly shit, Sir. You just have to know what you're doing…Sir!"

The Major, stifling a grin replied, "Yes you do, Private, and since you are here to learn to train, I'm giving you an acting rank of Corporal. You have to outrank your students."

He turned and left, hardly waiting to vacate to share the words of wisdom learned from the Outstanding Trainee of the Cycle.

At the end of the first day, Wally returned to his new quarters at the barracks. He was very proud of what he'd experienced, achieved and had the chance to talk to the Major and to give him some advice. He wanted to share it with Sarge, but Sarge wasn't there.

Later that night, Sarge knocked on his door and entered. He had finally received an answer to an inquiry he'd made.

"Wally, sit down. There is no easy way to say this, so I'll just say it: Charlie Yates was killed in Okinawa ,and Matt Carver is M.I.A."

The news hit Wally like a sledgehammer to the gut. He had never known the feelings he felt: anger, shock, sorrow, horror, fear, hurt, guilt, robbed, victimized, loneliness, all rolled into one. He wanted to scream, moan, yell, throw things, pound holes in the wall. He hated everyone…and no one. He didn't know what to do, he didn't know how to react. Never in his life had he ever felt anything close to what he was feeling.

Sarge was unsure what Wally would do or how he would react, so was prepared for about anything.

Wally sat there very stoically at the foot of his bunk staring into a void. Then tears welled up in his eyes and trickled down his face, joining the mucus running from his nose. His face crumbled into a pathetic and distorted look of agony. Finally, his mouth opened and he let out a quiet and gentle sob which slowly grew to a moan of anguish, "Those dumb sons-of-bitches, why did they have to go and get themselves killed?"

Wally's world had just collapsed around him.

Sarge sat down beside his friend, reached up and put his arm around Wally, who turned and leaned his face down into his mentor and friend's chest and wept. How long they sat there, neither remembers.

Death was a stranger to Sarge as well, and he too, began to cry. Although he knew and liked the two lost soldiers, he was grieving for this giant of a man he had grown to love like a brother. They both were facing the reality of war: a feeling far beyond hell.

Taps that night said it all. A fitting tribute to Charlie and Matt and the thousands of others who had died for our nation, and the thousands more who were yet to face the last full measure of devotion.

CHAPTER TWENTY-EIGHT

AND LIFE GOES ON

Wally arose promptly at 0600 hours and grabbed his Dopp kit and towel went to the latrine and showers. The same as any morning. He went to the Mess Hall, ate alone, and went to the Center to work.

He sat at his office desk, studying a manual on his duties, studied all the items on his agenda and began doing them. Sarge walked in and greeted him.

"How you doing?"

"I'm okay," replied Wally.

"Is there anything you want me to do?"

"No, I'm good."

"Are you sure you're okay?," asked Sarge.

"Last night, as you know, my life changed. I lost two good friends…you did too, I mean you would have been. But they're dead and there's nothing either of us can do about it. There's still a war going on and we got to get people trained so the same thing don't happen to them. That's something we can do," said Wally.

Sarge was amazed at Wally's attitude. For a nineteen year old to look at the world that way, was something else. Even he, at twenty- four couldn't do that.

Major Merriweather entered and both stood up at attention.

"At ease, guys, and you don't have to jump up every time I come around. Yes, I'm your superior, but I'm not god. We got a job to get started. Turner, I want you to work with Corporal Bearstone…" the Major stopped. "Where are your stripes, Corporal?"

"I forgot, Sir," responded Wally.

"My fault, Sir, I distracted him with some sad news," interjected Sarge.

"What kind of sad news, Sergeant?"

"We had a couple of good friends here who were called back to Fort Sill. They were sent to Okinawa and were killed," said Sarge.

"That's a tough break. Sorry to hear that," replied the Major, "Go take care of it now."

Wally, jumping up, "Yes, Sir."

The Major left for his office.

"You didn't tell me he gave you an acting position."

"We were too busy doing other things," retorted Wally.

They went to the PX and purchased corporal strips and they were able to sew them on then. He removed his fatigue shirt, and the girl sewing was having difficulty keeping her eyes on the fabric. Wally may have had a bad face, but he had a spectacular body. There were others working there there who also noticed and several found minor tasks to perform near where he was sitting. Wally was oblivious to it all. He said I have additional uniforms that I need to bring in.

"My name is Mitzy, and I'd be glad to take care of them for you."

"Thank you Mitzy, I'll bring them over after work... if you'll still be here...say 1630 hours?"

"I'll make sure I am here," said Mitzy.

Wally and Sarge left.

"Boy, was she flirting with you," said Sarge.

"What do you mean?" asked Wally.

"I'd be happy to do them for you," responded Sarge, imitating Mitzy. "I got too much work to do to get involved with a PX girl. Besides, her tits ain't big enough." replied Wally. End of subject.

They returned to the office where they faced a very heavy workload, which kept growing. They were preparing for the upcoming classes. Sarge now had only one stripe more than Wally. It made it easier for both to work together.

Wally was to become a heavy equipment instructor, replacing an older Sergeant who was retiring. He brought a new enthusiasm none had seen in many years.

April went by and they were into May. The battle in Okinawa kept raging; however, on May 8, the war in Germany was over. Hitler had poisoned himself in his bunker, the Allied forces found him and his wife, Eva Braun, lying side by side...or what was left of them. They'd been burned. Germany surrendered.

Wally had been spending more time at the PX. All of his uniforms were up to date, with Corporal stripes. He had been eyeing a new guitar in a case that was being sold there for $18.00...it was a beauty. They also had an instruction book for another $1.00. He thought he'd surprise Sarge, and so he bought it. Sarge never told him he could play or teach guitar, but music was music.

Wally would strum and strum, practicing chords, over and over, sometimes hitting the right ones. It could be heard throughout the first level of his barracks. Fortunately, like everything else he did, he began to master it. However, it took well into June.

On June 22, 1945, the battle of Okinawa became an Allied victory with heavy losses. Wally thought of Matt and Charlie and stared at their picture sitting on his desk. He uttered a little prayer for them, then went back to his guitar.

Fort Leonard Wood was still producing Field Engineers every ten weeks. Sarge and Wally had strengthened their bond, and each was the other's best friend. Wally had taken to instructing others like a duck takes to water. His level of expertise had increased by leaps and bounds. The trainees all liked him and respected what he said. Sarge was given another stripe (actually it was a rocker) and promoted to Staff Sergeant.

By later July, President Truman made an offer to Japan to come to a peaceful settlement, with the assurance that if they didn't he would destroy them. They wouldn't budge, so on August 6, 1945, on a top-secret mission, the *Enola Gay* dropped an atomic bomb on Hiroshima, killing 70,000 people and destroying five square miles of the city. Four days later, the US dropped another on the city of Nagasaki, killing another 40,000. There had never been a more devastating bomb on the face of the earth. Japan surrendered on August 14, 1945...Victory over Japan.

The entire country exploded with delight. Celebrations were everywhere. People were hugging and kissing each other whether they knew them or not. Wally and Sarge were at the USO Club and celebrated with everyone else. Beer and booze were flowing like never before.

"You ever had whiskey before?" asked Wally.

"No, have you?" replied Sarge.

"No. All I ever had was wine. My Pa used to drink it though" admitted Wally, "You want to do it?"

They agreed and ordered a couple of whiskeys. The waitress wanted to know how they wanted them.

When they told her they had never had it before, she suggested they have in with water on the rocks.

When they were served, both Wally and Sarge lifted them, and then Wally repeated a saying he had heard, "Over the lips and through the gums...look out belly, here it comes!"

Both took a big gulp of the alien stuff. Thanks to the waitress it was diluted with water, for had it been straight it would have choked them to oblivion.

They celebrated with a couple more each and were feeling the effects. They thought they better get back to the barracks and to bed. The two buddies, arm-in-arm, staggered back to their barracks. They were giggling like kids, tripping up the steps to the barracks, and staggering down the hallway to their rooms.

Wally looked at the picture of the four of them standing in front of the Chapel and began to weep, "We did it guys!" He kissed the picture and replaced it where it had been.

Japan officially surrendered to the Allied Supreme Commander, General Douglas MacArthur on 2 September 1945 on board the U.S. Navy battleship, *Missouri*, ending WWII.

The next several days were ones of celebration; however, the work went on. Wally thought the army had taken the Boy Scout motto, "Be Prepared."

Before they knew it, it was Christmas 1945. Sarge invited Wally to go to Louisville to visit his parents. Wally, naturally agreed. He'd like to see Louisville, the Churchill Downs and the bluegrass. They made travel plans and both were granted eleven days leave beginning on Saturday 22 December 1945. They had until Wednesday at midnight 1 January 1946.

Wally loaded with both uniform and civilian clothes, along with his guitar, and Sarge, with a travel bag, boarded the 1800 hour Greyhound Bus in front of the main gate. They were chattering about all sorts of things and arrived at the Union Station in St. Louis at 2030 hours. Their train wasn't until 2330 hours, but experience told Wally they better stay in the terminal. They located their departure gate for the train to Indianapolis, Indiana. They each had a cup of coffee and a donut and waited.

They boarded the train at 2315 hours and were off to Indianapolis' Union Station. They changed trains to the Monon Railway and departed for Louisville, Kentucky, where they were scheduled to arrive at 0800 hours on Sunday.

They were met by the Reverend and Mrs. Raymond Turner, who warmly greeted both boys with huge hugs and kisses. Sarge, whose name was changed at that point from Sarge to Josh, was short for Joshua. Wally, who had never known him by anything other than Sarge, was having difficulty in adjusting to the name change.

The Reverend was in his early sixties, with a rim of white hair circling a bald pate. He had a small pot-belly and a warm smile. Mrs. Turner was everyone's mom. She was warm, friendly, a little on the heavy side with grey hair as well. Wally liked them both immediately.

"Welcome home, Josh," said his father, "God has delivered you safe and sound, hasn't he mother?"

"He's answered our prayers for sure," replied Mrs. Turner.

"Mom, Dad, meet Wally Bearstone," said Sarge/Josh.

A grinning Wally said, "Glad to meet you... Reverend and Mrs. Turner."

"Please call us Mom and Dad," responded Mrs. Turner, "We don't answer to anything else. Besides, Josh has kept us well informed about you. We've been praying for you both."

Wally was totally caught off guard. Sarge had never mentioned that he wrote his parents. I guess it shouldn't be a surprise, but he had never mentioned it.

The Reverend said they had better be on the road as he had a 10:00 o'clock service. They left the terminal and soon located his 1941 green, four-door, Buick sedan. He drove them to Germantown, arriving at 0845 hours. Their home was in the parsonage next door to the First Christian Church. It was modest, but warmly decorated and made Wally feel welcome. Sarge/Josh took their luggage upstairs to their room.

"Go freshen up, guys," said Mrs. Turner/Mom, "I'll fix you a bite to eat." She put a couple of slices of bread in the toaster, took out some preserves from the refrigerator, made a couple of cups of coffee, and poured two small glasses of orange juice.

The Reverend asked both boys, "Would you please wear your uniforms? I want to introduce you to the congregation."

"Sure, Dad," replied Josh.

"Sure," said Wally.

The two went to the bathroom and got ready. They came down the stairs and went to the kitchen. There, on the table was the coffee, juice, and toast with strawberry preserves on it.

"Thanks, Mom."

"You're welcome, honey," she replied, "I'm so glad you're home."

"Wally, do you have family?" she said.

"No...just the ranch hands in Wyoming," he responded.

After they finished they went back upstairs, brushed their teeth, washed their hands and returned. Wally noticed that his guitar had been placed next to the piano in the living room. It looked like it had always been there.

Reverend Turner left for the church to do what he needed to do to get ready. A little before 1000 hours, Mrs. Turner, with her arm through Josh's, proudly walked out the door with Wally following.

They walked in the vestibule of the church and up the stairs. Wally ducking to avoid banging his head as he usually did. His immense size drew attention from all.

Most of the congregation knew Josh, no one knew Wally. When the Reverend proudly introduced them as War heroes the church broke out in applause. Some stood, some reached and patted them on their backs. Women walked across the aisle and hugged and kissed them both on their cheeks. Wally had never in his life felt more welcome anywhere. He felt like this was a home to come back to.

Reverend Turner was an excellent preacher and his congregation loved him. Wally was familiar with all the hymns they sang, but he didn't sing. He did, however, watch the music with intensity, trying to play them on his guitar.

After church, they were greeted by the entire congregation who wanted to hear everything about what they did. Many had watched Joshua grow up from a little boy into manhood. One in particular, a lovely young lady by the name of Becky Johnson. She approached Josh, all smiles.

"Welcome home, Josh. It's so good to see you." she said.

When she smiled, Wally had never seen a more beautiful smile. It lightened the whole room.

"Hi, Becky," smiled Josh back, "Meet Wally Bearstone...he's my army buddy."

"Hi Wally," she smiled, "I'm glad to meet you, too."

Wally noticed that she was happier to see Josh than she was to meet him. He also noticed it was returned by Josh.

"Hey guys, I'm going to let you two catch up with each other. I'm heading back to the house." He left to go home. No one objected either.

"Wally," called Mrs. Turner, "you going back to the house?"

"Yes'm," answered Wally.

"May I go with you?" she asked.

"Of Course."

She grabbed Wally's arm and proudly walked with her arm through his. The two created quite a sight, a mountain of a soldier towering over his friend's five-foot-tall mother.

Sunday night dinner was a time of togetherness. Mom had prepared a large roasted chicken with dressing, mashed potatoes and gravy, brussel sprouts floating in butter, and a large cherry pie.

Josh asked Becky to join the family gathering, and the five of them ate until they were stuffed. The evening was full of stories and laughter, sharing, joking and all in all, just having fun.

Josh played the piano, and very well. Soon everyone was singing. Wally played the guitar, and did surprisingly well and the evening turned into a song fest. Everyone was having a great time.

The evening was soon gone, and Becky bid farewell to all and left. The boys helped mom to clean up the dinner table, and after kissing her "Goodnight," left for bed.

They went to their bedroom, which had twin beds. Wally went to the bathroom, cleaned up, and changed into fresh skivvies and a T-shirt. He crawled into bed. When Josh was finished he did the same. Although the room was dark, neither went right to sleep.

Wally said, "I like your family, Sar....Josh."

"Thanks, Wally, I like them too." He paused for a while and said, "I like it when you call me Josh, too."

"You do?" questioned Wally.

"Yeah, Sarge always sounds so military. After all we've been through together, we're more than friends, you know. You're the brother I always wanted but never had. Someone to share with and talk to... about anything."

Wally was quiet for a long time, then spoke, "Josh... you're my brother too. I trust you more than anyone in the world, I'd trust you with my life. I know I'm just a big dumb hick from Wyoming, but you've helped me to become a different person. I'm still a hick, but not so dumb anymore. You took me as I was. You helped me be somebody. Nobody's ever done that before. All I want to do is to please you; to make you proud."

"I am proud of you, brother. Although there have been times I wondered?" he laughed.

"Asshole," said Wally.

They both laughed.

"Please call my mom, Mom and dad, Dad. It would thrill them to pieces," said Josh.

"I'll try. I've never called anyone that, so it's something I'll have to get used to saying."

"Take your time, Brother."

"Okay, thanks...I love you, Brother." This was the first time in Wally's life he had ever told anyone that he loved them. He doubted that Josh knew.

"I love you too, Brother. Goodnight."

CHAPTER TWENTY-NINE

CHRISTMAS, 1945

They slept a little longer than usual, but arose to the smell of fresh coffee and hot rolls. They had both slept well and slowly got up, each going to the bathroom, brushing their teeth, and slipped on their fatigues. Wearing socks only, they went downstairs and into the kitchen.

"Morning, Mom," said Josh.

"Morning boys," eyeing the fatigues, "Are those your pajamas?"

"No...they're our work clothes," said Wally.

Josh, much to Wally's surprise, said, "We're going to go cut a Christmas tree from the woods. You want to come along?"

"Land, no. I've got a lot of cooking to do, and Dad's already at the office getting his sermon ready for tonight."

Josh, pouring coffee, "You want coffee, Wally?"

"Sure, with cream and two sugars...Please."

Josh handed him a mug of coffee and said add your own stuff, you're at home now. I ain't waiting on you. Get your own rolls and butter too."

"Josh," corrected his mother, "that's no way to treat a guest."

Wally said, "I'm no guest, Mom, I'm home." It came so natural that he even shocked himself. He truly felt at home. All was natural, and he was surrounded by love.

The boys ate enough for double their number and then thanked Josh's mom and after carrying their dishes over to the sink, went upstairs and put on their boots. They grabbed their jackets and went back downstairs. Josh took keys from the side table at the front door and yelled to his mom.

"Mom, we're taking the car keys and going to the woods. Does Dad need the family car today?"

"No, Honey, he's working all day." She cautioned, "Drive careful."

The new brothers left, after withdrawing an axe, a saw, and a coil of rope from the basement. Josh threw them in the trunk, and off they went. They drove through the town along the parkway. Josh pointed out places of interest and recalled events of his school days. He pointed out where Becky lived.

"You like Becky?," Wally asked.

"We went to school together and we dated once in a while. We broke up when I joined the army. I didn't want her to miss out on an important phase of her life. She was too pretty and too sweet to let that happen."

"You still like her don't you?," asked Wally.

"Yeah, I do, but I don't know whether she still likes me."

"Yeah, she does. I watched her yesterday…she's still moony-eyed."

"You think so?"

Josh pulled into a wooded area, and they got out, each carrying a tool. They walked into the woods looking for a tree: the *perfect* tree. Josh related the story of how each year they did this. It was a family tradition that had been a part of his life…all his life. They found the one they were looking for, and after

Josh identified it, Wally grabbing the axe said, "Stand back."

With a couple of swings, the tree came down.

"My god," said Josh, "how'd you do that."

"It's an old tradition that Lon Bishop taught me on the ranch. This is how we build houses in Wyoming."

Wally picked up the tree, threw it over his shoulder, and started walking back toward the car.

"You don't even know your own strength, do you, Brother?"

"Guess not. On the ranch we had to cut trees, make fencing from it, dig holes, set the posts, string wire, make lumber, build buildings. We took stones from the land and used them to build foundations, and make fireplaces. I had to heave bales of hay up into the loft, and just about everything. You get muscles when you do all of that."

Josh was amazed to learn this. Wally had never shared life on the ranch.

Wally was amazed at how Josh drove, knew everything about Louisville and half the people in his neighborhood. He pointed out the school where he had gone, he showed him the University of Louisville, where he had gone. They drove along the Ohio River, where Josh talked about the great flood of '37, and they returned home.

There, they evened up the base of the tree and inserted it into a Christmas tree stand, strung lights, opened a box of ornaments that they saved from year to year. Mom joined them with a plate full of cookies and some milk and they withdrew an ornament. Wally learned that each had a story. They hung tinsel on the tree and Wally pronounced it was the most beautiful tree in the world. It was really a memory tree.

"We need to go shopping," he remarked to Josh.

"Yeah, we do, let's go."

"See you later Mom, we got errands to run."

Off they went in search of treasures. They spent the rest of the afternoon shopping in the department stores. They didn't have much money, and it had to last, so they shopped wisely.

After the boys split up, Wally picked out a beautiful brooch for Mom, a beautiful tie for Dad, and a nice pair of leather gloves for Josh, which would go with his army uniform. He'd never bought Christmas gifts and enjoyed it. He bought wrapping paper and three pretty cards to go on the package. He listened to the Christmas music playing on the speaker systems and enjoyed the decorations throughout the stores. They were beautiful, and the stores all smelled wonderful with Christmas candy and cologne and pine needles. It became the smell of Christmas.

They rejoined, and the two, with arms full of bags, went to the car and headed home. They went to their room and wrapped their packages...without peeking at the others. They took them down and placed them under the tree.

Dad came home from church, and they were joined around the dinner table. Wally had to admit, Mom was a better cook than the army...and said so. They all laughed, and Dad said grace, thanking the Almighty for sending his two sons to them and for the food.

They enjoyed a wonderful meal of ham and all that went with it. They had a hot apple pie. They helped with the dishes and all got ready to go for the Christmas Eve service next door.

It was glorious. The church was decorated with red bows and trails of holly and ivy. The choir sang Christmas songs, and Reverend Turner gave an exquisite sermon on the birth of the Christ child. So excited about the entire trip, Wally had forgotten it was his birthday as well.

Becky joined Josh in the pew, and it was like the family he had always wanted...the ones he had seen in magazines and had read about.

Christmas morning, they arose and went down to gather around the tree. There were a lot more gifts than when they went to bed. Dad had turned on the tree lights, and Mom had made fresh sticky buns and coffee. They all helped themselves and gathered around the tree. Dad played Santa Claus and sat on the floor in his pajamas. He read the cards and passed out the gifts, one at a time.

Wally, who hadn't expected any, was shocked when Dad said, "Here's one for Wally. It says, 'Happy Birthday to Wally...from Mom, Dad and Joshua.'" He handed the package to Wally.

Wally opened it carefully to find a black leather-bound study Bible with his name *"Wallace Bearstone,"* engraved in gold on the cover. The edges were gold leaf, and the entire Bible was exquisite. Wally opened it, and inside the cover was written:

Happy Birthday, Wally,
With love,
From your Dad, Mom and Brother Joshua,
Your family in Christ.

For the second time in his life, Wally's homely face distorted, and his eyes filled with tears. He was at a loss to say anything.

Mom reached over and taking the big guy in her arms, gave him a big hug, "God bless you child."

They all said they needed a break and broke up the little gathering to do whatever excuse they could think of. Josh brought back a glass of apple juice and after Wally was in control, Josh said, "I think Santa Klaus is getting impatient.

Dad went to the floor and it all began. Gifts were exchanged and there was one left. Dad reached for it and read, "To Wally, from the Groundhogs. Wally opened it and there was a black framed enlarged picture of the groups in front of the Chapel at Fort Leonard Wood. Josh had had it enlarged from his own copy he had sent home.

The image of this Christmas will go down in Wally's memory as the finest he will ever have of any Christmas, anywhere, ever. From this point forward, he had a Dad, a Mom and a brother which he truly loved.

The rest of the leave zoomed by. The boys were invited to attend a New Year's Eve celebration at a local restaurant with several of Josh's old friends. Josh took Becky and the three drove to the place a few miles from home. Wally sat and watched Josh and Becky dance and enjoyed it.

One of the local girls asked Wally if he wanted to dance with her, and after the usual excuses, he gave in. He was anxious not to have a repeat performance of last year. He didn't. Then another girl came up and asked him to dance. He did. He danced with seven different girls and was beginning to feel he had that special attraction back.

When midnight came, he caught Becky and Josh kissing on the stroke of midnight. Wally was feeling pride for his new brother when one of his dance partners came and planted a big kiss on Wally.

Wally, who was caught off guard said, "WOW, that was a surprise!"

"You deserved it big boy, anytime," said the cute little girl, "Happy New Year."

Wally didn't notice whether she had big tits or not. It didn't matter.

The next day, Wally and Josh prepared to leave for the trip back to Fort Leonard Wood. Mom, Dad and Becky drove them to the Union Station in Louisville where they awaited the Monon Train to Indianapolis and back. It was an emotional farewell, but one of hope and a brighter future.

The train arrived and after a round of hugs and kisses, Josh and Wally boarded the train which began to chug and left the station.

The brothers chattered and laughed and soon they pulled into Indianapolis. They switched trains and were on their way back to Leonard Wood.

They dozed a little, then talked a bit more. Wally felt as if he'd always known Josh. The feeling was mutual. They pulled into St. Louis and caught the last bus to the Fort. There, they gathered their gear and walked back to the barracks.

After mounting the steps to the barracks, they headed for their rooms. When they got to Wally's room, Josh stopped. "I want to come in, if it's okay?"

"Sure," Wally said.

They entered Wally's room. Wally put his stuff down and said, "What is it?"

"I'm in love with Becky. Guess I always have been. She said she's in love with me, too. What do I do?"

Wally replied,"You're asking me? Hell, I ain't ever been in love!"

"I mean, I've never been with a girl before and I want to marry her." said Josh, "but I don't think she'd want to be married to a soldier."

"Why not, it's a good life, Josh, you know that. Think about it, but you don't have to make a decision tonight. Go to bed."

Josh smiled, "Boy, the roles have changed, haven't they Brother?"

"You're still the smartest." Wally grumbled and grabbed Josh, gave him a big hug and kissed him on the cheek. "Night, Brother, thanks for the best Christmas ever."

It was now Wednesday morning, 2 January 1946.

CHAPTER THIRTY

CARPE DIEM

By March of 1946, Stalin's rise to power, and the spread of communism began to cause concern. The expansion of the Soviet Union throughout Europe and elsewhere began to threaten the peace of the world. Great Britain Prime Minister Winston Churchill made note of the rise of the growing threat in a speech in Fulton, Missouri. Churchill declared that the "anti-democratic 'Iron Curtain' a growing challenge and peril to Christian civilization" had descended across Europe.

Despite the desire for peace, one could feel that conflict was on the horizon. This was one of several factors influencing Josh's reenlistment decision. He had to make this decision by 1 August 1946. He was conflicted by his growing relationship with Becky, his duty to his family, his loyalty to Wally and his desire to teach.

He was offered a position at the University of Louisville, his alma mater. That would put him in his hometown near his mother and father and with the love of his life, Becky. There was really no decision to make. He had shared this with Wally, they spoke quite freely about everything. Wally had agreed, unselfishly, that he shouldn't reenlist.

Wally made several trips to Louisville, it was his adopted home. The last one that he made with Josh was to serve as Josh's best man for his wedding.

The years passed, and by 1949, Professor Josh and Becky had two children, a daughter whose nickname was Suzie and her little brother, Nick. Both called Wally, Uncle Wally. He was very much a part of their family. He felt right at home with Mom and Dad as well.

By 1950, Wally had risen to the rank of Sergeant First Class. His role in the Engineer School had varied and expanded. He focused on his own education and was nearing completion of getting his degree in civil engineering.

During June of 1950 the Korean conflict erupted. Mao Zedong controlled Communist China. The army's role expanded, and once again so did the need for field engineers. Wally's schedule rarely permitted trips to Louisville. They became less and less, and soon were nearly nonexistent. Letter writing and an occasional phone call kept him up to date. These too became less frequent.

Wally taught so many of the young men he couldn't remember how many. He couldn't remember how many were killed or wounded either. He converted his rank to Warrant Officer and also received a degree in Civil Engineering.

By 1965, the army was deeply invested in Viet Nam, and still he taught. Mom and Dad had both gone to be with their Saviour, Josh's and Becky's three children were in their teens. Wally was always welcomed, but rarely had seen them. They had their life, and Wally had his. The army was his life.

On Friday, 5 December 1975 at 1000 hours, Warrant Officer Wallace Bearstone, retired from the United States Army with full honors at Fort Leonard Wood, Missouri. Josh and Becky attended the ceremony after which there were the usual congratulations and a minor celebration. Wally thanked them for coming. There were hugs and kisses and promises to get together real soon. So, after a thirty year army career. Wally was a free man.

For thirty years he had been doing what he had been told, obeying orders, told how to act...which he did. His ass belonged to Uncle Sam whom he had served well. He loved his country and those whom he trained, and those who had loved him back. He had met the finest people he had ever known...Matt, Charlie and Josh. He loved his brother, Josh, and his wife Becky and their kids. He loved Josh's Mom and Dad, whom he considered his own. He was proud of his education and everything the army had enabled him to do. He loved Jesus and his guitar. He had loved every bit of life to date. But now, it was his time to do as he pleased. He was going to live life the way he wanted. He was going to live for the moment.

He had made up his mind that he was going to California, to Hollywood and live among the stars, and lie on a sunny beach to watch the waves from the Pacific Ocean roll in and out.

He had been planning on wearing a Spandex swimsuit, but realized that he probably shouldn't. He was nearly fifty and the sands of time had shifted. His hair was beginning to turn grey, his waist had expanded to support a pot belly. His super physique had gone with the tide.

He packed up his belongings which included an empty *Four Roses* bottle, a bar of lye soap, a picture of himself standing in front of the *Four Roses* Whiskey plant in Louisville, a picture of the Groundhogs, his Bible with his name on it, a guitar and instruction book with a lot of music books, a framed Degree in Civil Engineering, pictures of Josh, Becky and the kids, his camera and a few other odds and ends.

He also had a very large bank account, for those same thirty years, he only bought what he needed and he didn't need much. He now had his retirement as well. Wally was financially well off.

He bought a set of luggage from the PX and filled it all. He'd purchased a one-way ticket on American Airlines to LAX and was off. He was going to live for the moment.

As his flight approached Los Angeles it was dark. He couldn't believe his eyes. There were lights from horizon-to-horizon. As far as the eye could see, there were lights. It was the most beautiful sight he had ever seen.

The limousine to the Beverly Hills Hotel dropped him and his three suitcases at the entrance where he had a reservation. He was going to live big. He wanted to go to Disneyland, Busch Gardens, Knott's Berry Farm, Universal Studios…and go to the beach.

He bought a Hawaiian shirt, shorts and sandals and a Panama hat. He was no longer six foot, six inches tall, for due to poor posture and age he had shrunk. He was still a tall man, but only six foot and three inches tall...and still homely. His legs were snow white and slightly bowed. He'd lost a lot of muscle in his arms, which were also snow white. He had seen the long hair styles of the day and decided that was for him.

He hired a cab which took him to all the places he wanted to see. After two weeks at the Beverly Hills Hotel, and tallying up the bills, he decided he needed to find an apartment. He found a small rental unit in an older motel in Santa Monica. The cab driver was also costing a lot, so he went to Driving School and got his California Driver's License. He then purchased a used red, 1970 Ford Galaxie convertible which he kept in the parking lot of the old motel.

He was beginning to feel like a Californian. He walked a couple of blocks to the beach, and watched the tide and waves but learned that he also enjoyed watching the girls in bikinis more. Especially the ones with the big tits. He really liked to watch them play volleyball.

After several months, this too, was boring. He needed something to do. He decided he was still a young man…fifty isn't that old. He scanned the help wanted ads in the paper. He could find nothing that was even remotely interesting.

He discovered a steakhouse named *BJ's* which he frequented. He ate all of his meals out and being a creature of habit, he ate most of his meals at *BJ's*. They had a cocktail waitress named Jeannie that he enjoyed talking with. She had the most glorious tits he'd ever seen and Wally thought she was pretty in the face, too. He learned when the crowds were there and which times it was slow. He would go and dine during the slow times and she always came over and they would talk.

Jeannie had a great personality and loved to laugh. She would complement him on his Hawaiian shirts ,and he would buy more. He had a couple of dozen in his closet. Since he was used to wearing uniforms, he had never had to think about what to wear…you wore your uniform. The idea of matching colors or determining what went with what never crossed his mind. It showed.

He finally got up the nerve to ask Jeannie out. He was almost giddy when she said yes. She lived about thirty minutes from the restaurant and Wally figured how to get there.

He pulled up to her front door in his red convertible and a Hawaiian shirt. Jeannie had been waiting and she got in the car and they were going for a ride. Wally noticed that she was wearing a most revealing blouse.

"You know what, Wally?," she said, "I'd love to go to Thousand Oaks. I've read about it but never been there."

"All right, let's go to Thousand Oaks," replied Wally.

They drove on Interstate 5 North through the San Fernando Valley onto Interstate 101, heading north towards Ventura County. The views of the Valley were great and the road over the mountains into Ventura County revealed a view that was spectacular. Wally loved the entire area.

"Oh…it's beautiful," squealed Jeannie.

"It sure is," commented Wally.

"Don't you just love it?"

"I sure do," grinned Wally.

They arrived and drove all around Thousand Oaks. They did window shopping, ate lunch in a nice restaurant, looked at houses, shopping centers and became familiar with the entire area.

After several hours, they headed back to Santa Monica. Pulling up to Jeannie's house. Wally parked the car and shut off the engine. He was out of practice, but still a man and not stupid either.

"Would you like to come in for a night cap?," she smiled.

A grinning Wally replied, "Sure," like it was a surprise.

When they entered, Wally was pleasantly surprised. Her house was neat, clean and well decorated. It had a beautiful combination living, dining, and kitchen area and a well stocked bar with two stools.

"Have a seat, Wally," Jeannie said, "What would you like...to drink?"

He suavely said, "Oh, bourbon and water." He was not a drinker and knew of nothing else.

"Me too," said Jeannie.

They both had bourbon and water. Then another, and one after that. Then...they had each other. Wally spent the night.

The next morning, Jeannie, who was totally in love with Wally, made them breakfast. Then lunch. Then later she had to get ready for work. Wally followed her as they both drove back to Santa Monica. She went to work and he went to his apartment. He parked his car in the parking lot and entered an empty place with suitcases still mostly packed. He figured that he had subconsciously known he wasn't going to stay there.

He took a shower and shaved. He put on a clean Hawaiian shirt and shorts and walked to BJ's. He sat in his usual booth and watched as Jeannie came to him.

"You look nice," she said.

"You look beautiful," he said.

"Why, thank you, sir," she cooed.

There was no doubt, they were attracted to each other. Despite their backgrounds and circumstances, both were well educated. Jeannie had a degree in Financial Management and Wally, in Civil Engineering. They were both about the same age. Both were lonely. Both were at that stage in life where you have to make choices that a younger person wouldn't make so fast.

Three days later, Wally moved in with Jeannie. He played the guitar and Jeannie sang.

Trips to Thousand Oaks became frequent. On one trip, they stopped at a cocktail lounge and discovered it was for sale. It wasn't anything spectacular, but was something that Jeannie thought would make it financially. It wasn't that much initially and had great potential. Wally bought it. Jeannie managed it, and it prospered.

Wally would tend the bar, and Jeannie waited at the tables. Wally played the guitar, and Jeannie sang. Its very nature generated its own crowd and clientele. Within a year's time, it was packed most of the time.

Wally responded to an ad for a civilian logistics job in the Facility Management Division at nearby Port Hueneme Naval Base. He applied, was interviewed and offered a job. Jeannie opened the Bar at noon and ran the operation until Wally finished working, and he would run the operations at night. Both were hard workers.

Within a year, they learned of another lounge that was for sale in the Camarillo area, which was closer to Port Hueneme. After running some numbers, they bought the business. It was a classy place which served as the after work executive lounge for the headquarters of a large manufacturing company. It had burgundy leather booths, gold framed oil paintings, tasteful wall coverings and Persian looking carpeting. There were lots of brass fixtures and plants and leaded glass windows. All in all, a beautiful place.

With the success of the bar in Thousand Oaks, which was primarily a beer bar, and the associated clientele, it didn't take long for the classy Camarillo Cocktail Lounge to take on the lackluster appearance of the beer bar in Thousand Oaks.

Not surprisingly, Wally was not a slave to fashion. His full head of greying and kinky hair was now nearly shoulder length in the style of the 60's. He wore the polyester suits of the 70's...and it was 1980.

Jeannie didn't care, he had a big heart, among other things, was a good man, a good provider, and he worshiped her. What else could a woman ask for?

She loved him. He loved Jeannie, for she had everything he had ever wanted...actually, a pair of them. They were two peas in the same pod. They lived each day at a time to the fullest. They lived for the moment. Carpe diem.

CHAPTER THIRTY-ONE

A FAMILIAR FACE IN AN OLD CROWD

One night at the bar in Thousand Oaks, a man in a wheelchair was being pushed in by an attractive woman. He was in his fifties and wearing a patch over his left eye. It may have been a bit unusual for most places, but not for this bar. Its clientele consisted of a potpourri of people from all walks of life. Some people might call it a redneck bar. It was usually loud, raucous and sometimes a little crude. It also made a lot of money. Jeannie had been right.

Wally was tending the bar. Most of the regular customers were older, so a cripple with a patch over one eye didn't draw that much attention. The couple sat at a remote table in the corner.

Jeannie waited on them in her usual friendly manner, and as always, she visited briefly. They ordered. When she delivered their drinks, the gentleman in the wheelchair asked about the bartender. She told them it was her partner and left.

The stranger kept looking at Wally and thought he knew him, but wasn't positive. No one looked at Wally and wasn't sure who he was, but since the guy only had one eye, he had to be sure.

He sat there for thirty or forty minutes. He spoke to his companion who came in with him. When Jeannie returned to see if they needed anything, he asked if he might speak with the bartender...her partner.

"Sure thing, darlin', let me send him over," said Jeannie.

She went over and spoke with Wally. They both looked over at the stranger. Wally nodded and walked over to him. As he approached the man, he thought he looked familiar, but just couldn't connect him with a name, time or place. When he arrived at the table, the man smiled and said, "Hi, Groundhog, how've you been?"

Wally froze and drained as if he'd seen a ghost.

"My Gawd, Matt...is that you?

"What's left of me. I thought that was you, but only half sure...I only got one eye, you know," replied Matt.

Wally, who was still in shock, couldn't believe his eyes. There before him was his only connection to his native land and all his early days in the army, his trip to Chicago and everything. His very first friend.

"Matt Carver, where in hell did you come from...I thought you were dead?"

"Damn near was, but you can't keep a good man down," replied Matt.

Wally, now at least a little recovered from disbelief, suddenly lost all sense of his surroundings, reached down and grabbed Matt, lifting him nearly out of the wheelchair and hugged him like a kid hugging a teddy bear. Matt hugged him back, and both men had silent tears running down their distorted faces. All time stood still. It was pure and raw emotion that neither knew they had in them.

Finally, Wally set him back down, and wiping his own eyes with his shirt sleeve said without embarrassment, "My Gawd, it's good to see you. I'd heard you were dead!"

"Damn near was," commented Matt.

Jeannie came over and joking said, "You guys know each other?"

Wally, still overcome with emotion, responded, "Jeannie, this is Matt, my best friend from Wyoming and my best army buddy who we thought was killed."

Jeannie, who had never seen Wally so overwrought with emotion, now knew why. "Hi, Matt, I'm glad to meet you...and I'll be back, but right now I've got to get back to the bar." She turned and let.

Wally had a million questions, "Matt...we heard you were dead or missing, what's happened, where have you been, why haven't you written? Anything? Something.!" Wally squeezed Matt's hand. My Gawd man, it's damned near thirty years! It's great to see you. His eyes were still filled with tears.

Matt, too, had tears in his eye. Both men recovered a little. Matt introduced his wife, Sue, of twenty-eight years. Sue, a tall, slender lady was pretty, with dark brown, well-groomed hair. She appeared to be warm and comfortable to be around. She obviously was very much in love with Matt, and naturally extremely protective.

There were questions upon questions, but soon things began to settle down. Matt and Charlie were serving as forward observers in the first days of the Okinawa attack. They had just arrived and were ambushed.

"Charlie caught a shot in the temple and mine glazed my left eye. I caught another in my left hip. Of course Charlie was killed instantly...I figured I was dead too. I passed out. The next thing I remember, was being carried on a stretcher to a helicopter heading for a tent hospital. They patched me up as best they could and shipped me out to Honolulu. I was hospitalized there for many months."

"So you laid on the beach watching the hulu girls dance?" said Wally.

"Only half of them...I only got one eye."

Sue made a sarcastic comment and smiled. Only Matt hand heard it, and smiled back.

"They didn't leave me much leg either. That's why I'm in this chair. I get along pretty good in this chair, so much so, I began to train others. I got pretty strong arms from all my years of bailing hay on the ranch, you know, but now I really needed them. I taught others how to do the same thing. I met Sue in the hospital, she was my nurse. She still is and the reason I'm still alive" he said.

"He's full of malarkey too," commented Sue. "He did it all by himself. He's a true inspiration." She gave him a loving pat on the arm.

"Where did you end up, Wally?," asked Matt.

"Same place I started. Fort Leonard Wood." he said.

"At the Engineer School?"

"Yep, same place."

"The entire time?," asked an amazed Matt.

"I ended up training more than half of the field engineers in the army. Did that 'till I retired in 1975. Thirty years,"replied Wally.

"What about...Oh...what's his name? Sarge...what happened to him?"

"Sarge? His real name is Josh Turner, and he's kinda like my brother. He left the army, and married his wife Becky has three kids and teaches in the University of Louisville. Josh and me, became real buddies." replied Wally.

"Neat guy...I remember how he got us on that military hop back to Fort Sill?

"How the hell could I forget, you Goon, I was worried sick." said Wally, "and then we didn't hear nothing until Josh pulled some strings and found out. That damned near killed me, buddy, I can tell you that!"

"So, you're the bartender here?," hesitantly inquired Matt.

"Naw...We own the place...me and Jeannie," said Wally, "What are you doing in Thousand Oaks?"

"We live here? Moved here several years ago, after leaving Honolulu. Sue works at the Thousand Oaks Medical Center, has for years. I work in Physical Therapy."

"How long?," asked Wally.

"Hmm, several years now," said Matt, "When did you get here?"

"About three years ago...why haven't we seen each other?," asked Wally.

"Don't know. We don't go out much, what with work and all. We just thought tonight was a night we needed to get out. We've never been in here before," said Matt, "and look what happened. A one in a million chance."

"Well, we got two bars. One's here and the other's in Camarillo. I also got a full-time job at Port Hueneme. We call it Hue-enema!," grinned Wally with his characteristic left hand over his mouth.

There was a break in the crowd and Wally called over for Jeannie. "Hey Baby, come over here to meet my friend, Matt, the proper way."

Jeannie came over and was properly introduced.

"Hi Matt and Sue...welcome. I'm glad to meet Wally's friends and do hope we can all be friends." she said. "Sue...why don't we go and get acquainted. She and Sue sat at a different table. "Let them do their war talk, we got important stuff to talk about.

Matt was indeed an expert in the wheelchair. He could maneuver the wheelchair like no one else Wally had ever seen. A few more drinks and he was doing wheelies on the dance floor. Guess you can take the boy out of Wyoming, but you can't take Wyoming out of the boy!

Wally asked about his parents, who were both gone. They sold the ranch to be near to Matt and helped where they could. They had enjoyed Honolulu and Hawaii. It was a fitting tribute to both Matt and to his parents who had worked so hard all their lives.

Matt asked if Wally had ever gone back home? Wally said his adopted home and family lived in Louisville, Kentucky. He told of his brother-bond with Josh and how good his family was to him. He told of how Josh had helped him so often and then he told of getting a degree in Civil Engineering and converting to Warrant Officer.

Matt was once again Wally's anchor to his life. He was a part of his old and now his new life. He caused Wally to remember where he came from and how far he had gotten. He'd gone from nothing to being somebody and very comfortable. Matt had too. Neither were what one could call rich, but each had more than enough to live the rest of their lives...the way they wanted. They shared so many memories of people they both knew. It was what Wally needed. It was what they both needed.

The nice part was that Jeannie and Sue hit it right off and became friends as well.

Nightly get togethers were most of the time. All centered around the bar. It became a ritual. There were several others as well. All became friends.

Wally had always wanted a camper van to take trips in to see the world. He looked at Midas, Coach and several others. They were all very expensive, which he could afford, he just didn't want to spend the money to pay for them. All he wanted to do was have a way to get places and have a place to sleep and fix meals. They didn't need to be that fancy and Jeannie didn't think so either.

Wally saw in the paper where one of the local churches was selling a Blue Bird bus. It brought back a distant memory of him wanting to own a bus on his way to Fort Leonard Wood. This must be a sign that this was the one, and it was also cheap. He bought it. It had been well used and showed a lot of wear and tear, but Wally figured with a lot elbow grease and some plywood, he could have a real fine camper.

Resourcefulness has always been one of his strong suits. He tore out most of the school bus seats, replacing them with bunks he'd made from bent pipe which he screwed to the floor. He had created eight bunks. Jeannie found eight outdoor furniture pads that worked really well as mattresses. They found an old shower stall from a remodel job which proved to fit just about right, and Wally installed that.

Wally built a platform on the roof of the bus with an aluminum rail around it so they could sit in folding chairs as a sightseeing benefit. He also mounted a 55-gallon plastic water tub onto the platform for easy filling with a hose and to provide pressure for the shower below, while serving as a footstool or table for their cocktails while they were sightseeing. He found an old ladder which, when mounted, was perfect and gave them access to the roof, so he bolted it to the rear of the bus.

When they tore out the Persian looking carpet from the *Camarillo Bar* to make a dance floor, they used it to carpet the bus. It had only a few stains, and was beautiful. They went to *Goodwill Industries* and there found a bargain on a used stuffed sofa and a couple of stuffed chairs to set in. They added a four-set of metal TV trays for eating and cocktails.

He added kitchen cabinets he'd found at a *Lumber Liquidators* store and built-in an old kitchen sink and a used stove he found at the *Salvation Army*. He added an antique oak ice box where they could keep their food stuffs cool with a large block of ice. They had running water from the storage tank on top of the bus, which sometimes leaked but not enough to bother anyone. As an added bonus, Wally built a marvelous bar from the cabinet of an old *Stromberg-Carlson* radio and television unit, complete with a mirrored lift lid which showed their collection of booze bottles and glasses.

In the rear of the bus, which had an emergency door, he added a small room on one side with a flushable portable camping toilet with its own storage tank and a standing urinal which drained out the bottom of the bus. The other side of the rear exit, he built in plywood boxes and storage shelves. He also built-in a sliding ramp for Matt's wheelchair.

Wally hosed down the old bus, scrubbed it up, and although you could see Oxnard Baptist Church faintly remaining. It didn't show all that much. They were ready for the road. Wally climbed up the ladder in the back and added the final touch. A pair of oversized ladies drawers which he hung on the flag pole he had mounted on the roof platform.

Their total investment was no more than two thousand, three hundred dollars, and they had what was costing some people $55,000 on up.

They had friends who filled in for both bars and Wally, Jennie, Matt, and Sue took off for their first adventure. They were going to the beach and find a romantic spot to spend the weekend.

The bar was fully loaded. It had bottles in rows on shelves above the old *Stromberg-Carlson* cabinet, which had a mirrored background with wood strips painted with gold-gilt spray paint across the front to keep the bottles from falling. Stuff was protruding from every opening.

Second gear didn't work all that well, but they got along just fine. Wally drove his bus to the beach where they were camping. He pulled in and leveled the bus with pieces of lumber scraps. He got Matt down the ramp in his wheelchair and got out their folding camp chairs. Jeannie had fixed them all a drink and they were looking out over the Pacific ocean.

"Gawd, it don't get any better than this, does it?," asked Wally.

They all agreed. Jeannie and Sue got the eats out, the gents prepared the campfire, and they gathered around the campfire cooking a hot dog on some wire coat hangers Matt had stretched out. They had baked beans with bourbon and waters. The women had a Maraschino cherry in theirs. They topped the evening off with some *Smores* over the dwindling campfire.

After getting Matt and his wheelchair up the rear end of the bus on the ramp, they all got ready for bed...each finding a bunk, which Jeannie and Sue had made up.

They sat inside, as it was getting cold and damp outside, typical of California nights. Wally hauled out the Coleman lanterns, pumped them up and soon the interior of the bus was flooded with light. Jeannie pulled the curtains that she and Sue had made from flower patterned sheets to cover the windows and after a few more bourbons and water and hors d'oeuvre of pepperjack cheese on *Ritz* crackers, they decided to "hit the hay!"

Sometime during the night, Wally rolled over and farted. Matt instantly answered back...there were muffled giggles. So went the first night in their "Camper Blue Bird."

They used Camper Blue Bird on many occasions. They took it to wine festivals, Renaissance fairs, auto races. It soon was recognized by others on the circuit as well. Sometimes others joined them. It was certainly a curiosity.

The bar in Camarillo began to have the people from the Thousand Oaks bar come in and wanted to have fun there as well. Wally removed three of the burgundy leather booths, to clear an area large enough to accommodate a bowling machine. He also added a pinball machine. He removed a few of the gold-framed oil paintings and replaced them with electric beer signs. He had already removed a large area of the Persian-looking rug to install a dance floor.

He couldn't figure out why the attendance after work was dropping. He contracted a hard, metal rock band to perform during the Happy Hour. After three weeks, two of the three customers complained about the noise. Wally decided that wasn't his best idea. After investing a significant amount of cash into the Camarillo Bar, they closed it down. It was in a bad location.

The Thousand Oaks bar continued to flourish. Both Wally and Jeannie believed this was the style of night life that people wanted. Matt and Sue Carver agreed.

CHAPTER THIRTY-TWO

YOU CAN LEAD A HORSE TO WATER...

One day at Port Hueneme, he was talking to a coworker.

"You know, Jeannie and I have been together for several years now. I'm thinking I need to make an honest woman out of her. She's beautiful, she's smart, she's a hard worker..."

"She's got good taste in men," said the coworker.

"Yeah," replied Wally, missing the sarcasm.

"I'm thinking about getting married...what do you think?"

The coworker answered, "I certainly think you should give it some thought. I like Jeannie. She seems to be good for you. Keeps you out of trouble."

"Yeah. But I need your opinion…what do you think of getting married on Santa Catalina Island? They got a beautiful arch on top of the mountain there, overlooking the island and all the blue sea around it. It's beautiful."

"Sounds spectacular." Replied the coworker.

"We could take the morning ferry out there and meet the Justice of the Peace, and all the wedding party can walk up the trail to the arch and get married there. It's a bit of a walk so it will take a little while, but I want this to be special." said Wally.

"Oh, I'm sure it will be," replied the coworker.

Through the years, Wally had developed a pattern of speech which was slow, meditative, and expressed through an underslung jaw. It only expanded his homely appearance.

Wally went on, "We can stay at the hotel and change clothes from the ferry trip and have the reception after the wedding, across the street in the bar they have there. Of course, I'll get a block of rooms for our guests. Let's see, there's my buddy Glass-Eyed Matt (he's crippled) and his wife Sue; then there's Geezer and Janet, Harmonica Jake and Billie; there's Big Bertha and her girlfriend Shirley; there's Reed and Wilda Coons; and on and on…all told, 23 people."

"Sounds great…when are you thinking of having this?," asked the coworker?

"Oh, two or three weeks. Haven't thought about the date. I'll have to call the JP over there to see if she can do it." he replied.

"That would be a good idea," commented the coworker.

"I've ordered her wedding rings from a mail order diamond house, they are supposed to ship them soon. Paid a lot of money for them, too," he commented.

"Should be special."

"They were real pretty in the picture."

"I'll bet they'll still be pretty when they get here." commented the coworker.

Wally went back to his work. The following Monday, he returned to let the coworker know he had contacted the JP and she will do it.

"I've got the rooms reserved, the cake has been ordered for the bar and I've made arrangements for an open bar for the reception, the ferry is all lined up and the only thing that isn't going right, the rings still haven't come yet," he said.

"When is it, Wally?," asked the coworker.

"This Friday," said Wally.

"Well, bad goes to worse, you can always use those small brass curtain rings," joked the coworker.

"Yeah, that'd work if we had to," Wally agreed.

Wally said, "You know you're invited, don't you?"

"Aw...I already have other plans. I would love to, but can't. It all sounds so beautiful."

"I've even bought a new denim pants suit. It's got western cut leather pockets and all," he said.

"Have you asked Aggie to go?," asked the coworker.

"No, I hadn't thought of that. Do you think she would come?," he asked.

"Yeah, she's all alone, I'll bet she would be thrilled," he said.

Wally thought that was a good idea.

Later Aggie went to see the coworker and said she didn't know what to do. That Wally had invited her to go to his and Jeannie's wedding.

"What do you think I should do?," she asked.

"I think you'd enjoy it. Unfortunately, I have other plans and can't go, but would really like to see pictures of it. It sounds beautiful."

"Well, maybe I'll go. If you think it would be alright," said Aggie.

"Would you take pictures for me? You can use my camera and I'll buy the film?," asked the coworker.

"Sure."

"Great."

Friday, and both Aggie and Wally were on annual leave.

Aggie, dressed in a lovely suit, drove down to Thousand Oaks to Wally's and Jeannie's house, arriving at 7:00 a.m. Many of the guests were there and had been drinking beer. Aggie, who had never touched a drop of anything, was a little appalled, but went along to get along.

Wally appeared in a T-Shirt with a tuxedo painted on it, carrying a hanging clothes bag for his denim and leather wedding suit. He went into the bus and hung it along with Jeannie's dress.

Several more arrived, including Glass-Eyed Matt in his wheelchair and his wife Sue. Sue was a pretty woman dressed in a yellow suit and weaving spiked high heels. Matt's lap had a cover over it. Then Big Bertha and her girlfriend, Shirley arrived. Both had been drinking beer.

Soon the Camper Blue Bird was filled. People were sitting in the chairs, on the couch, on the bunk beds. All in all, it was crowded. Others, including Aggie, decided they would follow in their own cars. The caravan took off in a cloud of blue bus smoke and headed south towards Los Angeles on Interstate 101 at 7:30 a.m. on Friday morning...at the height of rush-hour traffic.

The Ventura Freeway, Interstate 101, is five and six lanes going in each direction and bumper to bumper all the way from Thousand Oaks, over the mountain and through the San Fernando Valley to Sepulveda Boulevard and Interstate 5, which leads to the Long Beach harbor.

The Blue Bird began having difficulty about six or seven miles into the Valley. It wouldn't shift from second gear, in either direction. It was stuck in second gear. Wally had been driving in the third lane from the right and had to get over to the exit ramp. The bus would chatter and bounce and die. He'd restart it, smoke pouring out the back of the bus.

Sue grabbed Big Bertha and Shirley, and the three exited the bus to direct traffic. Sue in her yellow suit and spiked heels, a slightly-intoxicated Big Bertha in her blue jeans, boots, and flannel shirt with a butch haircut, and little Shirley looking frightened out of her mind were staggering between the stalled cars, holding up their hands, clearing a path for Blue Bird to chatter, bounce, and eventually get to the exit.

When they got to the exit, they all got back in, and the incline helped them to get up to the second gear speed. They were off the freeway and heading for a garage. The caravan followed the smoke-streaking Blue Bird.

They found a repair place, only to discover that there was no hope of getting it repaired that day. They all piled in other cars as best they could, with the wheelchair, wedding dress, fancy denim wedding suit, and whatever luggage that they had brought. And they were off once more.

When they arrived at the terminal, the ferry had already left. They had to wait until the next one, which was two hours. Someone suggested they wait in a bar, and they did.

They finally boarded the ferry to take the twenty-six mile, one-hour trip to Santa Catalina Island. When they arrived, several were teetery, walking on a crushed shell roadway and walkways carrying their suitcases and whatever. They went to the hotel to check into the three rooms that Wally had reserved for them...for all twenty-three of them.

Wally and Jeannie changed into their wedding outfits and then walked up the street to the Justice of the Peace's house.

They were several hours late, so the Justice of the Peace, figured it was off and decided to clean her kitchen floor. She was stripping off old wax on the linoleum floor when there was a knock on the door. The Marjorie Main lookalike got up, wiped her hands on her apron, knocked away a hank of hair with the back of her hand, and opened the screen door.

"What do you want?," asked the crusty old lady.

"We're here to get married," replied Wally, "I'm Wally Bearstone."

"Oh Hell, I gave up on you hours ago. I'm scrubbing the kitchen floor."

"Our bus broke down on the way and we missed the ferry. Can you help us out...please?," pleaded Wally.

The JP hesitated and saw twenty-three people behind him, "Well, alright, but I'm not trudging up that mountain at this time of day. Go to the backyard."

There, standing in two feet high weeds and grass, among trash cans, a few chicken pot pie tins, and a couple of beer cans, the Justice of the Peace, in her apron covered with wax and soap suds, married Wallace Bearstone and Jeannie Evans.

After Wally slipped the small brass curtain ring on her finger, the Justice of Peace, by the powers invested in her by the State of California, pronounced them husband and wife.

Sue, who was crying more from the booze than the beauty of the moment said, "Oh, what a beautiful wedding."

When Aggie, who was taking pictures, heard Sue's remarks, she stopped and quietly said to herself, "Beautiful wedding, my ass!"

After the wedding ceremony, if one could call it that, they staggered down the street to the bar. Once entered, they were greeted by the proprietor, who led the way to the reception area which was located in the center of the bar.

There on a pool table, covered with a paper table cloth sat a beautiful three-layered wedding cake, complete with a plastic husband and bride on top. It was surrounded by paper wedding plates, white plastic forks, and wedding napkins in the rotary fashion of bar napkins.

Next to the pool table was a smaller table on which stood a four-tiered fountain of pink champagne gurgling out the top, surrounded by a pyramid of stacked plastic champagne glasses.

On each of the cocktail tables throughout the place including the main bar, there were bowls of peanuts and pretzels and each ashtray had a booklet of wedding matches with "Wally and Jeannie" printed on them.

Aggie observed a man sitting at the bar who left his seat on his way to the restroom just passed the table with the wedding cake. As he walked by, he swiped some of the icing with his finger and crammed it into his month.

They had pizza, hamburger sandwiches, and a choice of potato chips or *Frito-Lays* with dill-pickle chips. The guys were playing pool, some of the girls were dancing to the strains of the jukebox, and all but Aggie were drinking. Soon, she left to go to their rooms and find a bed.

The rooms were not big. She found one with a twin bed and quickly washed up, went to the toilet and lay down. In a while, Big Bertha and Shirley came in and took the adjoining room. Through the cracked door, she could see Bertha undressing and scratching herself.

Try as she might, Aggie couldn't keep from watching. The big woman scratched her stomach and her armpits and finished by picking her nose.

Aggie wasn't sure who she was sharing the room with, but the mystery was soon solved when a very drunken Wally came in with Jeannie.

He dropped his clothes and said, "Where's my bride?...It's time to do my manly duty."

Upon conclusion of his announcement, he passed out on his bed, missing Aggie, who was on a mattress on the floor beside it. Jeannie got him undressed and crawled in beside her husband.

Aggie lay there for hours trying to go to sleep, but the ceiling fan overhead was off balance and rocked above with squeaking sounds. About the time she started to drift off, a truck in the back alley began to pick up garbage cans clanging them against the truck sides. At this point, she arose, grabbed her things and headed to the ferry.

She made the early morning ferry and happily paid the fare to return. She got into her car and headed north towards Port Hueneme.

Monday morning, an incensed Aggie shared the whole disgusting experience with her coworker, who fought with everything he had to keep a straight face. It was as he had suspected it would be.

Wally is a good man who works hard and plays hard. He is well educated and a person of high integrity. He loves his God, his country and beautiful things. He is a kindly soul who would give you the shirt off of his back. He just hears a different drummer than most people.

CHAPTER THIRTY-THREE

PROUD TO BE AN AMERICAN

After their spectacular wedding in June, planning began for the Independence Day Parade in Thousand Oaks, California with all the pageantry and tradition of any Fourth of July parade in the country.

Other than our independence from Great Britain, the additional theme was to be Frontier Days. This might have presented a challenge to most but not those in the Thousand Oaks Bar.

This was going to be a float to set the standard for years to come. A real beauty, for Wally was proud to be reunited with Matt after all these years. A true hero, and one that needed to be honored. After all, they started out on the same bus to the same Fort Leonard Wood Army Base.

Matt was his oldest friend. He wanted to have Matt placed on a flatbed truck in his wheelchair surrounded by American flags, but Matt wanted nothing to do with that. He preferred to be doing wheelies and showing what a paraplegic can do, but Wally thought that was perhaps a bit too dangerous.

Jeannie came up with the theme of a gambling casino and dance hall in the Gold Rush days, complete with a honky tonk piano playing and everyone dancing.

Matt insisted he wanted to have his wheelchair decorated and be towed back of the flatbed. Wally, who was not a dancer, decided he wanted to pay tribute to his Cherokee heritage and wear western boots and a buckskin jacket with lots of fringe on the sleeves. He would stomp alongside the float like a sergeant.

At about the same time, he received a letter from Josh saying that he and Becky were coming to California on vacation and would like to spend a little time with them, if that were possible. They had started to periodically write to each other, but long periods of time would pass in between correspondence. Time had taken its toll on the relationship, and they had grown apart. They had gone from *Brothers* to brothers...to family...and were now a little like distant cousins.

Wally wrote back saying that they were certainly welcome and would be just in time for the Thousand Oaks Independence Day Parade on the Fourth of July. Wally said he would book them at *Motel 6*...if they got back to him right away.

Josh and Becky had gone to Wally's retirement ceremony, of course, but hadn't seen him since. It had been many years since either had seen the other, and Wally now had a new wife he wanted to introduce to them. Josh and Becky were now empty nesters with grandchildren, so maybe they once again had something in common.

Geezer had a 16-foot flatbed truck that they were using and brought it over to Wally's and Jeannie's house. They constructed a backboard out of fencing that looked like stacked logs, and they also constructed a skirt around the base of the truck and covered a good portion of the truck cab, leaving eye slots for Geezer to see through so he could drive it.

Next, they loaded an old upright piano onto the truck bed. This required all the men and Big Bertha to push the piano up the steep ramp made from a couple of 2-inch by 10-inch pieces of lumber, almost losing it once. They created end posts by using 2-inch by 6-

inch by 8-foot lumber into the side panel rack holes in the truck bed on the rear corners and two midway and up towards the front. From these, they attached wires with strings of lights interlaced with braided crepe paper in red, white and blue. These went in all directions and crisscrossed in the center to hang an imitation gaslight looking chandelier, which they hooked up to a generator. The upright posts and all the wood was painted dark brown to "reflect the look of olden times."

Wally hired their oftentimes-customer and the sometimes-ragtime piano player from the local pizza place to play honky tonk music for them all to dance to.

Sue, Jeannie and Shirley spent the last week getting their outfits ready, which were similar to Can Can dresses with glue-on rhinestones on ruffles. They had spangly tops, and the men had matching shirts...but black jeans and cowboy boots.

They had all rehearsed and made up a routine that was sure to please the crowd. Of that, they were all certain.

Wally had his outfit ready and helped Matt and Sue weave the crepe paper red, white and blue into the spokes of his wheelchair, with more yet to come. Matt was going to be outfitted in his Class-A WWII army uniform, with his Purple Heart medal pinned in the appropriate place on his chest.

They also added two American Flags on either side of the truck on the front, now-wooden fenders, and a gigantic one in the center of the truck cab roof.

Wally, standing back and taking it all in, remarked, "It's a beautiful float. I think we're looking at first place."

The others agreed. They went to the bar to celebrate. It was going full swing when Josh and Becky arrived. Josh, more than Becky, was better prepared to expect what they saw.

Wally looked up, saw Josh, and came rushing around the bar towards him.

"Hey, brother...how the hell are you?," he shouted.

Josh, grabbed Wally, hugged him and said, "It's been too long, brother."

Wally, seeing Becky, did likewise. The three were standing in the crowded bar hugging each other.

Jeannie walked over, and Wally, grabbing her around the waist, introduced her, "Here's Jeannie, my bride."

Josh responded, "Hi, Jeannie, I'm Josh, and this is my wife, Becky. Welcome to the family."

They went through the pleasantries, and Wally began to introduce them around. Jeannie, sensing that Becky wasn't all that comfortable in the bar, went to her and pulled her aside.

"Would you like to sit and talk a spell? You must be exhausted from the trip," she said.

"I'd love to," responded a relieved Becky.

When Wally got to Glass-Eyed Matt in his wheelchair, he said, "You might already know this cripple with a patch, Josh."

Josh stared at the smiling Matt, and then there was a glimmer of recognition. "Matt?...is that you?"

"Yep...in the flesh," he replied.

"My God, Matt...when did you show up?"

"Oh, 'bout a year ago...How are you Sarge?," he said.

Josh was stunned and at a loss for words, "I can't believe it...we heard you and Charlie were killed!"

"They were right about Charlie, but they saved what's left of me and here I am," said Matt.

The three sat and went through a litany of questions and answers. Wally noticed that Josh had gained a little weight, was graying at the temples, but all in all was a fine looking man. Becky too had aged, but her hair was still colored brown, she had gained a little weight, but she, too, looked good.

"Did you get settled into the motel?," Jeannie asked Becky.

"Oh, yes, it's fine," replied Becky, "The flight was a little tiring, but we're fine."

Wally said, "Well, tomorrow's the big day. "We got the float all ready and all we have to do is climb aboard, and we're on our way to first prize."

Josh observed later to Becky at the *Motel 6*, that Wally hasn't changed that much...just older and more lax than he used to be. He'd always been a character.

They both found the motel to be just adequate. It really wasn't what they were used to, but then perhaps they were being snobs. They came to an agreement to just roll with the punches!

They went to bed and Becky fell asleep. Josh lay there remembering all that he and Wally had gone through and the good times they had through the years. It was good to see him again...at long last. He was still a big, lovable character...larger than life, with absolutely no social graces. He fell asleep with a smile on his face.

Josh and Becky, after breakfast with Wally and Jeannie, were shown the best place to watch the parade. Wally took them two folding chairs to sit in on the curb. Jeannie brought two throws for their laps, as it is always cold on California mornings, even the fourth of July. Wally and Jeannie left the waiting couple.

When they got back to the house and walked to the backyard, to see the float, Jeannie screamed.

"Oh No! What's happened to our float?"

All of the crepe paper had absorbed the moisture of the California night and was drooping near the bed of the truck. The red, white and blue colors had run into a blend of purple and stained puce.

"We're ruined," she cried, "We're going to have to redo the whole thing!"

"I guess we should have covered it?," Wally brilliantly expressed, "Where'd you put the extra crepe paper?"

"We used it all."

"Where'd you buy it?"

"Sav-On Drugs!"

"Let's hope they're open today," remarked Wally as he headed for the car.

Luck was shining on them. They had several rolls left. Plus, they had some red, shiny metallic fringe, so he bought what they had. He returned with his treasures, and Jeannie and Sue had meanwhile stripped all of the old, damp crepe paper away. They strung up the new and duck-taped the fringe around the perimeter. The float was even better.

The rest of the bar crowd showed up, including the overweight piano player in his bright red, white and blue striped vest, string tie, and flowing white hair with his piano stool. They helped him up the portable steps, and he sat down, dried off the piano keys. The piano was only a little out of tune, and most of the keys worked. It was going to be a long parade.

They loaded the back of the log-like bar with a full keg of beer and beer mugs. Had to keep it authentic. Several of the guys had a flask as well. They were ready.

As Geezer backed the loaded truck out of the driveway, he couldn't see because of the new improvements. Wally, who had had a couple of shots of liquid courage, guided him back into the street.

There, they attached the twenty-five foot rope to Glass-Eyed Matt's wheelchair with a grouping of American flags on long wires sticking up in the air, attached to the back of his chair. Now Matt, in his army uniform and medal, was ready.

Wally, resplendent in his Cherokee buckskin jacket with lots of fringe, his tooled cowboy boots, black jeans, a black, ten-gallon cowboy hat with an imitation eagle feather protruding, holding an imitation rifle with *"Red Ryder"* visibly printed on the plastic butt, and in the other hand holding a flag pole with a large American flag, yelled out, "Tally Ho!" The spectacular float began to move.

They joined the other entries, and were placed behind the Thousand Oaks High School Marching Band. As they were lined up and were nearly ready, Wally pulled the starter cord on the generator, and it sprang into life. The noise was horrendous and the fumes worse; however, the lights on the float came to life and were beautiful. It was loud, but beautiful.

The parade began. The piano player began to play *"Buffalo Gals Won't You Come Out Tonight,"* and the hundred member Thousand Oaks High School Marching Band began *"The Stars and Stripes Forever."* The generator was loudly chugging, and the fumes were destined to overcome the piano player before the booze did.

Wally was proudly marching, stomping his boots just like Sergeant Swain, proud as a peacock. To the rear of the float was Glass-Eyed Matt, being pulled along and doing wheelies in his wheelchair. The dancers were doing a modified version of square dancing.

Josh and Becky were sitting in their folding chairs as the entire spectacle rolled before them. If they thought *Motel 6* was something, this was something else!

Neither could keep a straight face, the tears were pouring down their cheeks, and Josh could only think that his Mom and Dad would have loved it.

Matt, while doing wheelies, got twisted, and the rope tangled up in the wheels, pulling the wheelchair sideways so it began to chatter. The rubber runners on the chair were coming loose from the wire-spoked wheels, and the entire wheelchair and occupant were close to being pulled over and dragged through the streets of Thousand Oaks behind the smoking exhaust from the flat bed truck.

Wally, who was so proud to be an American, was strutting like a man through mud in galoshes to the strains of *"It's A Grand Old Flag"* with the band and was totally oblivious to everything going on behind him.

Josh saw what was happening, so quickly dashed into the street, grabbed the rope, and pulled it from around the wheel and righted the wheelchair. The crowd roared with applause and cheered with approval.

Wally marched and stepped even higher, believing the applause and cheering were for him and their float. He always knew he had that special something.

Matt said, "Thanks, Groundhog...it was nearly my day!"

Josh returned to his chair with many patting him on his back.

Becky had tears of laughter running down her face. She turned to him, reached up, and kissed him on the cheek. She patted him on his chest and said, "My hero."

Josh said to Becky, "Wally's finally found his element ,hasn't he? I just hope someone up there is looking out for him, 'cause somebody's got to."

"Don't you miss it?," she laughed.

"Maybe…a little."

THE END

Made in the USA
Middletown, DE
20 August 2022

71856162R00219